Art for Art's Sake:
Meredith's Story

ALSO BY BARBARA L. CLANTON

THE WHICKETT SERIES
Art for Art's Sake: Meredith's Story (Book One)
More Than Roommates: Dani's Story (Book Two)

THE CLARKSONVILLE SERIES
Out of Left Field: Marlee's Story (Book One)
Tools of Ignorance: Lisa's Story (Book Two)
Going, Going, Gone: Susie's Story (Book Three)
Stealing Second: Sam's Story (Book Four)
Out at Home (Book Five)
Tools of the Devil (Book Six)
Going Under (Book Seven)
Stealing Hope (Book Eight)

THE GRASSE RIVER SERIES
Quite an Undertaking: Devon's Story (Book One)
Rebecca's Story (Book Two) … <Coming Soon>

THE GIRLS' SPORTS SERIES (Children's Books Ages 9-12)
Bases Loaded
Side Out
Live, Love, Lacrosse

ART FOR ART'S SAKE
Meredith's Story

BOOK ONE IN THE WHICKETT SERIES

BARBARA L. CLANTON

Paperback ISBN   978-1-953734-35-8

Revised First Edition 2024
9 8 7 6 5 4 3 2 1

Cover design by Sarah (Forcoverservice)

Published by:
Bibi Books Publishing Company, LLC

Dedication

For my parents, Paul and JoAnne Clanton, who always put their children first. You encouraged me in everything I tried, and you let me learn my own life lessons, sometimes the hard way. Thanks for signing up to be my parents.

Acknowledgments

I must thank all of those kind people who took the time to give me their insights and suggestions on various drafts of *Meredith's Story*. Special thanks go out to my editors at Regal Crest, Marty Phillips and J. Robin Whitley, for guiding me through another one. Thanks to Andi Marquette, Sheri Milburn, Angela Perkins, Lori Hood, Carmen Roldan, the Cathys, Amy Gamber, Diana Schnitzer, and art experts Kymberly Moreland-Garnett and Irina Ashcraft. I naturally need to thank my parents, Paul and JoAnne Clanton, and my brothers, Paul Clanton, Jr. and John Clanton, and their respective families for their collective wisdom and support. Thanks also to my girl's folks, Mamie and Joe Weathers, who continue to encourage me. Grandma and Grandpa, take care of Shasta, Cody, Piglet, and Kisha, and thank you for your unconditional love through every phase of my life. And thanks, finally, to my foundation, Jackie Weathers, who pretends to understand why I spend so much time with my computer.

Author's Note to the Revised Edition

I have really enjoyed revisiting my earlier books. "Art for Art's Sake: Meredith's Story" is Book One in the Whickett Series, initially published in 2009. Originally, I'd meant for this to be a stand-alone book, but so many readers asked for Dani's story, so her story became Book Two, and a series was born.

This is a revised edition, not a second edition. Nothing major has changed in the story plot. Only the grammar, punctuation, and awkward stuff (to my current ears and eyes) have been changed, updated, or eliminated.

I must also make another note about phones and technology. When this was written in 2009, texting was just becoming a thing, and many households still had landlines. There was also no expectation for students to have their own individual computers in school. It seems odd to me now, but that's how it was a short time ago.

I'm hopeful that the emotions and situations will stand the test of time and that you will enjoy Meredith's self-discovery coming-out story.

Cheers,
Barb
Central Florida (March 2024)

Table of Contents

Chapter 1

The Outcast

All eyes were on her. Meredith Bedford cleared her throat and looked up from her notes. She coughed into her fist to hide her nerves. The other students in the classroom snickered. She heard someone say, "Freak." Another said, "Loser." Words. They were just words. Words she had heard a thousand times before. She sat up a little straighter at her desk in the back of Mr. Dalton's classroom, pushed her black-rimmed glasses up the bridge of her nose, and said tentatively, "They probably thought the capital should have been New York City."

Ben Kinsey sat two seats in front of her but in the next row over. He coughed into his hand and said, "Retard."

Meredith sighed softly and looked out the windows of the second-floor classroom. The gray January cold seeped through the glass and wrapped itself around her. Her long, black, wavy hair fell around her face and efficiently hid her from view. She knew her cheeks were turning a bright shade of crimson, but that was okay because blushing added color to her pale winter skin. But no one would see her blush behind her hair fortress, anyway.

She peeked out and saw Dani Lassiter, senior class president, whack her friend Ben in the arm and tell him to shut up. Meredith smiled and began another doodle in the margin of her notes. She was glad Dani stuck up for her. Dani had always been friendly, but

Meredith knew that, like the rest of them, Dani would never give her the time of day, so Meredith pretty much ignored her like she ignored everybody else. Meredith had just turned eighteen and couldn't wait to get out of high school. She had one more semester of senior year to go, and then she would shrug off these people like an old coat and move on.

Mr. Dalton nodded in her direction. "Meredith, that was a good answer. Many people thought New York City should have been the capital of the state instead of Albany. And many people still think that." He directed his next question to the entire class. "Now, people, why do you think they wanted New York City? Albany sits on the Hudson River just like New York does."

Meredith kept her eyes down like she always did because most teachers didn't notice you if you did that. Mr. Dalton was on to this trick, though, because he called on people who didn't even have their hands raised. That just didn't seem fair. Meredith knew he was trying to draw her out of her shell, but she didn't want to be drawn out. Her plans were to wait until college. That's when she would come out of her shell. That's when no one would know her or Mikey, and she could start her whole life over. She was done with these jerks at Whickett High School.

"Mr. Kinsey," Mr. Dalton directed the question to Ben. "Why New York City?"

Ben leaned back and put his hands in the pockets of his oversized army jacket that he wore every day, no matter what the weather. His short brown hair was unkempt as if he never combed it. Meredith wondered if his blue spiral was the only notebook he owned because she had never seen him with a book bag.

"Well, Mr. Dalton, it's obvious," Ben replied confidently. "People thought the capital should be where the Statue of Liberty was." The class burst into collective laughter at Ben's answer.

"Mr. Kinsey," Mr. Dalton said with a grin. "You have a textbook, don't you?"

"Yeah."

"Well, I suggest you read it once in a while." He held his hands out to the class as if conducting an orchestra.

"People, all together now, when was Albany made the capital of New York State?"

The collective response was "1797."

"And when did France give the United States the Statue of Liberty?"

"1885."

"Oh, almost a hundred years later. Mr. Kinsey, I suggest you brush up on your dates. This course is called 'The History of New York State,' not 'The Fiction of New York State.' I'm sure I don't need to remind you, Ben, but the semester exam is Tuesday."

Ben nodded and sank lower in his chair. He ran a hand over his hair to smooth his cowlick. It didn't work. He jammed his hands back into his jacket pockets.

Mr. Dalton directed his following comments to the entire class. "New York City, as all of you remember, was this great nation's first capital for about twelve years. So, although New York City may have been the country's capital, it never was the state's." He nodded in Ben's direction. Ben nodded back.

Meredith liked Mr. Dalton. She even thought he was handsome with his short black hair cut close around his ears and thick black mustache. He was probably still in his twenties, but he was very much in command of the class. Mr. Dalton was one of the few teachers who seemed to hear the hateful words constantly thrown her way, and he had probably embarrassed Ben in retribution for harassing her.

3

Although she was grateful he tried to defend her, she didn't like the extra attention it brought her.

~~~

Stepping into Mrs. Levine's sanctuary always helped Meredith shake off the rest of the school day. Bright and inspirational posters of works by Rembrandt, Monet, Cassatt, and Warhol covered the walls. Mrs. Levine had a strict rule about book bags in her art room, so Meredith placed hers in her assigned cubby. She could muddle through her other classes—English, Economics, Environmental Science, and Phys. Ed., but art was the only class of the day she actually enjoyed. She was grateful to Mrs. Levine for recommending her for Advanced Placement Studio Art. AP Art was a lot of work, but she was mostly free from her classmates' daily taunts and jeers in that class. The nine other students in the class pretty much left her alone. They were too busy with their own work to be bothered with her. Plus, mutual respect seemed to exist among artists. An honor among thieves, she decided. She had forty-three minutes to forget about the world before the long walk home in the frigid temperatures with her brother, Mikey.

Meredith lived for Thursdays because, for the next two days, Mrs. Levine let them work on whatever project they wanted to. And that day, Meredith planned to work on Mikey's portrait. She had to use a photograph of him, of course, because her brother could not sit still long enough for her to get anything on canvas. His face was contorted in concentration in the photograph. His karate class had been giving a demonstration during Whickett Days last May. Facial expressions were the focus of her required AP Art concentration, and she hoped this particular portrait would become part of her AP portfolio. She desperately hoped she could capture the intensity on his face. Meredith chuckled softly at the image. His tongue was sticking out, as usual. Typical Mikey.

Meredith had made a preliminary drawing of Mikey in her sketchbook with colored pencils, so she had a good idea how she wanted to approach the portrait with her acrylics. Sketching always helped her get a feel for her subject.

She pulled the rubber band off her wrist and raked her waves of jet-black hair into a bundle. She twirled the rubber band around her hair to keep it off her face and out of her eyes. She hid behind her hair most of the day, but in Art, she didn't care who saw her face. Her mother told her the acne scars on her cheeks weren't bad. Meredith wanted to believe her, but she wasn't completely convinced. And since she needed to see her artwork clearly, she couldn't worry about it.

She pulled Mikey's canvas from the rack and returned to her easel. She retrieved her plastic box of paints and brushes from her cubby and pulled her palette out of the box. When she painted portraits, she usually made a general pencil outline of the person to get a feel for the size of the subject on the canvas. Then, before painting facial features or other details, she concentrated on the clothing. Working the clothing let her get comfortable with her subject. Outlining and clothing usually took up the first session if she had an actual person sitting for her.

After costuming, she liked to work from the inside out. She would sketch the eyes, nose, and mouth with pencil and, when satisfied, would attempt to paint the features. Facial features were, in her opinion, the most important part of the person. She had painted enough portraits to believe that the eyes were, indeed, the link to the soul. The mouth, too, was crucial in conveying expressions. She assessed what she had done last week with her brother's mouth. She nodded in satisfaction. Yes, she had certainly captured the intensity on his face, especially in the way he pursed his lips.

But today was hair day. She liked to think of the hair as an extension of the face, so she planned to draw in the general shape of the hair, paint in the first layer, use slightly different shades for shadow, and then add a few lines for texture. She needed to capture the sunlight that came from behind his head by feathering the lighter colors into his dark brown hair. In real life, Mikey's hair was unruly, and she toyed with the idea of combing it for him in the portrait but decided that, no, Mikey was Mikey, and the world was going to get him as his usual disheveled self. With that firmly decided, she went about selecting tubes from her box of paints and placed them near her palette.

"Ah," Mrs. Levine said knowingly from behind her. "Hair day?"

Meredith smiled at her art teacher. "Yeah. I think I've got the right colors."

Meredith wished she could carry herself as confidently as her art teacher. Mrs. Levine wore her highlighted blond hair in a bun, but the old-fashioned hairstyle didn't make Mrs. Levine look old; it just made her look professional or business-like. Meredith wished she could keep her hair up, but that would be way too much exposure. Her art teacher's forest green smock was spattered with various paint colors, and Meredith wondered if the paint had come from student projects or her teacher's own artwork. Probably both.

Mrs. Levine nodded and smiled with her eyes. "Combed or wild?"

Meredith laughed. "I'm going for the natural look, so wild it is."

"Go for it. Holler if you need me." Mrs. Levine moved on to her next student. Although Thursdays and Fridays were free days, it didn't mean you could goof off. Mrs. Levine always made sure everyone worked productively.

Meredith pushed her glasses up the bridge of her nose and looked at the barely begun portrait of her brother. She didn't want to blame her troubles on him, but she couldn't help it sometimes. With a brother like Mikey, she couldn't help getting noticed, too. And getting noticed was the last thing she wanted. She knew that most people, including her classmates, thought that if Mikey was the way he was, then maybe she had a touch of it, too.

Meredith squeezed an inch of raw sienna onto her palette and then a half-inch of white. She mixed them together with her palette knife. Pleased with the results, she picked up her flat brush and dabbed it into her newly created color. She pushed up her glasses again and imagined the brush strokes she would use, sort of like a dress rehearsal. She took the plunge and used broad strokes to simulate his hair. She leaned back and nodded. Yes, the color was perfect. It's too bad that other aspects of her life weren't so perfect.

A year and a half ago, her parents decided to move from Greenspond, a small mountain town in the Catskill Mountains of central New York, to the sprawling suburbs of Albany. That was just before Meredith entered the eleventh grade. If she had stayed in Greenspond, her graduating class could have fit into two minivans. But her parents felt Mikey needed better opportunities for schooling, so they went off to Albany.

She missed Greenspond terribly. She had friends there. Not that many, but at least she'd had a few, and she wasn't the pariah there that she seemed to be at Whickett High School. At Whickett, she had absolutely no friends. Her classmates had not gone out of their way to welcome the new girl. In the beginning, Meredith tried desperately to shed her introverted nature. She worked up the courage to talk to some of the other kids in her classes, but after too many tear-filled nights, she gave up and locked herself away in the art room and stayed there. It was easier to be invisible.

Meredith slashed her brush across the canvas. She pulled it back in horror, and her eyes focused wide on the painting. She breathed a sigh of relief. The portrait was okay. She couldn't believe that here, in her sanctuary, she let those Whickett jerks intrude. Ben, Dani, and others could fall into the polluted Hudson River for all she cared. She closed her eyes, took a deep breath, and held it for a moment.

"What's up, kiddo?" Mrs. Levine was on her second trip around the room.

Meredith felt her face flush. "Oh, sorry. I just let the world intrude for a second."

"That happens to me, too, sometimes. Just breathe and let it go." She looked over Meredith's painting briefly and then continued, "Well, since you're taking a break anyway, I wanted to talk to you about the Senior Art Elective class in the second semester. Now, I know you probably don't need the credits to graduate, but I thought if you had room in your schedule during sixth period, you could take the course."

"Really?" Meredith was overjoyed. She didn't know she could take a second art course. "Yes, yes! A thousand times, yes. I have a study hall during sixth period now." Wow. Two periods of art out of eight. The day had just improved tenfold.

"I know you have extra responsibilities at home," her teacher gestured at the portrait in progress, "so I figured you could use the extra time to work on your AP portfolio. Of course, I'll require some kind of project from you for the elective course. Probably something to exhibit for Whickett Days in May."

"We went to Whickett Days last year. That was a lot of fun."

"I know. It's small-town stuff, but the Whickett townspeople love to celebrate their history." She smiled. "Okay, Meredith, I'll put your

8

name on my list and hand it in today." Mrs. Levine turned to walk away but then looked back. "I thought you might jump at the chance."

Meredith smiled. Now she was in the right frame of mind to work on Mikey's bad hair day. Once satisfied with the first go-around, she carefully put the still-wet painting in the rack, stored her supplies, and retrieved her book bag. When the bell rang to end the school day, she headed for her locker before picking up Mikey at his sixth-grade classroom in the middle school. Students jostled for position in the crowded hallways, but thankfully, no one noticed her, and she changed out her books easily. Meredith closed her locker just as Dani Lassiter opened hers. The senior lockers were randomly placed around the school, and for some reason, Meredith's locker was just three away from Dani's.

"Hey, Meredith." Dani stepped in front of her.

Meredith's stomach knotted. *Now what?*

"I'm sorry about Ben today," Dani said. "He's got a few marbles loose." She twirled a finger in a circle near her ear.

Why is she even talking to me? Practically no one spoke to her unless it was absolutely necessary. Meredith kept her guard up. "It's okay." She pushed past Dani to go down the hallway.

Dani caught her by the arm, and Meredith froze. She stared straight ahead and didn't turn around. She desperately hoped this wasn't the start of a new series of harassments from yet another person. She already had enough trouble from some tall guy on the basketball team. And now Ben Kinsey. He would probably do something to retaliate for the way Mr. Dalton had singled him out earlier. Maybe that's why Dani grabbed her arm. Dani and Ben were friends.

Meredith murmured, "What do you want?" She braced herself and waited for the worst.

Dani let go of Meredith's arm and said, "Uh, nothing except to apologize for Ben. Honest. It's not okay that Ben picks on you, and so, um...Look, I'm just sorry, okay?"

Meredith didn't know what to say. She looked back over her shoulder and muttered, "Thanks. I gotta go." She wasn't sure, but she thought she saw a genuine apology in Dani's eyes. But why would Dani apologize? Dani wasn't the one that called her a name. Meredith shrugged. Maybe Dani'd had enough, too. Having the senior class president as an ally might be nice. Not that Dani Lassiter would ever consider being her friend. No. No one at this school would ever claim that honor.

She rounded a corner and made her way toward the middle school that was attached to the high school by an enclosed walkway near the gymnasium. Meredith sometimes liked to surprise Mikey, so she paused outside the open door of his classroom. His resource teacher, Miss Stevens, was helping him get his coat on. Meredith smiled. Mikey's dark brown hair was wild as usual. Miss Stevens hadn't quite gotten his right arm in the sleeve when Mikey spotted her peeking around the door jamb. He ran toward her.

"Merry Berry," he yelled, running over to her, right sleeve dangling. He pronounced her name "Mewee Bewee" because he still had trouble wrapping his tongue around the "r" sound. And he had never been able to pronounce the name "Meredith," so they had settled on "Merry." He wrapped her in a big hug. He was in sixth grade and hadn't hit a growth spurt yet, so he only came as high as her chest, but he was strong, nonetheless. He gave her a sloppy kiss.

When she finally extracted herself from his grip, she said, "Hey, Mikey..." She searched her brain for something she hadn't used in a while. "...Bikey."

He seemed delighted with this play on his name. He jumped

around and shouted, "Mikey Bikey, Mikey Bikey, Mikey Bikey."

Miss Stevens laughed. "Hey, Mikey *Bikey*, come here and let me finish putting your coat on. His immediate compliance made both his teacher and Meredith laugh. Miss Stevens was a new teacher, and Meredith figured she wasn't much older than she was. Miss Stevens had a fresh, enthusiastic air about her that Meredith hoped she could recapture for herself when she went to Syracuse University in the fall. *If* she got in, that is.

Meredith walked into the classroom. "So, how did my baby brother behave today?"

"Oh, he was great. He always is. The other kids have warmed up to having a classmate with Down Syndrome, and he's a real charmer. Let me show you the book he started today. It's fourth-grade level." Miss Stevens finished getting Mikey's right arm in the sleeve of his winter coat and went over to his cubby. While his teacher pulled out the book, Meredith helped Mikey with his coat. She inserted the two ends of the zipper together and stood back. Mikey reached down and pulled the zipper up all on his own. Miss Stevens handed the book to Meredith and said, "It's about a dog named Harry who does detective work."

Meredith read the cover. *Harry, Dog Spy.* "I don't think he has this one."

"I think he had some real understanding today, too. We'll discuss the plot tomorrow, so I'll better understand his progress." She turned toward Mikey. "Mikey, do you want to take Harry home?"

The word Harry sent him into another jumping spree. He shouted, "Hawey, Hawey, Hawey."

Meredith laughed and took the book from the teacher. "I think that means yes." She put the book in his orange book bag. Actually, the color was leaning more toward cadmium orange. She looked for his lunch box but didn't see it. "Where's your lunch box?"

"Wunch box." He repeated, his demeanor suddenly serious. He turned in a complete circle and looked around the room. His face lit up. "Window." He pointed toward the row of windows.

"Window *sill*, Mikey. Windowsill."

"Windowsill, windowsill, windowsill," he said and skipped over to retrieve his lunchbox.

Miss Stevens smiled and said to Meredith, "I'll put this in my January report, but please tell your folks he's been enunciating more clearly. He's such a sweet little guy. I figure I'd spread the good news sooner."

"Thanks, Miss Stevens. I'll tell them. I think he likes having Resource with you." To Mikey, she said, "C'mon, Mikey Bikey, we have to hit the road. In the cold. To our abode." Meredith grimaced at her lousy attempt at rhyming.

Mikey threw his head back and laughed with his mouth wide open. "Merry, 'bode." He laughed again, even though he probably had no idea what the word 'abode' meant.

They left the classroom and made their way through the now deserted hallways to the front of the high school. Meredith stopped in front of the main doors and took a deep breath. She said to her brother, "Ready, Mikey? It's going to be cold."

"Weddy, Merry." His shoulders tightened, and Meredith could tell he was just as excited as she was to make the three-quarter mile trek home in the frigid January temperatures.

Meredith opened the door a crack and cringed. It had to be below freezing. "Let's do it, Mikey." A blast of cold air hit them as they left their sanctuary.

Chapter 2

The Sympathy Vote

Meredith sat in the auditorium with her sketchbook open. Mrs. Levine required a sketchbook for the AP Art class, so now was as good a time as any to add to it. Besides, she hated these senior class meetings. She hardly listened to anything spewing from the stage because, in the one and a half years since she had been at the school, she hadn't attended a single social event and didn't intend to start now. The senior class, over three hundred in total, met every other month in the school auditorium. Meredith looked up at the stage when Mr. Dalton, who sponsored the senior class, asked Dani to give an update on senior events.

Dani took the steps two at a time and practically leaped behind the podium. She was perfectly centered against the backdrop of the heavy green velvet curtains. Emerald green wasn't the best color for the large space, but she supposed the curtains made sense since green and yellow were the school colors. Dani looked out at her classmates as if taking them in individually. Some of the teachers at Whickett High School couldn't get their classes of thirty quiet, but here was Dani Lassiter keeping over three hundred plus seniors quiet with just a long glance. Meredith decided she had found a good subject to sketch.

During the first two senior class meetings of the year, she had sketched Mr. Dalton in profile, the back of some kid's head in front of her, and Mrs. Olsen, the secretary from the main office who took the minutes. She had tried to sketch her father from memory at one of these meetings but stopped when she couldn't quite recall how his brown eyes looked behind his glasses. She remembered how sad that had made her feel and quietly vowed to spend more time with her dad when he was home from his second shift job at Amalgamated Cardboard. She would be leaving home to head off for college soon enough.

Dani finally spoke. "My friends and fellow countrymen, you're probably wondering why I've gathered you all here today." The Whickett senior class chuckled. "I have some great news. We are only one fundraiser away from having enough money for the senior prom in May." Whoops and hollers sprang from the crowd. "And," Dani added with a sweeping motion, "I expect every one of you to participate in that fundraiser." The whoops and hollers turned to groans. Dani continued undaunted. "We'll probably have a car wash once it gets warmer. I'll give you more details at the next meeting."

Meredith swallowed hard. Was Dani looking right at her? No. No, it was just her imagination. Meredith turned the pad to a fresh sheet and began her sketch of Dani Lassiter, senior class president. Meredith decided that Dani was cute, pixie cute. Her blond hair was short like that woman who played Peter Pan on the Broadway DVD her mother had at home. Dani was the only girl in the senior class with short hair, but she was Dani, and no one gave her grief about it. Not that Meredith ever saw, anyway. Dani's skin was flawless, too, which made Meredith a little envious, even though she hadn't had a real acne outbreak since early summer. Her mother said her sporadic outbreaks the year before were probably due to nerves about starting at a new school.

Dani's nose was straight and thin. Meredith couldn't see Dani's blue eyes from her last-row seat in the auditorium, but she knew they would be playful and alert. Meredith smiled at the partial sketch. Yes, Dani was a good subject. Dani's expression behind the podium was serious but good-humored. Maybe Dani would pose for a portrait. Meredith tossed out the idea as quickly as it came. The likes of Dani Lassiter would never grant an audience to the likes of Meredith Bedford. She sighed but continued sketching.

Dani was in mid-sentence, "—so those of you going to the Winter Ball tomorrow, remember that it's formal. And we don't mean your best jeans." The class laughed, and a few names were thrown about the auditorium of classmates who clearly thought jeans were perfectly acceptable formal wear. Meredith wouldn't be caught dead at one of those formal functions. Who would she go with, anyway?

"And," Dani continued from the stage, "the senior class officers have okayed my proposal for our spring community service project. Participation is completely optional, as you know, but I hope most of you will help in one way or another. Some of you've already heard about it, but in case you haven't, let me spell it out. I call it 'Seniors for Seniors.' We're adopting the Hudson Pines Senior Center. A lot of senior citizens live at the facility, but a lot more go there for activities during the day and on weekends. And I think they have a convalescence wing, too, like a hospital. I'll get with some of you one-on-one, but I was hoping the chorus could drop by and spend an afternoon with them. Maybe the comedy club could come up with a routine. And maybe some of us could go by and read to the bedridden ones."

Meredith sensed the sudden unease of the students around her. Dani must have sensed it, too, because she said quietly, "Look, I understand this sort of thing might make you nervous. But think of these people like your grandparents. What if your grandmother lived at Hudson Pines, and all she had to do all day was watch TV? If you think about it that way, then it's not so scary. And, besides, once you meet the seniors, I think you'll be hooked."

Meredith sat up a little taller in her seat. She covered a smile when she noticed that many of the other students had done the same thing. Meredith thought maybe she might actually participate in one thing at the school. Maybe she would go to that senior center. She had no idea what she could do to help, but she had time to think about it because Dani told them the deadline for proposals would be in February, over a month away.

Meredith looked back up at Dani, who said, "Okay, if that's all, then—" The senior class booed their disapproval. Dani looked perplexed, but Meredith knew she was teasing them. Dani scratched her head. "What? What is it? Did I forget something?" She read her mental list of agenda items out loud, counting them on her fingers one by one. "Prom fundraiser, winter ball, community service project. Hmm, what else? I can't think of anything—" The senior class booed louder. Even Meredith anticipated Dani's announcement.

"Oh," Dani said as if realizing something for the first time, "you want to know how many days until..." She smiled the broadest grin Meredith had ever seen. "Lacrosse practice."

A collective groan of "Noooo" came from the students in the auditorium.

Dani laughed heartily into the microphone. She put her hand up as if to ward off the attack. "Okay, okay. Well, just so you know, there are twenty-five school days until lacrosse." More boos. "But there are less than one hundred days until graduation. We have—Drum roll, please."

The students stomped their feet and slapped their thighs. Even Meredith participated in the human drum roll.

"We have *ninety-eight* school days left of high school." Cheers exploded from the students.

Thank the Lord, Meredith thought as Dani banged the gavel, dismissing the senior class to their seventh-period classes.

Meredith didn't smile often at school but smiled on her way to Mr. Dalton's history class. Less than one hundred days of high school. What a concept. Less than one hundred days to freedom. She didn't even mind when some of the kids brushed her shoulder in the hallway, making her stumble. Well, she minded but had long ago stopped trying to decide if they did it on purpose. It didn't really matter. There were less than a hundred days of high school left.

She found her usual seat in the back of Mr. Dalton's classroom and put her book bag on the floor beside her desk. She examined the half-finished sketch of Dani and was pleased with her start. She had to get a better look at Dani's eyes, though. Many people had trouble drawing eyes. Meredith didn't, but she did need a good look at them to get a better feel. She decided to watch as Dani entered the room. She didn't have to wait long.

Dani must have walked from the auditorium with Mr. Dalton because they entered the room side-by-side. Dani's regular entourage of Ben, Jeff, and Sarah followed behind them. Sarah and Dani played on the girls' lacrosse team together. They were the co-captains of the team and seemed to be best friends. Sarah was one of those pretty girls. The kind who knew they were pretty. Jeff was Sarah's boyfriend, and they were supposedly the top couple in the school. They had apparently been crowned the homecoming king and queen. Meredith didn't really know because she didn't go to the homecoming football game or the dance afterward when that sort of thing was decided. Meredith heard the big announcement at school the following Monday. She wasn't sure, but she thought maybe Dani and Ben were going out. They were always together.

Meredith decided she didn't care to speculate on her classmates' relationships and sought out Dani instead. Dani's eyes sparkled with enthusiasm. The blue was so brilliant that Meredith wished she had her paints with her. Cerulean, that was just the right color. She watched the smile in Dani's eyes linger as she talked to Mr. Dalton. Yes, that was the look she had to capture. That smile.

Meredith was about to look back down at her sketch when she realized Dani was looking right at her. Meredith was mortified, and her eyes shot down to her drawing, but not before she saw the wide grin spread across Dani's face. Meredith knew she must be turning a bright shade of red or purple. She tilted her sketchbook to hide her face.

"All right, people. Settle down." Mr. Dalton leaned back against the front of his desk. "This is our last day of review before your exam on Tuesday. It's the morning session in the gym. Is everybody clear on that?" Heads nodded around the room. "Okay, before we get to the review, I want to set you up in groups for a project next semester." The students groaned. Ben smacked Dani, Jeff, and Sarah on the arms as if to claim them as members of his group.

Mr. Dalton rapped his knuckles on his desk. "C'mon now, settle down. You haven't even heard what you're doing yet." He paused for a moment and added, "Okay, fine. They tell you in teacher school that once you say 'get into groups,' students lose their hearing. So..." He walked to the front whiteboard and wrote in black marker, "Groups of two or three only. No groups of one. No groups of four or more."

He faced the students. "Okay, you have two minutes to figure it out." He turned his back to the class. Meredith dreaded moments like these. No one ever wanted to partner with her. Occasionally, Meredith would get the sympathy vote, and a group would ask her to join them.

But not today. She groaned because Mr. Dalton would have to assign her to a group again. It was better that way because her new group wouldn't feel responsible for choosing the class loser. She glanced at Dani. She and Ben had paired up after Mr. Dalton announced that groups of four weren't allowed. As expected, Jeff and Sarah were their own group.

Mr. Dalton held out his clipboard. He started in the front row and asked the students one by one who the group members were. When it became obvious that Meredith hadn't been invited to join any group, a few students laughed in her direction. Meredith looked out the window at the dreary January day. Less than one hundred days to go. Could she make it?

Ben was one of those students who laughed at her. He coughed into his hand and said, "Pathetic."

Dani slapped Ben on the arm and hissed, "Dude, what's wrong with you?"

"Ms. Lassiter?" Mr. Dalton addressed Dani. "Is there a problem?"

"Yes, there is." Dani then did something that surprised everyone, including Meredith. "Ben's on his own." She glared at Ben. "I'm going to work with Meredith Bedford on this project." Dani turned to face Meredith with storms flashing across her eyes. She asked, "That's okay, right?"

Meredith didn't dare say no, but she really didn't know what to make of Dani Lassiter, president of the senior class and captain of the girls' lacrosse team, asking her to partner up. She stammered, "Okay."

"All right then," Mr. Dalton said, writing down their names. "Ben, I guess this means you'll be joining Jeff and Sarah?"

Ben shot daggers at Meredith and said, "Yeah, sure, whatever."

Meredith hung her head and wondered what in the world had just happened. Mr. Dalton finished writing down the groups and then cleared his throat. "Okay," he said with mock seriousness, "now that we have the groups settled, the teacher school says I can explain the project to you. I'll give you a formal handout after exams, but I figured I'd plant the seed now to get you thinking. In this class, we're studying the History of New York State, but now it's time to specialize. We're going to study the history of the village of Whickett, that tiny little suburb of Albany that nobody ever heard of."

Some of the students groaned at the idea of studying their hometown. Meredith groaned, too, but inwardly. She didn't have enough nerve to be so outwardly rude to a teacher. Mr. Dalton seemed undaunted by their collective reaction. "Anyway," he said, raising his voice slightly to be heard over the groans. "Each group will present a piece of Whickett history to the class. Find a popular Whickett landmark or a long-term citizen. Find an old building or a park. Do some digging. Find the history of these places. Interview some of the senior citizens at Hudson Pines. Find out their stories. You may be surprised by what you find. This would fit in perfectly with the 'Seniors for Seniors' project."

Dani threw him a thumbs-up for plugging her community service project. Meredith smiled. It almost sounded like Dani and Mr. Dalton had contrived the history project together. Maybe having Dani as a partner would be okay because Dani probably had something already worked out, and they could get the whole thing over with quickly.

Mr. Dalton let the hum of anticipation die down. "Okay. Move your seats and get with your groupmates to discuss the project. Just ten minutes because we have that rather large quiz, er, semester exam, to prepare you for."

Meredith didn't move. She looked out from behind her hair curtain to see Dani hop up from behind her desk and bound toward her. The boy sitting beside her had gotten up to join his group, so

Dani slid into his newly vacated seat.

"Hey, Meredith." Dani faced her. "God. I hope that it was okay to tell Mr. Dalton we'd be partners. I mean, I didn't even ask you."

Since Dani had only volunteered to be her partner out of sympathy, what else could Meredith say besides, "That's okay."

"Cool. Well, like I said yesterday, Ben can be a jerk. I don't know why I hang out with him sometimes."

Meredith shrugged her shoulders as if to say, "Yeah, it's a real mystery." Of course, she said nothing of the sort to the senior class president.

Dani sighed.

Meredith noticed Dani's eyes again. As clear and sparkling blue as they had been at the start of the class, they were cloudy and almost gray now. What colors would she use for those eyes now? Light gray? Payne's gray? Something in between? Meredith hoped she could remember this troubled expression in Dani's eyes because she knew she would totally be sketching that anger later. Meredith felt Dani's real eyes burning through her.

"What?" Meredith swallowed hard. She hoped Dani didn't notice.

"Where were you? You looked miles away." Dani smiled.

Meredith knew her cheeks were flushing, but she couldn't do anything to stop her obvious embarrassment. "Oh, sorry. I was just thinking about an art project I want to start later."

"Right. You're into art." Dani straightened herself in her chair noticeably, "I'm going to take that Senior Art Elective. Me. In art. Can you imagine?"

Meredith could imagine. Not everyone had talent, but she knew how art could occupy your whole mind and take you away from the world. "Yeah, I can imagine you taking art. You can't?"

"Me? I'm a gym rat. A student government geek. I haven't done anything art-related since maybe seventh grade. Do you know that fine arts wheel they make you take in middle school? Oh, maybe you don't since you're new here."

Meredith smiled at Dani. Meredith had been at the school for over a year and a half. She wasn't exactly *new* anymore.

Dani continued. "In middle school, they make you take drawing, chorus, band, and drama. One each quarter. Anyway, I don't know my way around a paintbrush or a sketchpad. What in the world can I create that would be *art?*"

"Well, uh, I'm taking the class, too."

"You are? No way."

Meredith was shocked at how excited Dani sounded. "Yeah, Mrs. Levine asked me to take it—"

"But aren't you in AP Art?"

"Yeah, but she said I could take time out of the elective class to work on my AP stuff. I could, uh, show you stuff." Meredith couldn't believe she had just told Dani Lassiter she would help her. What could she, Meredith the loser, possibly show this larger-than-life senior class president? That was ridiculous. She had just lost her mind.

Dani beamed at her. "Oh, my God. You'd really show me what to do? That's awesome. Now I won't freak out so much. And I have to pass the course because I need a half credit of fine arts."

Meredith must have had a surprised look on her face because Dani said, "Yeah, yeah, I know. Stupid of me to wait so long."

"Well, I have the same thing. I have to take Health with a bunch of freshmen next semester."

"Why?"

"Because it's a graduation requirement, and I didn't take it at my old school."

"I can help you if you want, but I think you'll be helping me more with the art. And thanks in advance."

Dani put her hand on Meredith's. The shock of Dani's touch shot up her arm and sent her heart pounding. She swallowed hard again as she pulled her hand away. She said in a choked voice, "You're welcome." She couldn't squeak out any more words.

Mr. Dalton tapped on his desk and requested order. He said, "Okay, hopefully, you've all had the chance to get a preliminary start on your project. We'll talk more about them next semester."

Meredith felt Dani looking at her but was reluctant to meet her gaze. She knew she was still beet red. She wasn't sure if it was the physical touch that sent her pulse soaring or that somebody as nice and as important as the senior class president was treating her like a human being. Like a friend.

Dani whispered, "Crap, Meredith. We didn't even talk about the project. Here." She ripped a piece of paper from her spiral notebook and tore it in half. On one half, she neatly printed her name and phone number. She handed both halves to Meredith. "Give me your cell phone number, and I'll text you over the weekend so we can come up with something."

"Oh, I don't have a cell phone. I guess I'm one of the three people left in the world who doesn't own one. I'll have to give you my home phone number, okay?"

"Yeah, that's cool."

Meredith felt odd. Not a single soul at this school had ever asked for her phone number. When she first got to Whickett, she hoped some cute guy would ask her, but she gave up on that pipe dream when even casual friendships failed to materialize. But here was Dani asking for her phone number. Meredith was about to feel good when it dawned on her that Dani only wanted her number because of the project. She was not asking out of friendship. Meredith hastily scribbled her phone number on the other half-sheet and thrust it back at Dani.

~~~

Meredith found the familiar sound of pencil on paper comforting. She sat on her bed with the light from her bedside stand illuminating her sketchpad. She enjoyed Friday nights because she had the whole weekend to pretty much be by herself. The rest of her classmates were probably hanging out in town having a good time, but Meredith hadn't gone out on a Friday night in a long time. Well, she'd gone out to dinner with her family, but those had been her only Friday night dates. Ever.

Meredith looked at the storm she had drawn in Dani's eyes. She thought she had captured Dani's fiery expression quite well, but the best way to capture a person's essence was to have them sit right in front of her. Meredith suddenly felt the need to capture Dani on canvas in a way she had never felt about a subject before. Not even Mikey. She puzzled over the urge. She looked down and hoped the storm in her sketch never came her way.

If Meredith ever got up the nerve to ask Dani to sit for a portrait or two, she would use hot colors like reds, oranges, and yellows to capture the tempest in Dani's expression, but for the happier sketch, she'd use cool blues and greens.

Meredith grinned. Working on this history project with Dani might have benefits after all. Even though Dani asked to be her partner to get even with Ben and had maneuvered things so Meredith would help her pass the Senior Art Elective, two could play that game. She would help Dani all right, but Dani would have to help her, too. Dani would have to pose for at least one portrait.

A soft knock on her bedroom door startled Meredith out of her absorption.

"Merry?" Her mother was on the other side of the closed door. "Can I come in?"

"Sure, Mom. Come on in." Meredith closed the sketchbook and stretched.

The door creaked open, and her mother came in and sat on the edge of the bed. She still wore her nurses' scrubs. Meredith's mother, Leslie Bedford, worked as a licensed practical nurse at a local clinic in town. "How was your day, honey?"

Meredith couldn't tell her mother the truth. She couldn't tell her mother that no one at school liked her, that she had no friends. She could only say what she always said. "Okay, I guess." Then she remembered Mikey's portrait. "I've got Mikey on canvas. But he's not finished yet."

"Oh, honey. That's wonderful. I can't wait to see him when he's done." Her mother looked tired. Meredith noticed that her mother's formerly jet-black hair had recently taken on a fair amount of silver. Her mother pushed a lock of shoulder-length hair out of her face, but it fell back. Her mother sighed. "I've had a long day, and I've got an even longer one tomorrow."

Oh no, Meredith thought. Not another double.

"I've got to work a double at the clinic. Elizabeth's going to visit her parents downstate in Spring Valley, and I told her I'd take her shift." Her mother grinned sheepishly. Meredith knew what was coming. "Can you watch Mikey tomorrow?" She didn't wait for Meredith to answer. "He has karate at eleven."

"Oh, Mom," she whined the words, but it was a tired, resigned-to-her-fate whine.

"Please, honey? I know I owe you big time, but we can use the money, too. We're barely making it with what your dad makes at Amalgamated and what I make at the clinic. If I could just get my RN license." She patted Meredith's knee and said wistfully, "Ah, maybe when Mikey's a little older. So, would you watch him tomorrow?"

Meredith sighed and told her mother that, of course, she would look out for Mikey and take him to karate. Meredith understood that family came first. And that meant Mikey came first. When Meredith headed off for college, the heavier burden would fall back onto her parents. So, if she could do anything to help in the few months while she was still at home, she would.

"Thanks for being the best big sister in the world, Merry Berry."

Meredith smiled. She liked it when her mother used Mikey's nickname for her. "No problem, Mom. Oh, hey. I'm expecting a call this weekend from a classmate named Dani—"

"Danny? Really?" Her mother's eyebrows were raised about as high as humanly possible.

"Mom! Stop that. Dani's a girl. We have a project to do together in History, and she's going to call about it."

"Oh, okay. But I never heard of a girl named Danny before."

"D-a-n-i, Mom. Dani. It's short for Danielle."

"Okay. Gotcha." Meredith thought she heard disappointment in her mother's voice. Her mother stood up from the bed and said, "Okay, honey. I'm exhausted. Your dad is working overtime, so he'll probably get in around midnight." She leaned down and kissed Meredith on top of her head. "Goodnight, honey."

"'Night, Mom."

Meredith watched her bedroom door close. *Oh, well. There goes Mary.* Meredith had planned to spend most of her Saturday at the Whickett Public Library researching Mary Cassatt. Mrs. Levine recommended that Meredith study Cassatt's paintings to see how the

American Impressionist used the natural expressions of her subjects to convey emotion. Meredith reopened her sketchbook with a sigh. Maybe she would have time to go to the library after Mikey's karate class. She didn't want to use the slow family computer to search for websites on Cassatt. She preferred the tactile feel of an art book in her hands and the fact that she could take the book anywhere in the library to get just the proper lighting. The computer was too passive for her. Art was definitely *not* passive for Meredith.

She looked down at Dani's fiery eyes. You're not passive, either, Dani Lassiter, are you?

Chapter 3
The Scary House

Meredith sliced a sesame seed bagel and put the two halves in the four-slice toaster.

"Make one for your old man?"

Meredith jumped. She hadn't heard her father come into the kitchen. "Sure, Dad." She sliced a poppy seed bagel, his favorite kind, and placed the two halves alongside hers in the toaster.

Meredith's father poured himself a mug of coffee. The disappointed expression on his face told Meredith that the coffee was cold.

"So, daughter, what are you doing on this fine Saturday morning?" He put his coffee mug in the microwave.

"*Fine* morning, Dad? It's like twenty-five degrees outside."

John Bedford looked toward the kitchen window. "Ah, but it's sunny. And it's still morning, isn't it? I'm not acclimated to this second-shift business. I hope I didn't wake you when I came in last night."

"No. I was still up sketching."

"I thought I saw your light on." Her father took his now steaming cup of coffee out of the microwave and sat at the kitchen table.

Usually, Meredith would have taken her bagel and returned to her room, but she decided to spend the morning with her father until she had to wake Mikey up for karate. Her father looked tired. His thin face was gaunt, and he had dark circles under his eyes. His thinning hair was taking on as much silver as her mother's. Why hadn't she noticed before? She went to the refrigerator and pulled out a tub of butter and a tub of cream cheese. "Which do you want, Dad?"

"Oh, uh, how about both? Let's live on the wild side today."

Meredith laughed and brought both to the table. She went back to the refrigerator for orange juice. She put the carton on the table and got out cups and silverware. She plucked the bagels out of the toaster when it popped, put them on plates, and sat down to eat breakfast with her father.

Her father smiled. "Wow. To what do I owe this honor?"

"Oh, stop, Dad. I never see you, that's all."

"We're both busy, aren't we? How's school going? Don't you have exams coming up?"

"Yeah. English and Enviro on Monday, History on Tuesday, Econ on Thursday, and Math on Friday."

"I remember those days. I don't envy you at all, but then again, I wouldn't wish second shift on you, either." He pushed up his thin wire-framed glasses to sit on the bridge of his nose.

"Why do you work second shift, then?" Meredith stabbed into the cream cheese tub and lathered one side of her bagel.

"Well, I don't have a choice. Since I'm the new guy in town, I have to take the shift they give me. And, besides, I make a little more money this way." He stopped buttering his bagel long enough to give Meredith a teasing grin. "Somebody's got to pay for art supplies and karate lessons around here."

"Dad, c'mon." She pushed him on the arm.

"Is that all you've got, Merry? Maybe you should be the one taking karate."

Meredith knew he didn't mean to, but she detected a hint of

melancholy in his voice. When Mikey was born with Down Syndrome, her father's disappointment had been almost tangible. Meredith was only six years old then but still remembered her father's comment to her mother. He'd said, "There goes Pop Warner football." Meredith wasn't sure what he meant then, but she remembered his comment and years later realized that Mikey probably wouldn't be able to compete in sports the same way most other boys did. Her father was probably doubly disappointed when his attempts to interest her in sports failed miserably. She'd much rather hold a paintbrush than a bat or a basketball.

Meredith must have had a sad look on her face because her father said, "Oh, it's okay, Meredith. We both know that Mikey was the surprise package we didn't know we wanted, right?"

"Yeah." It was true. She loved her brother. Yeah, Mikey wasn't a *traditional* brother, a *normal* brother, but then again, Meredith didn't really know what *traditional* or *normal* were, anyway. Mikey was just Mikey. Whenever he mastered a difficult task, Meredith was proud right along with him. His smile alone made her heart soar.

"So…" Her father patted the back of her hand. "Who got tapped to take Mikey to karate?"

Meredith raised her hand as if she were in class. "That would be me."

"Yes!" He pumped a fist in the air.

"You can go, Dad. I don't mind."

"No, no," her father teased. "I wouldn't want to deprive you of the privilege."

"Thanks a lot. It's only freezing out there, and then I have to sit and listen to a herd of yelling eleven- and twelve-year-olds."

"They're tapping into their inner something-or-other, I guess. Mikey loves it."

"And Dr. Robinson said he's got to get more exercise, so off we'll go." Meredith took a sip of her orange juice. "Oh, Dad, do you want me to cook tonight, or can we just order pizza?"

"Pizza's fine. You have exams to get ready for. In fact, I'll even call DiGiovanni's myself."

"Whoa." Meredith chuckled. "Don't strain yourself, okay?"

"Not a chance."

"I have to go get Mikey out of bed. If Dani calls—"

"Danny? He would be the captain of the football team, hmm?" Her father loved to tease her about boys.

"No, actually," Meredith teased back, "the captain of the lacrosse team." She got up to put their now-dirty dishes in the dishwasher.

"Lacrosse. Is that a *real* sport?"

"Oh, come on, Dad. I've seen you watch lacrosse on ESPN."

"Yeah, because there weren't any real sports like football, basketball, baseball, or golf. Wait, golf isn't a real sport, either."

"I've seen you watch golf." Meredith feigned exasperation with her father. "I assume you'll be watching a sporting event this afternoon?"

"Naturally. Pro bowling, unless some kind of Syracuse game is on."

"What if Syracuse bowling is on opposite pro bowling?"

"Oh, then I'll be switching back and forth as fast as the clicker can take me."

Meredith couldn't help but smile at her father. Syracuse sports are all he ever thought about.

"Hey, Dad, when I return from karate, can you take over Mikey? I want to go to the library to study."

"Of course I will. Mikey likes bowling."

Just then, Mikey, obviously sleepy, lumbered down the stairs.

31

"Hey, Mikey," her father addressed his son. "What's shakin'?" Her father twisted and bounced in the kitchen chair.

Mikey laughed and twisted and bounced where he stood. "Dad's shakin'."

"And Mikey's shakin', too." Her father laughed with him.

Meredith laughed at both of them. "Hey, Mikey Likey. Do you want some cereal?"

"Yes, please." Her brother stopped his twisting and turning and sat with a grunt at the kitchen table. His short dark brown hair was, as usual, wild and uncombed. His glasses had slipped down his nose, but he didn't seem to care.

"Mikey, could you get your bowl and spoon?"

"Okay, Merry." He got up slowly, not fully awake, and pulled out his favorite bowl from the cupboard and opened the silverware drawer for a spoon.

"Don't forget that you've got karate in a little while."

He mumbled something she didn't understand. "More slowly, Mikey. What did you say?"

"Taekwondo."

"Oh, that's right. You take taekwondo, not karate. I keep forgetting. After breakfast, get your uniform on, and don't forget your belt this time, okay?"

"Okay."

Her father joined in. "And, hey, Mikey, do you think you could put on a little deodorant today? You were Stinky Mikey last time."

Mikey giggled at his father's teasing and grinned from ear to ear. "Stinky Mikey."

Meredith caught the wink her father sent her and smiled. She winked back at him and said, "And, by the way, Dad?"

"Yes, daughter?"

"Dani, the lacrosse captain that might call, is a girl. Dani's short for Danielle."

"Oh, okay then. And she's captain of the girls' lacrosse team?"

Meredith nodded.

"Very cool."

Meredith sensed intrigue about Dani, not disappointment, from her father. She was relieved.

Once Meredith got Mikey dressed and into their dad's rusty old pickup truck, she cranked up the heat. The pickup was old but thank goodness the heater still worked like it was brand new. Their five-mile trip to the Martial Arts Academy would take them down Center Street, the main thoroughfare through Whickett. Meredith marveled how the bedroom community for the city of Albany still managed to maintain a small-town feel. Many of the homes were older, but people seemed to take pride in their town and kept their houses up for the most part. Greenspond, where Meredith's family used to live, was smack in the middle of the Catskill Mountains. To get to the closest grocery store, they had to travel about fifteen miles to Deposit, although they sometimes went to a small convenience store a few miles down on the Quickway in a pinch. She missed the mountains, but there were definite benefits to living near a big city, and Meredith liked the convenience of the nearby stores.

"Scawey house," Mikey said as they stopped in front of the house that time had forgotten.

"Scary, isn't it, Mikey? I wonder who lives there."

The old Victorian house with its lacy ornamentation around the windows, doors, and roofline looked out of place along Center Street. She had learned about Victorian architecture from an art book she'd read at some point. She wondered what the four-gabled Victorian house looked like in its heyday. Meredith was sure that the peeling rose-colored paint had once looked grand. Three steps led up to a small landing surrounded by a darker rose-colored banister. Meredith admired the arched windows and the myriad geometric shapes that gave the house its old-time character. The trim surrounding the front picture window seemed to be waiting for one more snowstorm to smash it to its final resting place. She looked up at the second of three stories and imagined having an old-fashioned tea party on the balcony. She laughed. The balcony, overlooking the hustle and bustle of Center Street, would make for a noisy tea party.

Although Center Street was zoned for commercial businesses, the old house seemed to have dug in its heels, refusing to budge. Meredith wondered if people still lived in the old house, and if they did, they probably hated having an auto parts store on one side and a Mexican Restaurant on the other.

The traffic light turned green, and they continued toward the Martial Arts Academy. Meredith pulled the old pickup truck into the parking lot.

"Taekwondo, taekwondo." Mikey mushed the words together.

"All right, Mikey Pikey. Are you psyched?"

"Psych!" he shrieked.

She put the truck in park and was reluctant to turn off the engine because that would cut the heater, and they would have to brave the mid-twenties temperature. She did it anyway. A sister's duty. "Okay, little brother. Let's do it. Take off your seatbelt and watch out for cars, okay? Ready?"

"Yeah." He said with excitement. Once he got his seatbelt off, his hand flew to the truck's door handle. "Weddy."

"Okay." She grabbed her handle and yelled, "Go." They both jammed open their doors and jumped out of the truck. Mikey slammed his door first. He was beating her. Meredith slammed her door and ran after him into the Academy.

"I win. I win." Mikey giggled inside the Academy door.

"You always win, Mikey. I have to get in better shape if I'm going to beat you next time." Meredith shook her head. He really had beaten her that time. Usually, she let him win, but this time, she had all she could do to keep up. She wasn't in the best shape and even thought of herself as a little soft. Dani always looked strong and healthy, and for the briefest of seconds, Meredith considered starting some kind of exercise regimen but rejected the idea quickly. Exercising to her was as foreign as art seemed to be to Dani. She found a seat with the karate moms who sat in a line of fold-up chairs along the mirrored wall of the workout area.

One of the academy instructors helped Mikey take off his coat, but the bulky karate uniform underneath made the task more difficult than usual. Mikey had been so proud when he earned the yellow stripe on his white belt. The students in the class seemed to accept him as just another student, and Meredith was glad that her mother had found a positive and healthy way for Mikey to interact with other kids. It was too bad her mother couldn't help Meredith with that, too. But there were less than one hundred school days left, and Meredith figured she could hang on until Syracuse. She'd fallen in love with the idea of attending Syracuse after sitting through hours of the school's athletic games on television with her dad.

Some of the karate moms were reading magazines. Meredith never could concentrate when all the yelling started. She was rarely ready for that first spirit yell from the fifteen or so students. Their high-pitched voices almost tore her ears off, but she couldn't leave because Mikey would get panicky if he didn't see her. She loved it when he looked her way and smiled. She always flashed him a thumbs-up, which he returned, of course. Sometimes, they would keep flashing hand gestures, like the peace sign or the hang loose sign, until they were both giggling. Once, she pretended to pick her nose and flick the imaginary booger at him. They had both cracked up. This garnered a gentle reprimand to Mikey from the instructor and amused smiles from the karate moms.

The instructor worked the students through their warm-up moves. A collective spirit yell accompanied each move. Meredith cringed and readied herself for forty-five minutes of not-so-quiet torture.

"Am I stinky?" Mikey put his armpit in Meredith's face after his class was dismissed.

She playfully swatted him away and held her nose. "Phew. You *are* stinky!" She scrunched up her nose and made a distasteful noise. He was sweaty, but he wasn't really stinky. He still had that innocent smell of youth. That innocent smell that made Meredith fall in love with her little brother in the first place.

Mikey laughed, obviously pleased with his effect on his sister. "Show Daddy."

"Where's your coat?"

Mikey retrieved his coat from the hook and put it on. Meredith started the zipper for him, and he zipped it the rest of the way up. Winter coats back on, they raced to the truck, and this time Meredith wasn't playing. This time, Meredith had something to prove. This time, Meredith won.

"Cheat."

Meredith unlocked Mikey's door. "I did not cheat, Mikey. I won fair and square. You're just tired from all that karate. Oops, I mean taekwondo."

"Yeah." He got in the truck and snapped his seatbelt closed.

As they passed the four-gabled Victorian House again on their way home, she noticed the spotty front lawn and the mailbox out front as if it were in a suburban neighborhood. Meredith shook her head. What was such a grand house doing on a busy commercial street? Maybe she and Dani could research the house for their history project. Maybe they could find out who lived there and why the house was empty. Or *was* it empty? Maybe Dani knew about this side of town since she had lived in Whickett all her life. But then again, Dani probably had a project already worked out for them. Meredith decided she wouldn't suggest the scary house unless Dani hadn't come up with anything, and there was very little chance of that.

When she pulled into their driveway, Mikey ripped off his seatbelt, leaped out of the truck, and bolted toward the house before Meredith could get the truck turned off. She shouted out her now-opened driver's side door. "Hey, who's the cheater now?"

"I won. I won." Mikey did his famous happy dance on the front porch.

"Oh, come on, Mikey. You didn't even give me a chance."

Their father opened the front door. "Are you two going to come in or just argue in the cold?"

"I won," Mikey told his father.

"I gathered that. Good for you." He winked at Meredith, who slid by her father into the warmth of the house. He asked her, "How was karate?"

"Taekwondo, Dad," Meredith corrected with a smile. "We had a good time. He did really well today." She thought about the Victorian mansion on Center Street. "Hey, Dad? Do you know that old house next to Fiesta Loca? The one on Center that kind of doesn't belong?"

"Next to the auto parts store?"

"Yeah, that one."

"Scary old thing. What about it?"

"Do you know anything about it? Like, do people still live there?"

Her father laughed. "Why? Are you buying the place?"

"No, Dad," she said with sarcasm.

They walked to the kitchen, and Meredith's father opened the refrigerator to get a cold juice box for Mikey. "Want one?" He held a juice box out toward Meredith.

"No thanks. We might research the old house for our history project."

"Oh, yes, the history project. Your captain of the lacrosse team called." He went to the kitchen table and picked up the sports page. "Her number is right here next to the Superbowl predictions."

Dani called. She actually called. Meredith's heart raced, but out loud, she said calmly, "Okay. Can I take the whole sports section to my room?"

"Yeah, I'm done. She seemed very nice."

Something in his voice made Meredith suspicious. "No, Dad. You didn't."

He feigned a hurt expression. "What? What could your old man possibly do to embarrass you?"

"You didn't tell her that lacrosse wasn't a sport or anything like that, did you?"

"Of course not. I don't know her well enough." He smiled. "Yet."

And you're not going to get to know her because as soon as Dani can swing it, she'll be out of my life. Out loud, she said, "Okay, good. Please don't embarrass me if she calls back, okay?"

His tone turned more serious, and he said, "Okay, I'll be good. I promise. I just asked what her season looked like this year. She said they had a tough schedule, but they should finish in the top two in their division."

"You're such a sports nut." She shook her head, went back into the living room, and hung her heavy winter pea coat on the hook by the front door. She headed to the stairs and called back. "Hey, Dad, I'll call her from upstairs. But then I'd like to go to the library in about an hour. Okay?"

"Okay. The pro bowlers' tour is on. Mikey and I are going to watch a couple of games."

Meredith rolled her eyes at the prospect of her father and brother spending their afternoon watching bowling on television. She could think of a thousand more interesting things to do. Of course, she was planning to go to the library by herself. She laughed at the irony. What an exciting life, she thought.

She went upstairs to her room and wasn't sure what to do about the fact that Dani Lassiter had actually called her. She wasn't sure if she should call her back immediately or wait until after the library. She decided not to decide and plopped down on the bed. The early afternoon sun streamed through the window behind her, making it a perfect time for sketching. But then again, anytime was a good time for drawing.

She pulled out her sketchbook and turned to the first page. The first few sketches were quick, simple drawings of people who had posed like her mother, her father with more hair, and a couple of kids from her old school in Greenspond. Each of them had a rather bland, almost bored expression on their faces. The AP Art curriculum required that students not only have an in-depth exploration of something but also demonstrate growth in the pieces included in their portfolios. She had decided to explore facial expressions and the emotions displayed. Sure, "bored" was an emotion that could be sustained in the face for a long time. What about happiness? The smile she had seen in Dani's eyes the day before, just after the senior class meeting, had only lasted a few seconds. How could an artist capture a fleeting expression like that? And Dani's anger at Ben—that, too, had come and gone quickly. If she intended to show growth in her portraits, she would have to capture all those meteoric emotions of happiness, anger, and love.

Love. Meredith sighed. How was she going to capture love if she'd never experienced it? Well, that wasn't really true. Her parents loved her, and Mikey adored her, but she had never felt the all-consuming-grip-you-by-the-heart love she'd heard about in love songs or read about in senior English. Maybe it wasn't for her.

She took out her sketchbook and grabbed a few colored pencils. On a clean sheet of paper, she sketched a collage of images she had seen at the Martial Arts Academy. Mikey, face determined, making a high kick. The little girl with blond braids, face concentrated with effort, punching forward with one hand, pulling in with the other. She sketched the instructor, expression patient, leading his students through their rounds. Meredith was lost in her sketches when the phone on her bedside stand jangled her back to the real world.

She looked at the caller ID. Lassiter. She took a deep breath. This whole partner thing was going to be nerve-wracking.

"Hello?" Meredith said as if she didn't know who was calling.

"Meredith? This is Dani. Dani Lassiter."

Meredith almost laughed. How could Meredith *not* know who "Dani" was? As if the entire school didn't know who "Dani" was. "Oh, hi," she said coolly. "How are you?"

"Oh, great. I hope I'm not interrupting anything. Your dad said you'd be home from karate by now. What belt do you have?"

Meredith laughed into the phone. "Me? Oh, no. I'm not the one who takes karate. Mikey does. He takes taekwondo on Saturdays."

"Oh."

Meredith sensed the hesitation in Dani's voice.

Dani continued, "Mikey. That's your brother?"

"Yeah, he's in sixth grade."

"Oh, okay. That's nice of you to take him to his class."

Meredith stayed true to her decision to follow Dani's lead. They would talk about whatever Dani wanted to. That would be fine if Dani wanted to spend the next three hours talking about Mikey.

Meredith said, "Yeah, he has a good time in the class."

"Well, uh." Dani took a big breath. She sounded as nervous as Meredith was. "We should talk about our project."

"Okay. What did you have in mind?"

"Oh, well, I don't know. I've been so busy. The Winter Ball is tonight, and exams are coming up, so I haven't spent much time thinking about it. Well, except for thinking about calling you."

Meredith felt herself blush. Dani Lassiter was thinking about her. No, Dani wasn't thinking about her. Dani was thinking about the project, and Meredith was just a minuscule piece of that. Meredith said, "Oh, well, I haven't given it much thought, either." That wasn't exactly the truth, but she would stick to her plan to let Dani make all the decisions.

She heard Dani sigh on the other end of the phone. "Okay, well, I suppose we could interview someone at the Hudson Pines Senior Center."

"Yeah."

"But I bet a ton of people are going to do that. I mean, we *could* do that if you want to." Dani didn't sound enthused.

Was Dani Lassiter being indecisive? This was a new concept for Meredith. Confident, strong, and able Dani Lassiter wasn't sure of something. This was a surprise, but Meredith also surprised herself when she decided to run her idea by Dani. "You know, Mikey and I drove by an old house today. You know that old Victorian house near

Fiesta Loca?"

"The one by the auto parts store?"

Meredith suppressed a laugh. Dani sounded just like her father. "Yeah, that's the one. It creeps Mikey out. Could we research that? Find out who lives there or used to live there? Why does the rest of Center Street have stores but not there?"

"I don't know, but that's an awesome idea. I'm so used to seeing that house at the end of town that it's part of the background for me. All right, let's come up with some ideas for finding the owners. We can go to the village offices and see if they'll tell us. Maybe they'll show us land deeds or something. Is that where they keep that sort of thing, or do we have to go to the county or something? And, ooh, we could go down to the Senior Center. We could ask some of those folks what's up with the house. They've been around longer than we have and might know something about it."

Meredith smiled from ear to ear. Dani liked her idea. Meredith wasn't being railroaded into doing something Dani wanted to do. Maybe this project would work out after all.

Dani rambled on. Meredith fell back into her pillows and simply listened. "We could take pictures and make a PowerPoint presentation. And..." She seemed to run out of ideas. "Meredith? You still there?"

"Yeah, I'm here."

"Oh, okay. I just got excited and kept talking and talking. Hey, what if there's nothing to that old house?"

Meredith hadn't thought of that. "Well, then, I guess we just report that there's not much of a story to it. And then anybody who was curious doesn't have to wonder anymore."

"Ah, good thinking. I'm glad you're my partner. Okay, listen, I have to get ready for the Winter Ball. Are you going?"

Meredith suppressed a laugh. "Uh, no," she said with a touch of sarcasm.

"Oh, sorry. Maybe you can come to the next dance."

Meredith shook her head and laughed to herself. Dani had missed the sarcasm in her voice and acted as if Meredith had other obligations and *couldn't* go to the dance. The truth was, Meredith didn't want to go. Not that anyone had asked her, of course. She simply said, "Yeah, maybe next time."

"I'm going with Ben."

Meredith didn't know what Dani wanted her to say at that moment. So, she didn't say anything.

Dani broke the silence. "I don't know why I'm going with him." She sounded apologetic. "It's just that he's always been my best friend. I've known him since kindergarten."

Meredith still wasn't sure what she was supposed to say, so she just said, "Oh."

"Well, it'll be different once I go to college. I'm sure I'll find some different people to hang out with." Dani sighed loudly into the phone.

Meredith was shocked. *You're the president of the senior class and captain of the lacrosse team. Everybody loves you. What kind of change do you, of all people, need?* Maybe she and Dani had more in common than she thought.

Dani suggested they go to the house together to look it over. They agreed to wait until exams were over and decided to meet the following Friday evening, the last day of exams. Dani was going to pick her up. This was one for the books. Meredith was finally going out on a Friday night, and she was going out with the captain of the lacrosse team. Unfortunately, she was going out with the captain of the *girls'* lacrosse team. She laughed at the twist fate had brought her.

Chapter 4
Cumpnee

Meredith sat at the big open table in the art room, grateful that no other students thought to come by during exam week. Mrs. Levine let students work in the art room any time they wanted to, and Meredith always took advantage of that because the art room was the one place in the school where she felt safe.

She slipped out of the gym quickly after her History exam that morning so Dani wouldn't feel obligated to talk to her. They were doing a project together, and that was all. Meredith didn't want Dani to feel she actually had to go out of her way to be friendly. Once the history project was over, they would go their separate ways again. But then again, Meredith remembered with regret that she wanted to paint Dani for her AP Art portfolio. That would involve being friendly. She sighed. Life was getting complicated.

She didn't have any more exams that day, but she couldn't leave because she would only have to trudge back to walk Mikey home at three o'clock, and she didn't want to venture into the freezing temperature unless she had to. It was easier to simply stay at school and wait for Mikey's day to finish at 3:00.

She opened her sketchpad and turned to her first sketch. Well, it was a partial sketch of Dani. The one with the happy eyes. Yes, she firmly decided. She had to paint Dani no matter what. Dani's eyes were so expressive that she just had to get her to pose. Catching Dani Lassiter's fleeting emotions would be difficult, but Meredith knew she could do it. That is, if Dani didn't go running for the hills when Meredith asked. Nah, knowing Dani, she would be overly polite with her refusal, leaving Meredith feeling weird for asking in the first place.

Mrs. Levine walked into the room. She carried her mail in one hand and a steaming cup of what looked like coffee in the other. She smiled when she saw Meredith.

"It's good to see you here. All done with exams for the day?"

Meredith returned the smile. "Mm hmm. Just history today. My hand feels like it's going to fall off from writing so much."

"Mr. Dalton?"

Meredith laughed. "Yeah, how'd you know?"

"He has a reputation for making his students write a lot of essays. Good luck with his final exam in June." She lifted her coffee cup in salute.

"Thanks, I think."

"How many exams do you have left?"

"Nothing tomorrow. Econ on Thursday and math on Friday."

Mrs. Levine put her mail on the worktable. "I'm sure you'll do fine." She came up behind Meredith and looked at her sketchpad. Normally, Meredith didn't allow anyone to look at her sketches, but she trusted Mrs. Levine. Besides, the sketches were a requirement for the class, so Mrs. Levine would see them anyway.

"Meredith, this is wonderful. Look how you've captured the feeling in her expression. It's a *her*, right?"

Meredith nodded.

"The short hair almost fooled me, but you've definitely captured an expression of happiness or joy. Like something just went well in your subject's life."

Meredith smiled. "Thank you. I thought I'd captured the feeling but wasn't sure."

"Who is this person? If you don't mind me asking."

"Oh, that's Dani. Dani Lassiter." Meredith blushed and then wondered why talking about Dani Lassiter made her blush.

"Senior?" A look of realization crossed her face. "Oh, I know who she is. She's the president of the senior class, right?"

"Yeah."

"Pretty girl. Tall. High cheekbones. Amazing blue eyes, right?"

Meredith prayed Mrs. Levine wouldn't notice her red cheeks. "Yeah. I'm, uh, thinking about painting her as part of my AP portfolio."

"What a wonderful subject. You know—" Her art teacher pointed at Meredith and went back to her pile of mail. She tucked an escaped lock of blond hair behind her ear as she looked through the papers. "I think her name is on the roster for the Senior Art Elective." She found the class roster in the pile and ran her finger down the list. "Yes, here she is. Danielle A. Lassiter. I bet we can find some way to give you two time for painting and posing."

"Oh, but…"

"I know why you're hesitating. She might be embarrassed posing in front of the other kids. People can become self-conscious when posing, but you can use my private workroom in the back." She pointed to the door at the back of the classroom.

Meredith wasn't sure what to say. This was moving way too fast. "Thank you, but I haven't even asked her yet. She might not want to do it."

"Okay, okay. You're right. I'm getting ahead of myself. You go ahead and ask her."

"Thanks. And I did another one of her, too." Meredith turned to the sketch of Dani's eyes flaring at Ben. The anger seethed off the page.

"Wow," Mrs. Levine said slowly. "I would *not* want to be on the receiving end of that fury. She wasn't looking at *you* with that anger, was she?"

"No. She got mad at somebody one day, and I just caught her expression in my mind. I don't know how to describe it, but I took, like, a mental photograph. I did the sketch over the weekend."

"Meredith Bedford, you're telling me that you did this sketch of Dani Lassiter from memory?"

"Yeah."

Her art teacher shook her head slowly. "That's amazing. I wish I had your talent."

Meredith felt her cheeks burn again. Her art teacher had just given her the highest compliment anyone could have given her. She wasn't sure how to handle such high praise, so she said, "Thanks. But you're talented. All of us kids know that."

Mrs. Levine smiled. "And you're kind, too." She sighed. "Well, I'm going to sort through my mail. Let me know if this Dani says no to posing. I might be able to change her mind."

"Okay, thanks. I'll let you know what she says."

Meredith looked back at her sketch of Dani. The fire in her eyes scared her a little. Mrs. Levine was right. Meredith didn't ever want that expression shot her way.

~~~

Meredith sat on the couch in the living room, watching a SpongeBob DVD with Mikey. Mikey, mesmerized by the cartoon, sat planted on the carpet cross-legged with his elbows on his knees and his chin resting on both fists. Meredith barely registered the crazy antics of SpongeBob and Patrick the starfish because she was trying her very best not to be nervous. Dani was coming to pick her up to go to the old Victorian house in a matter of minutes.

Meredith's mother came into the living room from the kitchen. She wore a red-checkered apron around her waist and was drying a pot with a matching hand towel. "Oh, Meredith, you look so nice. I love that red sweater on you. Are you going to keep your hair back? You have such a pretty face. You should keep it back while you're working with your friend."

"Mom, c'mon," Meredith said through clenched teeth. "I have my hair pulled back because I used that new acne foam the dermatologist gave me. Stop fussing, okay? I'm just doing a project with her."

"Oh, honey, I know. I just wanted you to know that you look nice because you haven't had many friends come by the house since we moved here."

Meredith cringed. *That's because I don't have any friends.* Out loud, she said, "Okay, okay. I'll keep my hair back."

"And I'll let you be." She laughed and turned to Mikey. "Doesn't Merry look nice, Mikey?"

"Yeah," he said without turning around.

"See?" Her mother pointed toward Mikey with the pot in her hand.

"Oh, Mom."

Just then, a car door slammed in the driveway.

Her mother turned to go but said, "I'll be in the kitchen. Introduce your new friend when she comes in, okay?"

"Okay." Meredith decided to wait until Dani rang the bell. She didn't want to appear too eager.

When the doorbell rang, Mikey leaped up and yelled, "Cumpnee." This was his version of the word "company."

"I'll get it, Mikey." Meredith got up from the couch.

"No! Me." He raced to the door.

Okay, well, we might as well get this part over with first. Dani would meet Mikey right away, and then they would have that behind them.

Meredith sat on the edge of the couch and watched her brother pull the heavy front door open. He looked up at Dani, who stood outside on the stoop behind the glass storm door, and said, "Hi."

"Well, hi, right back." Dani looked down at Mikey. "Is Meredith home?"

Mikey did not open the storm door to let Dani in but turned and yelled, "Merry! Cumpnee!"

Meredith stood up from the couch. "Mikey, it's okay. You can let her in."

"Okay." He turned back to Dani and opened the storm door for her. "Come in, pwease."

"Thank you." Dani stepped into the house and smiled at Mikey and then at Meredith.

Dani looked nice in dark blue jeans and a yellow turtleneck that peeked out from under her green and yellow Whickett lacrosse jacket. The yellow complemented her blond hair. Dani didn't have a hat on, and Meredith thought she must be cold. No gloves, either. She must be superhuman.

Dani nodded her head toward Mikey. "Cute."

Meredith couldn't help but smile. "Thanks." Meredith thought that if everyone could just meet Mikey, they would immediately know how great he was. She said to her brother, "Mikey, close the front door, okay?"

"Okay." He closed the heavy door and stood beside Dani, staring up at her.

Meredith shook her head and laughed. "Mikey, I want you to meet Dani." She then looked at Dani and said, "Dani, this is my brother, Mikey."

Dani stuck out her hand. "Hey, dude. What's up?"

"What up?" Mikey laughed and put his hand in hers. They shook vigorously. "Dude," he added when he finally released Dani's hand.

Dani leaned down so Mikey wouldn't have to strain his neck to look up at her. "Hey, dude, I hear you're into karate."

He mumbled something, and Dani looked to Meredith for a translation.

"Oh," Meredith said, "he said, 'taekwondo.' Don't worry. I always get it wrong, too."

"Oh, okay." Dani turned back to Mikey. "Can you show me some of your taekwondo moves?"

Meredith motioned for Dani to back up. "Mikey, show her the warm-up routine you do with your instructor."

"Okay." He then proceeded to throw several punches and kicks, each one propelled by his spirit yell. He ended his routine and then bowed to Dani.

Dani bowed back with a look of utter disbelief on her face. "Mikey, dude, that was amazing. A lot of kicking and kind of loud, but amazing." She looked at Meredith. "He's great."

"Thanks. I can use him for protection if I ever need it." Meredith meant it as a joke, but when Dani's face turned serious, she realized she had hit a little close to home. Dani had, after all, protected her from Ben's verbal abuse the other day in class. And Dani, with their lockers so close, must have seen all the times kids *accidentally* knocked into her in the hallway.

Dani said thoughtfully, "Well, let's hope it never comes to that."

Meredith knew she was probably blushing, so she rushed past Dani to grab her coat off the hook near the front door.

"Comes to what?" Meredith's mother asked as she stepped into the living room.

Meredith swallowed hard. "Oh, nothing. Mikey was showing us his moves."

"Yeah, I heard." She turned toward Dani and said, "You must be Danielle. I'm Meredith's mom."

"Nice to meet you." Dani offered her hand. Meredith's mother shook it and nodded.

"I hope you girls—"

She stopped her sentence short because Mikey rushed over to Dani. Apparently, he wanted another handshake, too. Dani smiled at him and stuck out her hand. As they shook hands, Dani said again, "Nice to meet you, dude."

"Meet cha, dude," he mimicked and gave Dani another tight hug around the waist.

"Oof." Dani coughed and changed her voice to sound as if Mikey had knocked the wind out of her. "Strong, too." In a normal voice, she said to Meredith's mother, "He's great."

"Yeah, we like him. We think we'll keep him."

At Dani's perplexed expression, Meredith's mother added, "That was just a joke, Danielle. You two girls have fun and stay warm. Meredith, do you have your gloves?"

Meredith nodded.

"And your hat?"

"Yeah, Mom. I'll be fine. I don't think we'll be gone that long." Meredith just wanted to look at the house, divvy up the work, and then come home. She didn't want Dani to be subjected to her any longer than necessary.

"Okay, you girls have a good time." Meredith's mother headed back into the kitchen.

"Bye, Mom." To Mikey, she said, "And you have fun watching SpongeBob. I think you missed some. Do you want me to start it over?"

He didn't say anything but just stared blankly at his sister. He then looked at Dani and said, "Ki come?"

Dani looked perplexed again and said to Meredith, "I need a translator, I think."

"He wants to come."

"Oh, he can come if it's okay with your mom."

"Are you sure?"

"Yeah, I have three seat belts in the front of the pickup."

"Okay, let me go ask. We won't be too long, right?" Meredith tried to keep her smile hidden. Dani had a pickup like her dad. Meredith knew she would be in trouble if Dani and her Dad ever met. And it almost sounded like Dani didn't mind hanging out with her. *And* with Mikey. Confused by this apparent turn of events, Meredith went to check with her mother.

Meredith returned to the living room with two thumbs up and handed Mikey his coat.

Dani smiled at Mikey. "Yeah, dude! You can come."

"Yeah, dude!" Mikey said and waited for his big sister to start the zipper to his coat.

Dani said to Meredith under her breath, "And if we need any protecting," she pointed to Mikey, "we'll be all set."

"Absolutely. Let's go."

Dani's pickup truck was a lot newer than Meredith's father's. The white exterior looked freshly washed, and the burgundy interior looked and smelled like someone had recently cleaned with Armor All. Mikey sat in the middle of the truck's front seat, which comfortably held the three of them.

"Nice truck," Meredith said once they were buckled in and on their way down Center Street.

Dani looked at Meredith over the top of Mikey's head. "Thanks. It's my dad's, but he usually drives his Honda to and from work. He lets me use his truck if he doesn't need it, so I basically use it all the time. Someday, I'll get my own, though."

"You really want a truck? Not a sports car or something?"

"Nah. You sit high up in a truck. And if you have to haul cargo, you've got the room."

"Okay." Meredith thought about it for a moment and asked, "What *cargo* do you plan on hauling?"

Dani laughed, and Meredith smiled because she liked the sound.

Dani looked at her and said, "Well, you got me on that one. I don't know. I've just always liked trucks. Probably because my dad does."

"That's cool, I guess. Oh, I brought my digital camera, by the way. My grandparents gave it to me for Christmas. We might be able to get some good pictures with the flash, seeing as it's dark."

"Yeah, I know. We didn't think about the fact that the sun goes down early, did we? Did we, Mikey?"

"No," he said and smiled up at Dani.

Dani looked at him and said, "But we're going to be okay because Center Street is so lit up, they can see us from space."

Meredith chuckled and squeezed her brother's hand. He had grabbed her hand the moment they got in the truck. He was probably a little nervous about the new truck and the new person in his sister's life.

Mikey reached up and grabbed at Dani's hand on the steering wheel. Dani looked at Meredith, presumably for a translation of his gesture. "I think he wants to hold your hand, too."

"Oh, okay. Gee, I'm a little slow."

Meredith watched Dani cringe.

"Oh, Meredith. I'm sorry. I didn't mean that. That came out wrong." Dani took Mikey's hand in hers.

Meredith couldn't see but figured Dani was probably turning red. "It's okay. You didn't mean it. And hey, he's heard worse." Although Meredith felt bad that Dani was embarrassed by her slip, she couldn't help but turn her artist's eye toward Dani's new expression. She hadn't seen this one before. Embarrassment. She took a mental photograph of the moment and knew she was going to add one more sketch to her growing collection of the many moods of Dani Lassiter.

They pulled into the parking lot of the auto parts store. Mikey fumbled with his seatbelt and said, "Weddy, Merry?" He wanted to race.

They stepped out of the truck, and Meredith grabbed him by the shoulders. She said, "No, Mikey, we're not going to the store."

She looked toward the store and saw three guys, probably in their mid- to late twenties, hovering over the open hood of a blue sports car. One of the guys, the one with the weak mustache, leaned into the engine with a cigarette dangling from his mouth. Meredith thought that probably wasn't the safest thing to do, and she wanted to get as far away from them as possible. One of the other guys, the one with the dark complexion and dark hair, pointed to something deep in the engine and told the cigarette guy how to do something. The third guy wore a red checkered hunter's jacket and just looked bored. Meredith turned away, but something about them made her uneasy.

Meredith shrugged off her unease and turned Mikey to face the dark, four-gabled Victorian House. "We're going to take pictures of that house."

"Scawey house."

"What?" Dani had come around to their side of the truck.

"Oh, we always pass this old house on the way to kar—. Oops, taekwondo, and he calls it the scary house."

"Yeah, it does look kind of scary. Is he going to be okay with this?"

"We'll find out, won't we? Hey, Mikey. Let's go take some pictures, okay?"

He took a big breath and exhaled loudly. "Okay, Merry." He reached up for her hand.

Dani went to his other side and held out her hand. He grabbed it without looking. He just stared at the scary house looming in front of them. As they headed down the sidewalk to the front gate, Meredith was overcome with emotion at the kindness Dani showed her brother. She looked at Dani through a slight haze of tears in her eyes. When Dani looked back and smiled, Meredith blinked back her tears and mouthed, "Thank you." She dropped her chin slightly to indicate Mikey.

Dani continued to smile. She said in a low voice, "No problem. He's sweet."

Meredith could have sworn Dani was blushing again. Maybe Dani was sincere after all.

With no lights and no signs of life, the house was positively creepy. The chain link fence around the property stood like a metal sentry warning passersby to stay out. Lights from the neighboring stores created eerie shadows across the face of the dark house and yard. The upstairs balcony, quaint by day, was gloomy and foreboding by night. The dark house now seemed cold and inhospitable, and

Meredith didn't much feel like a tea party anymore.

The century-old oak tree that towered over the house creaked and moaned, and Meredith felt a chill go up her spine at the sound. In the dark, she couldn't make out the wonderful rose color of the exterior, but she held onto the fact that the bright color was there because otherwise, she might lose her nerve and run back to the truck. Why had they come in the dark?

They stopped in front of the gate that opened to a concrete walkway leading to the front porch. Meredith let go of Mikey's hand to take her camera out of its case. "Let me take a couple of pictures. I can zoom in on anything you want, so if you see something, point it out." She turned on the flash and snapped a few pictures of the front of the house. She took wide shots to include the yard and a couple of close-ups. "It's such a beautiful house, you know?"

Dani grunted in disbelief. "Yeah, well, it's kind of creepy right now. We should have come in the daytime."

"Yeah, duh. Live and learn, I guess."

Dani said, "Hey, Mikey. You want to go up to the house with me?"

"No." He pulled her away from the gate that she had just unlatched.

"How about you?" Dani asked Meredith. "Do you want to go up?"

"I'd better stay here with the scaredy-cat."

"Would that be him or you?" Dani laughed and extracted her hand from Mikey's. She stopped laughing as soon as she stepped inside the yard. The dark shadows seemed to suck away her bravada. The long path to the house was choked with dead grass. As she picked her way carefully over the terrain, she turned her head and said to Meredith, "We should have brought some flashlights."

Meredith fidgeted where she stood on the sidewalk. They didn't have permission to take pictures of someone's private property, let alone trespass in the yard. "Dani," she pleaded, her voice barely above a whisper, "maybe you should come back."

"No," Dani called back, "it's cool. I'm just going to check out the front porch. Maybe look in the windows. If the coast is clear, you guys should come up. Okay?"

"Okay," Meredith said with resignation. "Hey, Mikey Spikey, let's get ready to walk up to the front door."

"Scawey."

"Oh, I know it's scary, but Dani's up there, and she's very brave. And, besides, Mikey, *you* are the only one of us who knows taekwondo. What if Dani needs you?"

He looked at her as if considering this and said, "Okay, Merry, c'mon." He pulled her by the hand through the open gate and practically dragged her up the walkway.

Meredith called, "I hope the coast is clear because we're on our way."

"I see you had no choice." Dani smiled.

"None."

"Hey, Meredith. Take my picture on the landing."

"Okay." She pulled Mikey to a stop. "Wait a second, Mikey. Let me take Dani's picture."

Dani held the banister with one hand while the other was shoved deep in her bulky letterman's jacket. Meredith snapped the picture. She zoomed in a little and snapped another but watched in horror as Dani and the banister tumbled to the ground.

"Dani!" Meredith screeched and ran to her. Dani sat in the wilds of what used to be a flower garden. The flowers were long dead from the winter cold.

"Oh, my God. Dani, are you okay?" Meredith searched for breaks and bruises. She grabbed Dani by the arm and patted her up and down. She even felt Dani's forehead as if Dani had a fever. She stopped when she saw Dani grinning at her.

Meredith smacked her in the arm. "Cut it out. I thought you were hurt."

"Is that all you've got? We've got to get you into some kind of weight training program. Gee whiz."

With that comment, Dani could have been her father's clone, but Meredith ignored it and said, "Are you okay?"

Dani locked eyes with Meredith and said, "You're cute when you're worried."

Meredith felt her face grow hot. "Oh, stop that. I was afraid you got hurt."

"I may have bruised my ego a little, but I'm okay." Dani reached a hand toward Meredith's face. "You're very pretty with your hair pulled back, you know."

Meredith leaned back out of reach, mortified. Dani had almost touched her acne scars. Meredith knew she was blushing furiously, and if she didn't know better, she would have thought that Dani Lassiter was flirting with her.

Dani pulled her hand back. "Why don't you wear your hair back at school?"

"I don't know," she stammered. "I guess I don't want to be seen." She instantly regretted saying it. She never thought she would admit that to anyone. She barely admitted it to herself.

Dani brushed herself off and stood up. "Well, I think you need to be seen from now on. Starting on Monday."

Meredith started to protest, but their conversation abruptly ended when Mikey launched himself at Dani, sending them both sprawling back to the ground. "You 'kay, Dani?"

Dani laughed. "Mikey, I'm okay. Really." To Meredith, she said, "He said my name. Did you hear that?"

"Yeah, he's quick like that."

Dani smiled and got up. "Hey, let's go get hot chocolate and cookies. This ground is cold." She stopped and looked at Meredith. "Oh, can he have sweets?"

"Sure, why not? Let's get out of here. Cookies, Mikey?"

"Cookies! Yeah." Mikey heartily agreed with the change in plans for the evening.

They stood up to go, but something caught Dani's eye. "Hey, look at this banister I broke." Dani pointed to something in the shadowy darkness. "It looks cut at the base, like with a hacksaw or something. See where it's smooth all the way around except right here in the middle, where it's all splintery? It wasn't cut all the way through. It almost looks like someone meant for the banister to break like it did."

Meredith looked at Dani with concern. "There may be more to this house than we bargained for. Let's get out of here."

Halfway down the overgrown walkway, a loud bang shattered the quiet air. Meredith knocked into Dani, who in turn grabbed onto Meredith's coat sleeve to keep her balance.

Meredith whispered urgently, "Did you hear that?"

"Yeah," Dani said, still holding onto Meredith's sleeve. "It came from inside the house. Let's get out of here."

Meredith grabbed Mikey's hand, and the three of them ran down the concrete steps and through the open gate. They didn't stop running until they reached the pickup truck. Meredith's eyes grew wide when she realized that the blue sports car was still there, but not a single one of the three guys was in sight.

Chapter 5
The Protector

The first half of Meredith's senior year was finally over. What a relief. But when one thing ended, another began; in this case, that was second semester. She sat at the big worktable in the art room and waited for her new course, Senior Art Elective, to start. The art class was filled with mostly seniors who needed to fulfill the fine arts half-credit required for graduation. Meredith hoped she'd learn something new even though this was a beginner's course. Art was ever-evolving, and Meredith knew she'd be learning all her life.

Four tables placed together formed the large student work area. Naturally, she had plenty of space around her because the other seniors in the new class, about twenty or so, crammed themselves into the chairs well away from where Meredith sat by the windows. She sighed when she realized what was happening again. In fact, she had an empty seat on either side of her. Clearly, the other students did not want to be associated with her. Less than one hundred days of high school left. She could make it. Endings created beginnings, after all. And after high school, she would create a new beginning at Syracuse University. If she got in, that is.

Mrs. Levine bustled around the room, getting ready for the new semester. She reached around Meredith to place a basket of fruit in the middle of the work area. The bananas had definitely seen better days because several had brown spots. And some kind of genetic engineering had gone into creating the orange because it was an almost unworldly color. The huge, Delicious apples looked so shiny. Meredith figured they could make candles from the wax.

"What do you think, Meredith? Think this bunch is ready for a still life?"

Meredith laughed. "I'm not sure about that, but I guess they have to start somewhere, right?"

Mrs. Levine patted Meredith on the shoulder, and Meredith saw the other students look her way. She sensed their confusion with Mrs. Levine's obvious familiarity with her. Most students didn't know that Meredith was in the AP Art class, but that was because most students didn't know Meredith at all. How Dani knew she took AP Art was a real mystery. She smiled in spite of herself. In this class, at least, she was in her element. Maybe she wouldn't have to hide so much. She couldn't make up her mind that morning whether or not to pull her hair back in a ponytail like Dani wanted her to, but ultimately decided against it. She would pull it back for Art like always, but then she'd yank out the rubber band before heading to Mr. Dalton's seventh-period history class.

And where was Dani? She was supposed to be in this art class. Maybe she decided to drop. Maybe she didn't want to spend so much time with Meredith after all. By the time Meredith had almost convinced herself that Dani was trying to get out of her life, a blur of Whickett green and yellow barreled through the door.

"Am I late?" Dani asked no one in particular. "We went out for lunch, and I forgot when sixth period started." The bell rang. "Ah, I made it." She looked up and saw Meredith at the far end of the art room near the windows. "Meredith! Long time no see." Dani sauntered over to Meredith, threw her book bag on the floor, and plopped down in an empty chair beside her.

Meredith saw the other students turn their heads again and whisper to each other. *Yeah, that's right. The president of the senior class is sitting next to me.* Meredith sat a little higher in her chair. She hoped that Dani wouldn't take too much flak for associating with the class outcast. She nodded hello.

"Did we start yet?" Dani whispered.

Meredith shook her head no.

"Hey, how's my dude, Mikey?"

"Oh, he's fine." Meredith smiled. She remembered how great Dani had been with her brother when they had gone out for hot chocolate and cookies the Friday before. "He kept talking about you all weekend. Dani this and Dani that."

"Yeah? He did? Tell him I said, 'Hi.' No, wait. Tell him I said, 'Hi, dude.'" Dani reached into her book bag but then stopped. She looked perplexed. "What do we need for this class?"

Meredith laughed at Dani's confusion. "Mrs. Levine will probably give us supplies today, but eventually, you'll have to buy your own. We'll probably use graphite pencils for the still life." She gestured at the fruit.

"Still life. What does that mean? Life that is still?"

Meredith smiled at Dani's ignorance. "You really haven't been around an art room since middle school, have you?"

"I told you I was inept. You're supposed to help me."

Meredith couldn't help it and actually smiled. "A *still life* is a piece of art that depicts inanimate objects. You can take anything, like the fruit Mrs. Levine put out or shells or kitchen utensils or whatever and draw them."

"Why would you want to do that?" Dani blinked several times in apparent disbelief.

"Well, for one thing, the artist has control over the objects in a still life. But with, say, a landscape, you draw what's already there. You can't manipulate the scenery. Here, though, Mrs. Levine could have put the bananas in the back instead of on top. Do you see? And each one of us has a slightly different perspective on the bowl. Those kids across from us can see the full orange, while we only see the top. We see the entire apple—"

"While they only see part of it. Okay, I get that. But what makes this art? Why do I want a picture of fruit on my wall?"

Meredith laughed again. "You're funny, but at least you're asking questions. Most people don't get it at all. Sometimes, it's just art for art's sake."

"Oh, now that's clear...not."

Meredith smiled. "Sometimes we do art just for the sake of doing art and not for any other reason. Artists just enjoy the process. Mrs. Levine told the AP class that art doesn't always have to make a big moral or historical statement. And the art doesn't even have to be displayed once it's done. But Mrs. Levine will probably display our still lifes on one of the bulletin boards. When we look at everybody else's stuff, we'll see how differently people see the same objects. Some people will focus on the colors. Some on the shapes. And some will focus on the contrast—the interplay of light and dark."

"I think I just got schooled." Dani grinned at her.

Meredith wondered if she had gone too far. "Oh, sorry." She dropped her gaze, embarrassed.

"Oh, my God, Meredith. Don't be sorry for being smart. You really know what you're talking about."

"Thanks, I think."

"What, uh, focus are you going to use?"

"Mainly the interplay of light and dark, but I'll keep all three in mind." Meredith unzipped her vinyl pencil case and took out a handful of colored pencils.

"Well, that's why you're in the AP Art class, I guess."

"I guess. Anyway, Mrs. Levine told us the ancient Egyptians hung still life paintings in the tombs of their dead because they believed the stuff in the paintings would become real and feed the dead person in the afterlife."

"Oh, now that's gross."

Meredith giggled. "No, it's not. I think it's fascinating."

Mrs. Levine called the class to order and had the students put their book bags in their newly-assigned cubbies. Meredith had already stored hers, so she opened up the fresh sketchpad she'd bought over the weekend because she didn't want to mix up her AP art sketches with the sketches for this class. She raked her hair back with both hands and pulled her dark waves into a bundle. She held her hair back with her left hand and, feeling playful, held her right wrist out to Dani. Dani looked at her perplexed, but then realization hit her face. She pulled the rubber band off Meredith's wrist and placed it in her open palm. Meredith smiled and put the rubber band around her hair. Dani nodded at her in approval.

As expected, Mrs. Levine wanted the students to draw the still life using graphite pencils. Before she let them start, however, she explained the concept of composition. She wanted them to find just the right balance, not too big and not too small, for the objects on their paper. She also reminded them to keep the size relationship realistic among the objects. No huge bananas. That brought a snicker from several of the boys in the class.

When Dani reached for one of Meredith's colored pencils, Meredith shook her head. Dani then slowly reached for one of the 2B graphite pencils, and Meredith nodded. Colored pencils would have been too overwhelming for Dani's first attempt at drawing since middle school.

Still lifes were not her favorite type of drawing because Meredith preferred portraits, but she didn't mind because she was happy whenever she was drawing. In fact, she had been so absorbed with her sketch that she was shocked when Mrs. Levine announced that the class was almost over.

Mrs. Levine told them they would continue working on their still life sketches the next day. Of course, by that time, the bananas would look even worse. Meredith laughed and thought Mrs. Levine should have used plastic fruit, especially in a beginner's course.

Dani leaned against Meredith's arm to see Meredith's drawing. She fell back in her chair, defeated. "Meredith. Oh, my God. Yours is so good. It looks just like a bowl of fruit. Look at mine." She slid her drawing toward Meredith.

Meredith covered her mouth with her hand. "Oh, umm, well, uh, that's...Sure, that's a good start." The composition was awkward. The tiny blob of fruit looked as if an evil scientist had shrunk it. Meredith pointed this out to Dani, who looked utterly defeated.

Dani sighed. "I have a lot to learn, I guess. But I have the best teacher right here sitting next to me. Should I start over tomorrow?"

Meredith nodded. "Probably." And by "probably," she meant "definitely."

Dani sounded helpless. "I don't even know where to start."

"No problem. Tomorrow's a new day."

The bell rang, and Meredith put her colored pencils back in their case. She still wasn't sure if Dani's friendliness was genuine or if she was just trying to get help passing the class. Meredith didn't care. Not really. She would share her expertise willingly. Even if Dani was using her, at least it kind of felt like friendship.

Meredith pulled the rubber band out of her hair and slipped it back over her wrist. She shook her long hair free so it fell around her face.

"Meredith, don't do that." Dani looked disappointed. "You promised."

Meredith shrugged and looked away. She had never *promised* anything. She ripped the still life out of her sketchbook and got up to get her book bag.

Mrs. Levine came by to collect their sketches. She picked up Dani's and said, "Thank you, Danielle." She glanced at the drawing and said, "Okay, tomorrow, we'll talk about composition, okay?"

Dani blushed. "Okay. I'm new at this stuff."

"That's fine," Mrs. Levine said.

With a sigh, Dani went to her cubby and yanked out her yellow and green book bag. She hiked it over her right shoulder. The book bag matched her letterman's jacket.

Mrs. Levine looked at Meredith and asked, "So, have you asked her yet?" Her teacher looked from Meredith to Dani and back again.

The look of mortification on Meredith's face must have been obvious because Mrs. Levine hastened to cover her error. "Oops, sorry. Never mind. You two had better get on to class. I'll see you both tomorrow." Flustered, she looked at Meredith and added, "Well, actually, I'll see *you* back here in about forty-five minutes." She picked up Meredith's still life and scampered to her private workroom.

Dani looked at her with questions in her eyes. "What did you want to ask me?" She turned toward the classroom door.

Meredith followed, "Oh, nothing. Nothing."

"Are you sure? You can ask me anything."

"I...no. It's nothing." Meredith didn't feel like getting rejected. She'd just had a good art class and didn't want to have the mood spoiled.

Meredith was pleased that she had two periods of art for an entire semester, but, unfortunately, she had to schlep to Mr. Dalton's history class in between. Dani led the way out the door and into the bustling hallway, but Meredith lagged behind to give Dani time and space to get away. She wanted Dani to know that she wasn't obliged to walk all the way to Mr. Dalton's second-floor classroom with her. She wanted Dani to know that she didn't presume they were friends just because they were in the same art class and doing a history project together. She silently wished for those less-than-one-hundred days of school to speed along so she could get out and start her life over.

"Hey, slowpoke," Dani called back to her. "Are you coming?"

Meredith looked up from behind her hair curtain. She sighed and quickened her pace to catch up to the mighty Dani Lassiter.

"I thought you were taking the scenic route or something. Hey, I have to stop at my locker. Can you wait?"

"Uh, sure." They reached their row of lockers just as a group of junior guys, basketball players, came roaring down the hall. One of the guys veered from his path, and Meredith braced herself. She was only sorry that Dani had to witness it. The tall, beefy basketball player lowered his shoulder and sent Meredith crashing into the lockers. Luckily, her book bag took most of the force. She heard the guys congratulate their friend on his "direct hit." Meredith willed herself not to cry. Less than one hundred days.

"Hey," Dani called after them. They didn't turn around and were soon out of earshot. "Jerk!" She turned to face Meredith. "Oh, my God, Meredith. Are you okay? That idiot did that on purpose. Why didn't you do something? Why did you just take that?"

The million-dollar question. Meredith didn't know what to say. The silence between them in the noisy hallway was deafening.

"Meredith, we have to report them."

Meredith knew a look of fear took over her face. "No." Her voice came out a little too high-pitched, so she cleared her throat and tried again. "No, Dani. That'll just make it worse."

"Worse? How? They can't do that to you." Dani sounded shocked that this sort of thing happened in her school, but this was Meredith's everyday existence at wonderful Whickett High.

Meredith steeled her chin and said, "Yes, they can, Dani. And they do. And we're going to be late." Meredith pushed past her and headed toward their history class.

The late bell marked Meredith's entrance into Mr. Dalton's classroom.

"You just made it, Miss Bedford," Mr. Dalton said from behind his desk.

Meredith smiled sheepishly and made her way, head down, to her usual seat in the back of the room. Dani burst through the door seconds later.

"Nice of you to join us, Miss Lassiter. We're not keeping you from anything, are we?"

"Sorry, Mr. D., it won't happen again."

"See that it doesn't."

Dani nodded and slid into her usual seat. She dropped her book bag on the floor. Ben patted Dani on the shoulder a couple of times as if to say, "Way to be late, loser."

Meredith took her history spiral from her book bag and opened it to a fresh page. A new semester, a new page. She wished she could do that with her own life. A new semester, a new life. Ah, but that new semester would have to wait until Syracuse. In September. Too many days away to count. She rested her head on a closed fist and looked out the second-floor window on another gray January day.

Mr. Dalton handed back their semester exams. Meredith was

pleased. She had gotten a *B*+. She wasn't one of those students who needed an *A* in every class. She was happy if she had tried her best and passed the class. Well, unless it was an art class. She had to get at least an A in her art classes, or she wouldn't be happy with herself. She couldn't see Dani's grade, but Ben had gotten a *C*-. A generous *C*- from Mr. Dalton, no doubt.

Mr. Dalton paced in the front of the classroom as the discussion about the exam took about half the period. He collected the exams back from them because they had to go into permanent storage or something. Meredith figured the permanent storage was the landfill on the Northway. What was the point of hanging onto them? What was done was done like the guy who smacked her into the lockers right before class. It was done and over with, and there was no sense worrying about it. If she turned him in, then he'd get back at her somehow. She decided to count the days and try to remain invisible.

"Ladies and gentlemen," Mr. Dalton rapped his knuckles on his desk. "May I have your attention, please?"

The students cut short whatever conversations they had started during the short handing-back-in-of-the-exams time. Meredith, of course, spoke to no one during that short time, and no one spoke to her. Instead, under the cover of her hair, she listened to Dani and Sarah, the co-captains of the lacrosse team, talk about the lacrosse workouts starting later that day in the weight room. Sarah complained about having to do the workouts. She whined that they shouldn't have to start working out now because the actual practices with lacrosse sticks weren't even starting until early March, over two months away. Meredith wondered how someone with an attitude like Sarah's was elected captain of a team. It must have been a popularity contest. Meredith instantly felt bad about her quick judgment because that would imply that Dani had been elected on popularity alone.

Meredith knew differently. Dani was popular, all right, but with good reason. She was a natural leader. Meredith was sure that Dani had earned her captainship.

Meredith looked up when Mr. Dalton passed out the handouts for the second-semester project. Without turning around, the boy in front of her held the paper high over his head and let it fall back toward Meredith's desk. Instead of looking foolish trying to catch it, Meredith waited until the paper floated gently to the floor by the heater under the window. She heard some stifled snickering but ignored it and got up to retrieve her handout.

"Okay, people, settle down." Mr. Dalton reached for a dry-erase marker and wrote "The History of Whickett" on the whiteboard. "As promised, we're going to explore your home town. We're going to find out how Whickett got to be, well, Whickett. If you refer to your handout, you'll see that I want you to find a person, landmark, or event that is or was significant to the history of the village. You can look for something that Whickett is well known for. Has anything of historical significance happened here? Are there any famous people from Whickett? Perhaps your own family has been part of Whickett's long history. Tell us about that. Interview some of the seniors at Hudson Pines. Maybe some of those folks can give you a better idea what Whickett was like back in the day." Mr. Dalton paced in front of the class as he read from the handout.

Meredith noted that her classmates were fairly attentive during the project description, probably because the project was worth one-quarter of their second-semester grade.

Mr. Dalton paced on. "Find an old building in town or on the outskirts. Anywhere. Go to the village offices and find out anything you can."

Dani turned and nodded to Meredith at the mention of an old

building. Meredith nodded back. She listened to her history teacher explain the requirements. When he mentioned a PowerPoint presentation, Dani turned around again and smiled at her. Dani had suggested they do a PowerPoint. She wasn't sure why, but Dani's attention made her uneasy. Usually, when she got attention at school, it wasn't good. She shifted in her seat, looked down, and pretended to focus on the handout. She didn't want to catch any more of Dani's acknowledgments if she could help it.

Mr. Dalton stopped pacing and sat on the edge of his desk. He smoothed down the ends of his dark mustache and looked at his students. "I've contacted the Hudson Pines Senior Center, and they're quite pleased to be included in our project. They're expecting a bunch of Whickett High seniors this Saturday at around three o'clock. They told me you could stay as long as you like. So just show up and tell them who you are, and they'll hook you up with someone to talk to."

Meredith looked up to catch Dani's mouth, "You want to go?" Meredith nodded and looked down when Ben, Sarah, and Jeff turned her way.

Ben leaned over to Dani and whispered, "Make sure you de-flea your truck after."

Sarah and Jeff laughed openly. Dani sank lower in her seat. She did not acknowledge Ben's attempt at humor.

Sarah whispered, "C'mon, Dani. He was just kidding." Dani didn't acknowledge Sarah, either.

"So," Mr. Dalton concluded, "your project proposals are due in two weeks. Those are to be typed, by the way." He waited for the groans to die down. "Two weeks after that, I'll need a detailed outline. That should take us through February. During March, I'll meet with each group to make sure you're staying on track. This is all on the handout, but I just wanted to say it out loud. The final project, including the five-to-ten page write-up, five or more photographs, the PowerPoint presentation, and your list of resources, will be due on April 18." He scanned the room. "Any questions? We have about five minutes."

A few students asked for clarifications, but Meredith felt the project was fair and understandable. She and Dani had picked a good subject. Getting pictures wouldn't be a problem; they already had some, but finding out who owned the scary Victorian house might be an issue. A shiver ran up her spine when she remembered the loud bang they'd heard at the house the Friday before. Maybe the house wasn't abandoned after all.

Mr. Dalton closed his lesson plan book and said, "Okay then. We have about one minute until the bell. Go ahead and pack up."

The students sprang into motion. A cacophony of student conversations erupted in Mr. Dalton's usually quiet classroom as students stashed notebooks and pens in their book bags. Meredith carefully put her history spiral away and pulled her AP Art sketchbook to the front. She would probably need it during the next period.

Meredith closed the zipper of her bag and heard Ben ask Dani, "So, how's the project going? Catch anything yet?" He roared at his joke. Sarah high-fived him and laughed just as loud, if not louder.

Meredith sighed in anger. What had she ever done to Ben or Sarah? Why did they constantly make fun of her? But just as she looked out the second-floor window, wishing everyone would leave her alone, Dani bolted out of her desk and towered over Ben in his seat.

Dani hissed, "Would you just shut up? What's wrong with you? Both of you." Her fiery gaze included Sarah.

The entire class grew quiet, hospital quiet, and all movement ceased. Meredith was mortified that Dani reprimanded her friends so publicly. She closed her eyes and prayed for the ability to teleport. The bell rang, and most of the students got up to leave, but Meredith sat in her seat as if glued to it. She wanted to wait until every single one of the other students left before she did. That way, she wouldn't have to face more ridicule. She would be late for AP Art, but that couldn't be helped.

As the other students in the class quietly and carefully picked their way out of the room, Dani and Ben continued to glare at each other. Dani took a deep breath and stepped away. She sat back down in her seat, even though the class period was over. Ben sprang up and smacked Dani's desk with his opened palm. The violence of it startled Meredith. Mr. Dalton stood behind his desk with his mouth hanging open.

Dani turned toward Meredith. With sympathy in her expression and tone, she said, "I'm sorry about him, Meredith."

Meredith stood up quickly and tried to rush past Dani, but Dani scrambled to her feet and caught Meredith by the arm at the classroom door. "Meredith, c'mon," Dani said again, blinking back angry tears.

Without sympathy, Meredith said, "Look, Dani. We're working on this project together. Can we just leave it at that? You don't have to defend me. You're, you're not my protector." She wrestled her arm free and ran out of the classroom.

Chapter 6

Hudson Pines

The cab of Dani's truck smelled like Armor All again, and Meredith wondered if Dani cleaned the truck every day or something. The Hudson Pines Senior Center expected the Whickett High School students around three o'clock, and it looked like they would be right on time. An uncomfortable but now familiar silence engulfed them as they drove. The silence had started five days earlier on the Monday of their blow up in Mr. Dalton's class.

They had acted as if nothing was wrong in front of Mikey, but besides this small semblance of friendship for Mikey's sake, they had barely spoken during the entire week. For whatever reason, Dani still sat next to Meredith during their art class, but Meredith had coldly suggested that Dani ask Mrs. Levine for help.

Meredith was sure that creating distance between them was in Dani's best interest. Dani surely understood this because she had gotten a small dose of how it felt to be Meredith when her supposed friends Ben and Sarah turned on her. If Meredith kept her distance, then Dani wouldn't get the kind of teasing Meredith got regularly. Yes, it was better to simply do the history project together and then be out of each other's lives for good. Meredith couldn't help feeling a bit of loss, though, because Dani was the first person to make even the slightest overture at friendship.

Meredith snuck a peek at Dani out of the corner of her eye as they traveled down Center Street. Ignoring Dani wouldn't be easy because Dani had found a way to get beyond Meredith's outer layer of protection.

Meredith figured she could easily find another subject to paint for the AP Art portfolio. Well, maybe not so easily. That stung a little bit, too. She snuck another guilty glance at Dani's profile and then looked out the passenger window at the stores going by. They passed the bakery Dani had taken them to for hot chocolate the weekend before. Mikey always said he hated rainbow sprinkles, but when Dani gave him some on his whipped cream, he loved them and asked for more. Mikey would definitely be disappointed when Dani didn't come around anymore. She sighed. Her sigh must have been audible because Dani cleared her throat.

"Meredith? I called Hudson Pines, and we've got someone to talk to about the old house. A Mrs. Randall, I think."

Dani kept the conversation confined to the project. Good. She must understand that friendship between them was not an option. But why did it feel so horrible?

Meredith tried to keep her voice even. "Okay. It's good to have a lead."

"Yeah." They lapsed into silence again.

Meredith knew she should apologize and at least get that behind them before they went into the senior center. As Dani pulled the truck into the crowded parking lot, Meredith was amazed at how popular the center seemed to be on Saturdays. Dani pulled the truck into the only open spot she could find. She turned off the engine but didn't move to get out. Neither did Meredith.

"Dani—" "Meredith—."

They laughed when they said each other's names at the same time.

"Go ahead," Dani offered. "What were you going to say?"

"I..." She wasn't sure how to begin. "No, you go ahead."

Dani's hands remained locked onto the steering wheel. She smiled at Meredith with closed lips as if afraid to begin. "Okay. Look, I'm sorry for coming across too protective the other day. You know, acting like your bodyguard or something."

Meredith looked down at her hands, slightly embarrassed.

"But," Dani continued, "I can't sit by and listen to my jerk friends make fun of you. They don't even know you. I mean, I hardly know you, but in the short amount of time I've spent with you, I think you're really nice. Mikey and your parents, too." Meredith looked up and caught a pleading look in Dani's eyes. Meredith held her gaze but didn't say anything. "Meredith, I just want to be your friend. But you make it kind of hard."

Meredith felt her own cheeks color, but not from the cold creeping into the cab of the truck. She looked down at her hands again and took a deep breath. "Dani, I...First of all, thanks for being so nice to my brother. And..." She hesitated before adding, "And to me, too. I've had such a hard time fitting in here. I don't know why." She picked at a loose thread on her gloves.

"I know why. It's because you hide. You hide behind your hair. You walk through the halls with your head down. You never make eye contact with anyone."

"I know. I know. It's just that Whickett is such a big school, and when I got here, I didn't know how to fit in. I'm kind of shy, in case you haven't noticed. You guys have all been together since kindergarten, and when I tried to make friends, no one seemed to want to know me."

"Why not? They're crazy."

"Well, maybe..."

Dani waited. When Meredith didn't continue, she asked, "Maybe what?"

"I don't know. Maybe my insecurity turned them off. But I also had really bad acne when I first got here. I felt ugly and freakish and insecure about it." She was a little embarrassed to admit this to Dani, but letting some of it out felt good. "And I don't know. I wasn't...I'm not very outgoing, I guess."

"It must be hard being so shy."

"You're not shy."

Dani laughed. "Not really. I don't know how you can let them pick on you."

"Dani, come on. I'm the *new girl*. It's easy for everyone to pick on me. You saw how that kid pushed me in the hallway. And Ben. He's *your* friend, and even he picks on me." Meredith cringed. She hadn't meant it to come out so scathing.

Dani just rolled her eyes. "I'm not sure I can claim him. He's his own person, you know?"

"I guess. And then there's..." Meredith paused. She wasn't sure if she should finish her thought out loud.

"What?"

Meredith took another deep breath. This, especially, she had never admitted to anyone. She looked up at Dani and searched for the trust she hoped to find. She needn't have worried because the look she found in Dani's eyes made her heart melt. Compassion, caring, and understanding. This time, she didn't think about capturing Dani's expression for her AP Art portfolio. No, this time, she wanted to keep those feelings all to herself. She blinked hard to stave off tears. She was losing the battle, so she looked away quickly.

"Meredith, what? And then there's *what*?"

"Mikey."

"Mikey? My dude? What about him?"

"People can't deal with things that are different. *People* that are different."

"No kidding." Dani nodded as if she had experienced being different.

"He and I took a lot of harassment that first year we got here. People always stare at him. They still do. And you heard those kids call me names like 'retard.' I'm not blaming my troubles on him. Don't get me wrong, okay? I love my Mikey Bikey, but he's just one more thing to add to the list that makes me different."

"But if people could just meet him—"

"I know. You know it now, too. But admit it. You were a little uneasy that first time you came over."

Dani shifted in her seat. "Yeah, I was. But that was just because I didn't know what to expect. I'd never met anyone with Down Syndrome before."

"And you survived, right? Most people don't even try like you did. Most people are scared, I guess, and they use insults to deal with their fear." Meredith sighed. "It's just easier to be invisible."

"You can't be very happy."

Dani hit a major nerve, which started a sudden flow of tears. Meredith cried quietly behind her hands for a few moments, but when she tried to get herself under control, a sob escaped.

Dani flung off her seatbelt and slid across the bench seat. She put a hand on Meredith's and pulled her toward her. Meredith resisted at first but then let herself be consoled. She cried into Dani's shoulder while Dani rubbed her back. Meredith finally managed to catch her breath. "Oh, God, Dani. I'm sorry."

"No, I'm the one who should apologize. I didn't mean to hurt your feelings."

Meredith sat up and pulled a tissue out of her coat pocket. She dabbed at her nose. "You didn't hurt my feelings. You just hit a nerve. I'm not happy. Not really."

"Can I ask you something?"

"Okay."

"What did you want to ask me in Mrs. Levine's class?"

"Oh. Well..."

Dani flashed her a smile. "C'mon. I said you can trust me."

"Okay. I sketched you at the last senior class meeting."

Dani smiled. "You did?"

"Yeah, and Mrs. Levine thought it was good. She thought I should ask you to pose for me. For my AP Art portfolio." Actually, Meredith had come up with the posing idea, but just in case Dani turned her down, she didn't have to take too much of the hit. "But you can say no," she added quickly.

Dani looked surprised. "I, uh, don't know what to say. Of course, I'll pose if you want me to. Can I see your sketch?"

"Sketches." She emphasized the plural.

"More than one?"

"Uh, yeah. I'll show you when you drop me home later."

"Cool. What do I have to do to pose?"

"Well, I'm concentrating on facial expressions and the emotions they show. Your part would be easy. All you have to do is sit. Sit still. Think you can do that?" Meredith teased.

Dani laughed. "I think I can handle that. I'd be honored to pose for you. And the emotion I'm expressing now is probably embarrassment."

"Yeah, I've seen that one before." Meredith smiled. "And thank you."

"No problem."

79

"No, I mean, thanks for sticking by me. I was mean to you on Monday in Mr. Dalton's class. I guess I forgot what having a friend was like."

Dani smiled. "Friends. Yes. I'd like to be friends."

Meredith looked at her. "Being my friend is gonna be hard."

"Why?"

"A lot of people don't seem to like me."

"I kind of know the feeling."

"You? No. No, you don't."

Dani just smiled and said, "Well, I'm going to be your friend anyway. I can handle it. Meredith, I gotta tell you, it was killing me not talking to you during art."

"Yeah, me, too. I'm sorry. And I really do want to help you understand art. On Monday, I promise we'll start over, okay? I'll be the best art tutor you've ever had."

"Deal." Dani looked at her watch. "I think we'd better get inside because I'm starting to freeze out here. Somebody cried all over my jacket."

Meredith feigned a hurt look and said, "And Mrs. Randall, whoever she is, is probably waiting for us."

They signed in at the front reception desk with a tall attendant named Rudy, who pointed them toward the convalescence wing. They passed a couple of other Whickett students in the hallway. Dani nodded to them, but Meredith ignored them completely.

Rudy said the maze to the convalescent wing was kind of tricky. He was right, but they persevered.

On the way, Dani said, "Meredith? Did you see just now when Mark and Kevin passed us?"

"Yeah."

"Did you see how I looked them in the eye and nodded to them?"

"Yeah."

"I want you to do that next time we pass somebody. Don't hide. Keep your head up. It shows people that you've seen them. It just, I don't know, shows them that you're equal. Maybe that doesn't make sense, but we've got to find a way to make you lose that invisibility cloak you've had on for the past year and a half."

"I don't know if I can."

Dani looked at her softly. "You'll just do what you can, okay? You can't beat shyness overnight, right?"

"I guess."

They reached an intersection in the hallways, and Dani pointed left. "How about this? When we get to Mrs. Randall's room, you introduce yourself first. Okay? I did all the talking to Rudy back there, so now it's your turn."

"All right. But wait." Meredith pulled her hair into a bundle and held her wrist out to Dani. Dani smiled. She knew what to do this time. She pulled the rubber band off and handed it to Meredith.

"Thank you." Meredith finished tying back her hair and took a deep breath. "Ready."

"Let's go."

They rounded another corner and found a microscopic sign indicating the Rose M. Rothschild Memorial Convalescence wing.

"This is it," Dani said. "Okay, look for room 129."

"Here." Meredith pointed to the room coming up on their left. She didn't know why she was so nervous, but she sensed that having Dani in her life would mean significant changes. Dani wanted her to take charge? Fine, she had three seconds to figure out how to do that.

Meredith knocked lightly on the propped-open door of room 129 and saw three people in the room. The woman in the bed had snow-white hair and looked to be in her seventies. This was, presumably,

Mrs. Randall. A rather good-looking guy with rust-colored hair sat on the edge of the bed. He wore a dark blue suit, a crisp white shirt, and a striped blue tie. He looked to be in his mid-twenties. Another woman, who also looked to be in her seventies, was seated in an overstuffed armchair on the other side of the bed. This woman had short silver hair and wore a long-sleeved red flannel shirt with dark blue jeans.

The woman in the bed looked up and said, "Oh, hello, girls. Are you from the high school?" When they nodded, the woman said, "Come in. Come in. What are your names?"

Meredith went into the room first. She kept her head up and nodded to the rusty-haired man and then to the woman seated in the armchair. She held out her hand to the woman in the bed and said, "I'm Meredith Bedford, and this is my friend, Dani Lassiter." Friend. She liked the sound of it. Meredith shook the invalid woman's hand gently and stepped aside so Dani could reach in.

The woman in the bed had the whitest hair Meredith had ever seen. The color of fresh snow. Her complexion was pale, but the sparkle in her eye made Meredith smile.

"Girls, this is so nice of you to visit. Rudy said some children from the high school might come by today." She smoothed her covers and said, "This is my nephew. Well, I guess you'd call him my grandnephew. Right, Millie?" She consulted with the woman in the armchair, who nodded. "This is my grandnephew, Gregory. My sister Bernice's grandson."

Gregory nodded at them and stood up. "Aunt Esther, I'm going to head out. It's a long drive back to Pearl River." He leaned in to kiss her on the forehead. "You take care of yourself, okay? I'll be back up next weekend to see how you're doing. And, uh, think about what we talked about."

"Okay, sweetie. Tell everyone I'm fine. I'll be up dancing a jig any time now."

Grandnephew Gregory turned and nodded curtly toward the woman in the armchair. The woman in the armchair barely nodded back. He seemed nice enough and was kind of cute, too, but Meredith got the distinct feeling that the woman in the armchair didn't like him. She made a mental note to ask Dani later what she thought of him.

"Oh, girls, I'm so sorry. I'm Esther Randall, and this is Millie Bradley." She gestured to the woman in the armchair, who bounded out of the chair and shook hands vigorously with Dani and Meredith.

"Girls, good to see you." The woman named Millie seemed genuinely glad to see them. She turned to Esther and said, "Glad he's gone." She rolled her eyes.

"Millie, come on. He's family." Esther scolded.

"He's your family. Not mine. And what's with the suit? I don't trust him for a second."

"Millie. We have company."

"Okay, okay. Sorry, girls. Carry on." Millie sat back down in the armchair and opened a crossword puzzle book Meredith had not seen earlier. The woman looked back up abruptly and said, "Oh, girls, Rudy brought in a couple of folding chairs for you."

Dani was on the chairs in an instant. She opened one up and gestured for Meredith to sit first. She then opened up the other and set it down next to Meredith.

Meredith took the lead. She had to. She had promised. She cleared her throat and said, "Thank you so much for seeing us today. We're doing a school project about the history of Whickett, and I, I mean, we thought that you might be able to tell us something about the old Victorian house on Center Street."

Esther's eyes lit up, and she exchanged a glance with Millie.

Esther said, "The old painted lady. Right, Millie?"

"Yup, that's her, all right."

Meredith was perplexed. "Painted lady?"

Esther looked at Millie and said, "They're too young, aren't they, dearest?"

"Yup."

Esther looked back at Meredith and said, "Sometimes Victorian houses were called painted ladies because of the pretty colors used to paint them."

"Rose," Meredith said.

Dani shot a questioning glance her way.

"Oh, I noticed the color the other day when I took Mikey to taekwondo." Meredith turned back to Esther. "That shade of rose, leaning toward pink, is just lovely."

"I do love it. The paint's all chipping and peeling now. Isn't it, Millie?"

"Yup. Been a long time since I've been able to do any work on her."

Meredith looked at Millie. "Do you own the house?"

Millie laughed a hearty laugh. Meredith suddenly got a crazy mental picture of Millie sitting in a rocking chair, smoking a pipe, and telling tall tales of days gone by. She shook the thought out of her head and wondered where such a warped idea of this sweet older woman came from.

"Me? Own the house?" Millie leaned her head back and laughed again. "Not me." She nodded her head toward Esther in the bed.

Meredith turned toward Esther. "Mrs. Randall? Do you own the house?"

Esther scowled. "No, and yes. No to the *Mrs.*, but yes to owning the house."

Meredith didn't quite know how to interpret her response. Millie seemed to pick up on that and said, "My Esther here isn't married. Well, not in the legal sense anyway."

"Millie!" Esther scolded her again. Meredith got the feeling that Esther scolded Millie often.

"Okay, okay. Sorry. I'll just sit here and do my puzzle." Millie leaned back in the armchair. Meredith smiled when she pictured the pipe and rocking chair again.

"Oh, girls, don't mind her." Esther flipped her hand in dismissal at Millie. "She's just crazy bored sitting here all day while my hip heals."

"How rude of us, Miss Randall. How are you feeling?" Meredith was careful not to use the word *Mrs.*

"I've seen better days, my dear, but they tell me my hip wasn't fractured too badly. It's not broken all the way through and should heal pretty much on its own. Rudy told me they're going to start me on physical therapy next week. I can even get around a little with that walker. Hate using it. I'm not old enough for a walker. Am I Millie?"

"Nope." She didn't look up from the crossword.

"Rudy said I was lucky, but I sure don't feel lucky. I've never tripped like that before, have I, Millie?"

"Nope."

"Honestly, I don't know what happened. I slipped on something in the front hallway and tripped over the rug. That's when I fell. Thank goodness Gregory was visiting over the weekend. He was such a big help, but he didn't find anything when he checked around the rug. We were already at Albany Medical by that time. Millie was by my side the whole time. Right, Millie?"

"Yup."

"Anyway," Esther continued, "they moved me here to Hudson

Pines for bed rest and some really fun pain medication. I'll be here for about two or three weeks. That's right, Millie, isn't it?"

"Yup."

Meredith smiled sympathetically at Esther. "Well, we sure hope you feel better soon."

"Yeah," Dani added, "I think there's a jig you're supposed to be doing soon, right?"

Esther laughed. "You girls are fun. So, what can we tell you about our old painted lady?"

Meredith cleared her throat. She wasn't sure what to ask. Before they left that afternoon, she figured Dani would do all the talking. "Um, can you tell us a little bit about the history of your house? Do you still live there?"

Dani jotted down notes while Meredith and Esther talked about the house. For almost an hour, Esther Randall, with some help from her friend Millie Bradley, relayed the story of the Victorian House. The Randall House was well over a hundred years old, built in the early 1890s by Esther's great-grandfather, Charles Bickford Randall. Large tracts of land had once surrounded the property, but as Whickett grew, the property shrank.

Esther talked about her days as a young girl growing up in Whickett. She had been born in 1936 during the Great Depression but couldn't claim to remember much about it. She had been too young. World War II, however, did make a big impression on her, and she told them about her volunteer work collecting nylon stockings, used cooking grease, and old tires for the war effort.

Meredith found that she wasn't shy around these two strangers. She wasn't normally outgoing by nature, but she felt good talking with Esther and Millie. Her self-imposed bindings had loosened a little. She knew it was temporary, but she could almost understand why Dani was perplexed at her introverted nature.

Meredith asked, "So you inherited the house when your father passed?"

"Yes. That was a sad time. It was just Daddy and me then. Mama had passed about ten years earlier. My sister Bernice had already moved out and lived downstate in Pearl River. That's near New Jersey. We never understood why she wanted to live there, but her new husband wanted to be near the city. New York City that is. So, when Daddy passed on, Bernice sold me her share of the house. I was thirty-five at the time. And it was right about then I met my Millie. Right, Millie?"

Meredith thought Millie had fallen asleep in the armchair, but Millie's eyes flew open. She leaned forward and poked the air. "Best damn day of my life."

"Millie!"

Millie just smiled and leaned back in the armchair.

Meredith smiled at Millie and turned to smile at Dani. She was surprised to see Dani grinning like a cat.

"Anyway, girls," Esther continued. "We decided after my hip accident that the house was just too big for us. Well, to be honest, we'd been thinking that way for a while now, so my Millie hired some movers to take our things to a one-bedroom first-floor apartment over on Grove Street we'd been looking at. It's one of those over fifty-five housing complexes. I'm sure you've never heard of it."

Meredith looked sheepish. "I have to say that I haven't. Sorry."

Just then, Esther yawned. "Oh, I'm sorry, girls. This is my usual nap time."

Meredith stood up, "We've tired you out. We should be going." Meredith was mortified that they had tired out the convalescing older woman. "Would you mind if we took a couple of quick pictures of you for our project?"

Esther sat up and smoothed her hair. "Of course you can, honey. I'm not looking my best these days, but sure, go ahead." She turned to face Millie. "We have some old pictures of the house the girls can use, don't we, Millie?"

"Yup. I was going to unpack that box when I got home tonight."

Meredith smiled. "Thank you so much, both of you. This will help our project. We're putting together a PowerPoint for our class, a kind of slide show, and some old pictures would be perfect."

Dani leaned forward and said, "I'll scan them on my computer and get your pictures back to you right away."

Meredith pulled her coat off the back of the fold-up chair and patted down the pockets for her digital camera. "Oh, shoot. I think I left my camera in the truck. Let me go—"

"I'll get it." Dani sprang to her feet. "I'll be right back." She grabbed her letterman's jacket and shrugged it on as she bolted from the room.

Millie leaned forward. She gestured toward the open door and said to Meredith, "She's quite a catch."

"Millie!" Esther reprimanded.

"Cute, too." Millie teased. "Those pretty blue eyes. That golden blond hair. I used to have hair like that. Okay, I was six at the time, but still."

"Don't mind, Millie," Esther said to Meredith. "What she means is that you're very lucky to have such an attentive girlfriend."

Meredith cleared her throat and asked, "What do you mean?"

Millie gestured at the chairs. "Well, she put your chair out for you. She let you introduce yourself first and waited in the background. Then she jumps up and runs." She turned to Esther. "Did you see her run?"

"Reminds me of you, Millie."

Millie smiled and looked back at Meredith. "Yeah, she's a keeper, all right. I have an intuition about these things."

Meredith's confusion must have shown because Esther changed the subject with a nervous laugh. "Did we tell you our plans for the house?"

"Uh, no. No, you didn't." Meredith was relieved the subject had turned.

"We have big plans. We'll wait for your friend to return, but I hope we can pull this off. Right, Millie?"

"Yup."

Just then, Dani raced back into the room, a little out of breath. She handed the camera to Meredith.

Meredith thanked her and took the camera out of its case. "We took some pictures of the house last weekend. I hope you don't mind."

Esther said, "No, of course not, honey. You girls take as many pictures as you like. Millie, do you still have a key under the flower pot?"

"Yup."

Esther looked back at them. "If you girls want to look inside, Millie keeps a key hidden under the clay pot on the front landing. Go ahead and let yourself in any time you want. The heat's on but set low, so turn it up when you get inside. Just remember to turn it back down when you leave."

Meredith couldn't believe these strangers they had just met would give them a key to their house. "No one lives there now?"

"No, honey. I haven't been there since my hip, and Millie hasn't been there in weeks."

"That's probably why it looked so lonely the other day." Meredith smiled sympathetically.

Millie frowned. "It's lonely without my Esther and with the furniture gone. It kind of gives me the heebie-jeebies. That's why I stay away."

"And I live here at majestic Hudson Pines for now. Millie's at our new place on Grove Street with all our things. No one's at the house to bother you, so you girls take all the pictures you need."

"Thank you both so much." Meredith put a hand to her heart. "I promise we'll take good care of your painted lady."

Millie stood up and said, "Hey, anything for a sister."

"Millie!"

Meredith had no idea what Millie meant by her comment, so she just laughed at the silly antics of the two older women. She smiled and turned on her camera. "Here are the pictures we took of your house the other night. She stood up and leaned toward the older woman in the bed. Millie, already standing, leaned in from the other side. Dani moved in behind Meredith to look over her shoulder.

Meredith said, "We haven't even looked at them ourselves." When Meredith scrolled to the last picture, she laughed. "And this one is just before the banister broke, and Dani fell off the landing."

"I'll pay for it," Dani said quickly.

Esther reached for Dani. "Don't worry about that, honey. Are you all right?" Esther didn't wait for an answer and turned to Millie. "See? I told you that old place is cursed. The old painted lady reached out and hurt this child, too."

"Pah," Millie said. "The old painted lady is just old. She's not cursed."

While Esther and Millie bantered back and forth, Meredith looked more closely at the photograph. She held the camera out so Dani could see the image. They looked at each other wide-eyed.

Meredith whispered, "Is that a face in the window?"

Chapter 7

The Old Painted Lady

The trip from the Hudson Pines Senior Center to the Victorian house took ten minutes. Meredith felt bad staying warm in the truck while Dani pulled up the metal latch holding the drive gate shut, but Dani had jumped out of the truck as soon as they pulled into the small length of driveway in front of the gate. Dani walked the gate open and pushed the metal rod into the ground so it wouldn't swing shut as they drove through. Dani turned and gave Meredith a thumbs-up. Meredith smiled but motioned for Dani to get back into the truck quickly.

Dani opened the driver's side door and jumped back in. "What's the hurry? Esther and Millie said we could check out the house whenever we wanted." She pulled the truck up the long, narrow driveway alongside the old house.

"I know, but it's getting dark, and I don't want to be around this house in the dark." Meredith shivered. "I still say that was a face in the window of that picture."

"Maybe it was a trick of the light, or..."

"Or what?"

With an evil laugh, Dani said, "Maybe the house is cursed."

"Danielle Lassiter. You cut that out. That's not funny." Meredith crossed her arms.

"Okay, okay." Dani's voice took on a more serious tone. "I was just kidding. And, by the way, my middle name is Anne. It sounds more threatening if you say 'Danielle Anne Lassiter' like my mom does when she's pissed at me."

"Well," Meredith said, unfolding her arms, "Miss Danielle *Anne* Lassiter, I suggest we get going because the light is fading. And if I were painting, I'd have to use deep reds and blood orange to paint the sunset at this point. So, chop, chop. Let's go."

"Yes, ma'am." Dani put the truck in park and turned off the engine. She opened her door and hopped out. Meredith met her in front of the truck.

"Can you go see if that key is up there? I'm going to wait here. Just in case."

"Chicken." Dani laughed. Her feet crunched the frozen grass as she cut from the driveway to the front porch. The house stood higher than the surrounding buildings, giving it a look of superiority over the rest of Center Street.

The late afternoon shadows reminded Meredith of the scare they had the first time they checked out the house. The loud slamming door, the face in the window. Maybe someone had been trying to scare them.

What was taking her so long? Meredith tried to keep the nerves out of her voice when she called, "Dani? Is it there?"

"Yeah, right here. Come on up."

Meredith steeled herself and headed toward the house. "Are you sure?"

"Yeah, c'mon."

"Do you really think we should? Shouldn't we wait until Miss Randall or Miss Bradley are here? It's their house, after all."

"Meredith, come on. They gave us permission to look around, and it'll be great for our project. I know you're scared, but they said that no one will be here and..."

"What?"

"Well, after meeting them, I kind of want to see where they lived. I want to see what their life was like in their *old painted lady*. You know?"

Meredith took comfort in that because she, too, was curious about the two older women and their house. "Okay, let's go before I change my mind. But let's not break anything this time, okay?" She attempted a smile and pointed to the banister lying on the front lawn.

"Go ahead. Rub that in." Dani smiled back.

They turned toward the front door and looked through the windows flanking it. Meredith heard Dani exhale loudly. Meredith smiled. Dani was nervous, too.

Dani said, "Looks clear. No ghosts."

Meredith smacked her playfully on the arm. "Just unlock it."

Dani unlocked the heavy wooden door and pushed it. The door swung open wide into the front foyer. The slow squeak of the hinges made Meredith cringe. The eerie sound was something out of a bad horror movie.

They crossed over the threshold in silence. Once inside, Meredith closed the massive door, making sure it latched tightly against the cold. The house was chilly inside, yet despite that, a warm and homey feeling enveloped her. The house had been loved. She was sure of it. She looked to the left. "Hey, look at this room. This must have been the sitting room where Miss Randall and Miss Bradley entertained their guests."

"Esther and Millie," Dani said.

"I can't call them that. It seems, I don't know, disrespectful somehow."

"They insisted we call them that when we left just now."

"I know, but wow, look at this fireplace." The decorative stone and wooden mantle were in such good condition they looked brand new. "I bet they had wonderful evenings sitting in here by the fire."

"Yeah, Esther knitting and Millie...Hmm, what would Millie be doing?"

"Smoking her pipe," Meredith said confidently.

"Smoking her pipe? Where'd you come up with that?"

"I don't know, really." Meredith ran her fingers along the fine wood of the mantle. "I just kind of pictured her with a pipe. Weird, I know. None of the old ladies I know smoke pipes."

Meredith noticed the thermostat on the wall. "Hey, Miss Randall said we could turn up the heat."

"Esther."

"Okay, fine. *Esther* said we could turn up the heat, right?"

"Go for it."

Meredith turned the dial. "How high should I set it?"

"Uh, I don't know. Sixty-eight, maybe?"

"That sounds good. Anything's better than the fifty degrees it's set on now."

Meredith turned back toward the wide staircase that wound to the second floor. "So, Esther has a sister named Bernice, right?"

"Yeah, why?"

"Which means Millie isn't Esther's sister?"

"No, they're definitely not sisters." Dani walked to the other side of the sitting room and stood beside the window overlooking the auto parts store.

Meredith realized her error. "Oh, yeah, if Millie were Esther's sister, then Gregory would be Millie's grandnephew, too. But Millie denied being related to him. Esther and Millie seemed so close, you know? Like sisters. Maybe they're two old spinsters living together because they never found husbands."

Dani laughed loudly, and Meredith shot her a glance. "Why are you laughing at me?"

Dani pulled herself together and said, "I'm not laughing at you. I'm laughing near you." She poked Meredith lightly on the arm and shouted, "Tag. You're it." She bolted past Meredith and up the stairs to the second floor.

"Hey, don't leave me alone down here." Meredith chased after her fleeing friend. "Wait."

Meredith was slightly winded when she got to the top of the stairs. She found Dani in one of the smaller bedrooms. This one overlooked Fiesta Loca, the Mexican restaurant next door.

Dani seemed wistful when she said, "I wonder what they used to see out this window back in the day. You know, like, cow pastures or meadows?"

Meredith stood next to her at the window. She blocked the brightly colored restaurant from her mind's eye and said, "I bet there were big open meadows where Esther played with her big sister Bernice. Their mother would call them in for supper, but they wouldn't want to come in yet, so they'd hide in the tall grass and stay really, really quiet. But after a while, they could tell by their mother's tone that they were going to get in trouble if they didn't come in. Then, but only then, would they leave the field and go in for supper."

Meredith felt Dani looking at her. She turned her head slightly to return the look. "What?"

"That was nice. You made that sound so real."

Meredith smiled. "And, you know what?"

"What?"

"If I lived here, in the old painted lady, this would be my studio. The light is fantastic right now. I'd be up here all day painting, and you'd be downstairs making supper and call up to tell me it was ready."

"Why am I the one making supper?"

"Because I'm up here painting, obviously."

"But I'll be out coaching lacrosse somewhere and won't be home, woman."

"You'd stay away all day? And leave me alone?" Meredith flashed a hurt look.

Dani's expression changed from playful to serious. "Never."

Meredith caught Dani's serious expression and felt her cheeks color. They had just decided to become friends, and Meredith couldn't understand why she'd imagined Dani in the house with her. She must be lonelier than she realized. That must be it. Flustered, she turned away and moved into the hallway toward the biggest of the three bedrooms on the second floor. "Hey Dani," she called, "which bedroom was Esther's? Which one was Millie's?"

Dani joined Meredith in the largest bedroom—the one with the balcony overlooking Center Street. "This one."

"This one, what?"

"...was Esther's. Yeah, this would have been Esther's room."

"And Millie's was my art studio."

"Yeah, okay." Dani grinned.

Meredith moved to the french doors leading out to the second-floor balcony. She looked out to Center Street. "You know what, Dani?"

"What?"

"I want to paint their portraits."

"Esther and Millie?"

"Yeah. I think their portraits should hang in the entryway downstairs. I mean, they want to call this the Randall-Bradley House, right? They'll need something permanent in the front hall to remind everyone who created the Randall-Bradley House for Women."

"That's awesome. You'd really do that?" Dani moved closer to Meredith near the closed doors.

"I do. It'll be my community service project."

Dani's smile went straight to Meredith's heart.

"Meredith, that's awesome. Wait, I just said that, but it's true. I wanted the senior class to get involved in the community somehow, but what you want to do is above and beyond. I mean, I just wanted our classmates to go down and read to some of the seniors at the center."

Meredith wasn't sure, but it almost looked as if stoic Dani Lassiter had tears in her eyes. Meredith said quietly, "What I'm going to do is small, really small, compared to what Esther and Millie have planned for this house."

Dani turned to face her. "I know. A house for, how did they phrase it, women in need?"

"Yeah, I think so. You know, I feel so out of touch. I didn't realize Whickett had women who were homeless and needed housing. Even women with kids."

"I know, and honestly, I've never thought about it. That just shows you what a cocoon we live in, you know? But Esther said there are lots of women who need help. I think it's so cool they're donating the house and property. Did Esther say she was still going to own it?"

Meredith shrugged her shoulders. "She said something about creating a trust or something like that, so the house and land will become the property of some corporation they create. Hey, does Millie own the house, too?"

This time, Dani shrugged her shoulders. "I don't know what legal rights Millie has in the house. But Esther talked as if it was both of theirs."

Meredith's thoughts turned serious. "You and I are so lucky we have two parents who love each other and us."

Dani seemed to understand Meredith's train of thought. "Yeah, I can't imagine a family having to run off in the middle of the night." She swallowed hard. "All because the mother was getting beaten up. That makes me sick." Her shoulders drooped.

"I know. Me, too. But Esther said it's more common than people think. It's nice to know there'll be a place like this, the old painted lady, where those women and kids can come to get back on their feet."

Dani looked out the windows of the french doors leading to the balcony. Remember how Esther said she wants to help them find jobs and get counseling and stuff? That's so cool." Dani nodded. "I'm so glad we met them."

"Yeah, they're two modern old ladies, you know? They moved out to make room for people who need help." Meredith looked around and then looked back at Dani. "How big is this place anyway?"

"I think there's a third floor. We can check it out later. But first..." Dani turned the deadbolt to the french doors and opened one. She extended her arm toward the balcony in an after-you gesture. "Join me?"

Meredith nodded graciously and walked past Dani onto the wooden landing. A gust of icy wind hit her, and she pulled her coat tighter. "Oh, this is so neat. I wish I had a balcony off my bedroom." She imagined a world without the neon and noise of the present age. Two plastic resin chairs and a small table sat on the balcony, sure signs of a modern era, but Meredith didn't care. She pulled a chair out for Dani, who stepped onto the balcony behind her and said, "Miss Lassiter, will you join me for tea?"

"Well, I would be delighted, Miss Bedford." Dani took the offered chair and looked expectantly at Meredith.

Meredith sat in the other plastic chair. She did her best to ignore the surprisingly cold plastic and pretended to pour hot tea into a pretend fine china teacup. She held out the teacup and saucer. Her fine companion, Miss Danielle Anne Lassiter from Whickett, New York, graciously accepted the tea. She then poured her own cup and said, "Thank you so much for joining me on this fine afternoon. The fields should be ready for planting soon. Don't you think, Miss Lassiter?" She held her pinky out and took an elegant imaginary sip.

"Uh, yeah, sure. Uh, I mean, why yes, Miss Bedford. What a wonderful spring we're having here in the country without cars or streetlights or Mexican restaurants." Dani started to giggle, and Meredith couldn't help herself. She began to giggle, too. After all, it was, maybe, thirty degrees as they sat in cold plastic chairs, talking as if the spring planting was imminent.

Meredith pretended to spill her tea on the table. "Oops. How clumsy of me." She grabbed her pretend napkin and reached down to wipe up the spill at the same time Dani did. Their hands touched, startling Meredith back into the present. She looked up at her friend. Dani's serious expression made Meredith uneasy, but she wasn't sure why. She realized their hands still touched and jerked hers away.

Dani cleared her throat and broke into a smile. "Um, Miss Bedford? Think we can take this party inside? My tea is frozen." She looked into her imaginary cup.

Meredith smiled and got back in character. "Why absolutely, Miss Lassiter. Please, lead the way."

Dani led them back into the bedroom, and Meredith locked the balcony doors securely behind her. Something had happened on the balcony, and the mood between them had shifted. Meredith couldn't figure out what was wrong with her today. Their hands had touched.

So what? A shared moment between friends shouldn't make her uneasy. Meredith figured she was just out of practice when it came to friendship. It was, after all, only a few scant hours since she had decided to let her guard down around Dani.

They made their way toward the staircase to go up to the third floor but froze in their tracks. The distinctive groan of the front door opening shattered the serenity of the house.

Meredith grabbed Dani's arm through her letterman's jacket. "Dani!" She whispered.

"I hear it." Dani leaned over the railing toward the front door, but Meredith knew she couldn't see anything since the staircase reversed direction after a small landing in the middle and blocked any view of the front foyer and door.

Dani whispered, "I can't see anything."

"What do we do? What do we do?" Meredith squeezed Dani's arm tighter.

"I don't know. Maybe we left the door open, and the wind got hold of it."

Meredith wanted to believe that, but she was the one who had closed the door. She had heard it click shut. She was sure of it. She hadn't turned the deadbolt, though. Maybe it was those guys she'd seen at the auto parts store the other night. Or, she prayed, maybe it was just some kids playing around.

Dani whispered, "Wait here. I'll go check it out."

Meredith didn't want to be separated from her but decided she didn't want to go downstairs more, so she murmured, "Okay. I'll look out the windows and see if I can spot anyone."

"Okay." Dani squeezed Meredith's forearm to reassure her everything would be fine. Meredith reluctantly let go of Dani's arm and headed back toward the primary bedroom.

Meredith thought Mikey was right. *This is a scary house.*

Meredith crept to the windows in the bedroom. She looked out the french doors to the front of the house. The sun had already gone down, but she could still make things out in the dim shadows. Several cars were stopped in the traffic in front of the house, but nothing looked out of the ordinary. She looked at the driveway. The gate was still wide open with Dani's truck on guard. Meredith checked the property from the windows on the second floor and found nothing strange except that she hadn't heard Dani for several minutes. A cold shiver ran through her. She rushed to the top of the stairs and hesitated.

"Dani?" she whispered but realized that unless Dani had been standing right next to her, she wouldn't have heard. She was just about to call out to Dani a little louder when the front door slammed shut, making her jump. She slunk back toward the wall and swallowed around the stone in her throat. She looked from left to right, not knowing which way to run. She heard the slow creak of a footstep on the bottom stair and was propelled into action. She slowly backed her way into the primary bedroom. She had nothing to defend herself with. No fireplace poker or anything remotely useful. She could have opened the balcony doors and grabbed one of the plastic chairs, but it was way too late for that. And the noise would give her away. Wait. Her camera. In the darkening late afternoon, she could set the flash to blind whoever was messing with them. And if that didn't work, she would hurl the camera at him, fly down the stairs, find Dani, and get out of the house.

She heard another slow creak on the stairs. Closer. She fumbled with her coat pocket, trying to find her camera. *Where is it? Where is it?* Panic rose in her throat when she couldn't feel it. Was it in the truck? She somehow willed herself to slow down. She finally found the camera in her coat pocket and yanked it out. She hit the flash switch and heard the familiar whir as it charged. Another creak. This time at the top of the landing, right outside the bedroom door. *C'mon, c'mon,* she willed the flash to charge. Why was it taking so long? She squatted just inside the doorway, hiding the camera from view. Her heart was pounding so hard she knew anyone could hear it. She prayed that whoever was outside the doorway would think the second floor was empty and would just go back down the stairs. No such luck. A shadow moved across the doorway. *Don't snap too soon. Wait. Wait.* The shadowy figure took a step into the room, and Meredith reacted. Snap! The camera flashed.

The figure took one startled step backward, and Meredith darted out the door and into the hallway.

"Meredith, what are you doing?" Dani blinked repeatedly. "I can't see a thing."

"Oh, my God." Meredith stood up and threw her arms around Dani's neck. "Oh, my God. I thought you were Jack the Ripper." Her heart was still pounding.

Dani returned Meredith's hug but continued to blink furiously. "What had you so spooked? It was just the front door. We didn't close it all the way." With a laugh, she asked, "Are you okay?"

Meredith pulled away. Her heart slowed down, but nowhere near normal speed. "I got myself all worked up. Can we get out of here? This house *is* cursed."

"What? You and Esther. You both think the house is cursed. Come on, let's go back down. We'll check out the third floor another day."

"Fine by me."

Meredith wanted to bolt down the stairs and out of the house, but she didn't want to be first, so she clutched the sleeve of Dani's lacrosse jacket. She didn't care if Dani thought she was a coward.

When they got to the bottom of the stairs, Dani pointed to a sizeable discolored area on the floor. "This must be where the rug was. The one Esther tripped on."

"Yeah. She said she slipped right before she tripped."

They inspected the wood floor but didn't find anything odd.

"Hey, wait. Look over here." Dani knelt on all fours and inspected a spot on the floor. "The wood looks different here."

"Hmm, that's about the size of my sketchpad."

Dani looked up.

Meredith shrugged. "What? You'd probably say it was the size of the net in your lacrosse bat or something. We all have our points of reference."

"Stick."

"What?"

"Lacrosse stick. And, yeah, you're right. The stain's about as long as my lacrosse head."

Meredith looked at her friend knowingly.

"What?"

"See? Like I said, we all have our own reference points."

Dani sat back on her heels and laughed. "Okay, you got me there." She leaned forward again and put her nose to the stain.

"What are you doing?"

"Grease."

"Grease? Like for french fries?"

"No. Axle."

"Axle? Axle grease?"

"Yeah. I have a truck, remember? I know axle grease."

Meredith exchanged a puzzled look with Dani. She got on her knees next to Dani and smelled the stained wood. The stain smelled like the garage when her father worked on his truck. "Why would someone put axle grease on the floor?"

Dani just shook her head. "I don't know," she said slowly. "Ah, come on. The movers probably dropped something there." She stood up and put her hand out to help Meredith up.

Meredith accepted Dani's help. "Yeah, you're probably right. Now, can we get out of here?"

Dani swept her arm toward the front door. "Why, yes, indeed, Miss Bedford. Your chariot awaits."

Chapter 8

John Casey

Mrs. Levine placed a silver pair of scissors between Meredith and Dani. She said, "It's Monday, which means a new project." To Meredith, she said, "I want you to help Dani see the interplay of light and dark, shadow and reflection."

Meredith nodded her understanding. "Okay. That shouldn't be too hard." She looked at Dani and chuckled because Dani had a look on her face that said, "Easy for you to say."

"I'm promoting you to private tutor so you can get started on Dani's portrait on Friday. You can use my workroom, okay?"

"Thanks, Mrs. Levine." Meredith nodded. "I think we'll start with her happy eyes portrait first."

Mrs. Levine smiled. "Perfect." She moved on to another student.

Meredith was surprised to see Dani's flaming red cheeks. "Now, don't worry. I'll take good care of you." She flashed what she hoped was a reassuring smile.

"I know. It's just embarrassing."

"What is?"

Dani looked down, obviously flustered. She stammered, "I don't know. I've just never had anybody talk about my 'happy eyes.' It's weird."

"I didn't mean to embarrass you. But you do have a very expressive face sometimes."

Meredith reached under her sketchpad and pulled out a brand new vinyl pencil case she'd hidden at the beginning of class. She pushed the case over to Dani.

"What's this?"

"I, uh, got you some pencils."

"For me?" Dani picked up the case and ran a finger along the tiny green bow Meredith had attached with scotch tape.

"Yeah. You're a real artist now, and you need professional supplies. And…"

"And, what?"

"And I wanted to say thanks for being my friend."

Dani beamed and looked down at the pencil case as if embarrassed. "Thanks. This is so nice." She opened the case and pulled out a sealed pack of graphite pencils along with a professional set of colored pencils. She grinned when she pulled out the green and yellow pencil sharpener with 'WHS' printed on the side. "Oh, sweet. Did you get this at the school store?"

"Yeah. I thought you might need a Whickett High souvenir."

"I do. Thank you."

"You're welcome." Meredith smiled and opened her sketchbook. Having a friend felt amazing.

Dani unwrapped her brand-new pencils. "That's awesome. Mrs. Levine is going to let us work on the portrait during class. I mean, we're still doing art, right? But it's *you* doing the art."

"And I appreciate you giving up your own art time for my project." Meredith smiled at her friend. She held out her wrist so Dani could take off the rubber band. When Dani didn't reach over for it, Meredith looked up bewildered.

Dani smiled. She whipped up her own sleeve to reveal six colored hair bands, each about a half-inch wide. She held them out and said with a grin, "You're not the only one with something up her sleeve. My sister helped me pick them out yesterday. I had no clue what kind to get for you."

"You got these for me?" Meredith was stunned.

"Yeah." Dani dropped her gaze but then looked back up.

"That's so sweet. Thank you." She looked over the selections and chose the second one in line—the red one. "Look, this one matches my sweater."

"You're pretty in red. And I still think you should keep your hair back all the time."

Meredith felt a slight blush creep across her face. She looked at Dani. "Maybe I will." She cleared her throat. "But, um, I think we should get going on these scissors."

Meredith pulled her sketchpad toward her, picked up her pencil, and began teaching Dani how to see the scissors in light and shadow. Meredith showed her how to subtly shade the sketch so the scissors took on a three-dimensional look. Dani caught on quickly, so Meredith went back to her own sketch.

They worked silently for a bit, but then Dani stopped sketching and sat back.

Meredith stopped her work and looked up.

"Meredith?"

"Yeah?"

"That kid's name is John Casey."

"What kid?"

"You know, the basketball player." When Meredith still didn't understand who she meant, Dani continued, "You know, that jerk that tackled you in the hallway the other day."

"Oh, him." Meredith looked down at her sketch. She didn't want to think about him.

"I asked my friend Lisa, who plays on the girls' team who he was. And here's what I think you should do."

Meredith remained silent, still sketching.

"Next time he starts to bother you, call him by his name. Knowing someone's name gives you an advantage. He won't expect it, and you'll surprise him. Maybe he'll leave you alone."

"Just by using his name?"

"Yeah. You should say something like, 'John Casey, I've had it up to here with you.'"

Meredith laughed. She couldn't say something like that to him.

Dani laughed with her. "Okay. Maybe not. That sounds like something my mom would say. But I don't know. Say something to him."

"Okay," Meredith said pensively. Easier said than done, Dani. Easier said than done.

They went back to their drawings. She was touched that Dani was trying to find a way to help her cope with the abuse she got from the other students. She knew that, and the hair bands were small gestures on Dani's part, but they were huge in Meredith's heart.

At the end of the class period, Meredith looked at Dani's drawing and nodded her approval at the very lifelike sketch of scissors on the paper. Dani proudly handed the work to their art teacher.

Dani was still beaming when they walked out the door. "Did you hear what Mrs. Levine said about my scissors?"

Meredith laughed softly. "Yeah. They are the best scissors ever. I think you've made a little progress since those middle school art days."

Dani laughed loudly. "Yeah, I think so. Hey, I need to get my history book. Hang out and wait for me, okay?"

As Dani worked the combination to her locker, Meredith took a deep breath and hoped she wouldn't have to implement Dani's plan for the overly-aggressive boys on the basketball team. She rehearsed the boy's name, John Casey, as she waited for Dani. Her hopes were dashed when she first heard and then saw the tall basketball player and his equally tall entourage saunter toward them down the hallway. She automatically steeled herself for the inevitable. But then something shifted inside of her. She decided she was tired of getting picked on every day. Today, she would stand up for herself. Well, she would try anyway. She pulled her book bag higher on her shoulder, and instead of cringing and waiting for him to push her, she stood tall and lifted her chin high. She didn't have time to wonder if Dani was watching because she had to look the junior basketball player John Casey in the eye.

She watched him take his now familiar path away from his friends toward her. When he was within about two yards, he must have noticed something different about her because he hesitated.

Meredith stood firm, pointed her finger at his face, and said calmly but forcefully, "John Casey, I've had enough of your shit. So, keep going and leave me alone." She pointed down the hallway.

The tall basketball player, obviously surprised, stopped dead in his tracks, put both hands up in defense, and said, "Okay. Okay." He stepped backward and made a wide berth around Meredith to catch up to his friends. They gave him no end of grief and said things like, "Ooh, you got schooled" and "Way to go, stud."

Meredith's heart was pounding as she covered a smile. She slowly turned to face Dani, whose jaw had dropped open. Dani stared wide-eyed at her.

Meredith grinned again. "Did I just do that?"

Dani nodded slowly. "Uh, huh. I'm pretty sure that was you."

Meredith blew out a sigh. "Oh, my God."

"Guess we won't need Mikey's taekwondo after all. Will we?" Dani grinned and shook her head to match Meredith's own oh-my-God reaction.

They headed toward the stairwell that would take them to their history class. Meredith smiled inside and out.

~~~

That same evening, Meredith sat at the desk in her room, typing notes about Esther and Millie's house. She still hadn't gotten comfortable referring to the two older women as Esther and Millie, but they had insisted, so she'd given in. She thought of Dani and smiled. On Saturday, in the parking lot of the senior center, she had told Dani that she had forgotten what having a friend was like. But that wasn't right. She had *never* known what having a friend like Dani Lassiter was like.

Meredith reached behind her head and felt for the red hair band Dani had given her earlier in the day. She had never had a friend buy her a gift for no particular reason. And Meredith had rarely experienced anyone who took the time to wait for her to speak like Dani did. Most people just kept talking because they didn't have the patience to wait for her to respond. But Dani wasn't like that. Dani waited and didn't railroad her into taking on her opinions.

The phone rang, jolting Meredith out of her thoughts. She looked at the caller ID. Lassiter. Dani must have sensed Meredith thinking about her. She picked up the phone but heard her father's voice before she could say hello.

"Well, what do you know? It's the captain of the lacrosse team," he said. "How are the practices going?"

Dani answered, "Well, sir, we're still in pre-season workouts, but our first game will be on March twenty-first. I'm pretty sure that's a Friday. Can I expect you in the stands?"

Meredith was amazed that Dani talked to her father so easily. She would simply have asked for Dani if Dani's father answered.

Her father said, "I'll circle the date on the calendar. I'm sure the whole Bedford clan would love to go."

Meredith smiled. She hadn't thought that far ahead in their friendship, but yes, she'd like to go to Dani's first game. And Mikey would absolutely love to see his dude play lacrosse.

"Glad to hear it, Mr. Bedford. So, who'd you have in the Superbowl yesterday?"

Oh, no. More sports. Meredith tuned out at this point and waited for her father to call up the stairs. Eventually, after what seemed like an hour, he yelled up that she had a phone call. She didn't want them to know she'd been on the line all along, so she hit the on/off button once to hang up her extension. She hoped she wouldn't disconnect Dani in the process. She tapped the button again to reconnect.

"Thanks, Dad," she called out her open bedroom door. "I've got it." She closed her door and said into the phone, "Dani?"

"Yeah, it's me. How's it going?"

"I'm working on our project proposal, actually."

"Oh, yeah. That's due on Friday, right?"

Meredith saved the file on her computer. "Yeah. Just the proposal, but I'm outlining it, too, since that's due in about three weeks. Right around mid-winter recess, I think. I figure we should start with a report about how the house looked in its heyday. Millie said she had pictures for us, so when we get those, we'll ask them for more history of the house."

"Yeah, cool."

"Should we put in the part about the new Randall-Bradley House for Women?" Meredith asked but then answered her own question. "Yeah, we should put that in."

"Definitely." Dani's voice sounded strong and sure. "I mean, like, we can talk about how the house used to look and about Esther and Millie—we'll put pictures of them into our PowerPoint—and then we'll talk about their plans for the women's shelter."

"And maybe we could put in statistics about domestic violence or something because I found some horrifying statistics online like this one. A woman is battered every nine seconds. That's from the Department of Justice. And can you believe what Esther said? If a woman tries to leave an abusive man, he's likely to kill her? That's crazy. I'll have to find documentation on that somewhere. I mean, obviously, it's not *all* men, but..."

Dani was quiet on the other end of the line.

"Dani? Are you still there?"

"Yeah." There was a sad tone to her voice. "I'm still amazed that there's so much abuse in the world, and I've been completely oblivious to it."

"I know. Me, too. But I think Mr. Dalton would want us to include stuff like this. Don't you think?"

"Oh, yeah. I think we've uncovered an amazing story. I'm so glad you came up with this project. And Esther and Millie are so cool. I'm glad we met them."

"Yeah, me, too," Meredith said. "Hey, I forgot to ask. What did you think about Esther's grandnephew?"

"Her grandnephew?" Dani sounded puzzled. "What was his name again?"

Meredith stood up from her desk to sit on her bed. "Uh, Gregory, I think."

"Oh, yeah. I guess he was okay. Why? Did you think he was cute or something?"

"What?" That was the farthest thing from her mind. "Well, okay. He is cute, but I got the distinct feeling Millie didn't like him."

"Oh, yeah, I got that feeling, too. I don't know, though. He seemed okay to me."

"I guess."

Dani cleared her throat. "Hey, Meredith? What are you doing during Winter Recess the week after next?"

"Besides working on my portfolio? I don't know. My folks are working, so I'll be in charge of Mikey the whole week. I'll probably take him to the movies or something."

"Can we take him bowling, too?"

Meredith smiled. Dani wanted to take her and her brother out. She was kind of overwhelmed. She'd never had a friend to do things with. She fell back snugly into her pillows. "Sure, but I don't think you realize what you're getting yourself into. I'm no athlete, and Mikey's, well, Mikey, but if you can handle both of us, then, sure, we'd love to go bowling with you."

"Cool. And maybe we could go back to the old house with Mikey afterward. I mean, now that we can go inside any time we want, we could get subs and have a picnic or something."

"That would be fun. I bet that would help Mikey overcome his fear of the house."

Dani laughed heartily into the phone. "And yours, too, I imagine."

Meredith joined in her laughter. "Yeah, I think you're right. I'm so sorry I almost blinded you with the flash on my camera on Saturday, but that house gives me the creeps. Even though we've met Esther and Millie, and they're just wonderful, I still think Esther's right. I still think that house is cursed or haunted or something."

"Okay. I'll be like Millie." Dani changed her voice to sound gruff. "'Pah, the old painted lady's not cursed; she's just old.'" She laughed and switched back to her normal voice. "Hey, when are you starting their portraits?"

Meredith took a deep breath. She hadn't thought that far ahead. "Um, well, I have to finish most of my AP portfolio first, then I can start their portraits."

"Do they have to pose for you like I am?"

"Well, that might be an issue because I want to paint them slightly younger. You know, like in their fifties or something. So, I have to use photographs for that, but I guess I should ask them what era they want depicted. You know? Having yourself preserved in paint is kind of a personal thing."

Dani laughed. "Believe me, I know."

Meredith laughed but realized she was also a little nervous about painting Dani's portrait. She wanted to depict Dani's expression perfectly. That smile. Her eyes. She wanted to capture the essence that was Dani Lassiter. Getting that personal with a subject was difficult, but Meredith had a willing subject, which was half the battle sometimes.

Meredith attempted to sound reassuring. "You'll be fine. All you have to do is sit. In fact, you'll probably be bored in less than five minutes. I'm the one who has to do all the work."

"Yeah, I guess you're right. You do have the hard part. Well, I guess I should get going. I just called to say hi."

Meredith smiled as they said their goodbyes and hung up. She liked having a friend who called just to say hi.

Chapter 9

Hot Chocolate

Meredith held her hair back with her left hand while Dani slid the blue hair band off Meredith's wrist and placed it in her open palm. Meredith put the band around her thick hair and took a deep breath. She had spent a good part of the previous evening going over the sketch she had made of Dani, so her plan of attack would be firmly planted in her mind before she applied paint to the canvas.

Mrs. Levine's small workroom had two large windows that helped the room seem less claustrophobic. The afternoon sun managed to show itself between the gray clouds, and Meredith welcomed the natural sunlight. Mrs. Levine had provided a couple of adjustable floor lamps for additional lighting if they needed it. Meredith assumed her teacher used these for her own projects. Meredith pushed her glasses up the bridge of her nose and then worked for several minutes on a general head and shoulders outline of Dani on the canvas. Once satisfied with the positioning, she added a squeeze of cerulean blue and a squeeze of zinc white acrylic paint to her palette. She used her palette knife to mix them.

Before applying the paint, Meredith asked, "Still comfy?"

Dani shifted in Mrs. Levine's desk chair. "I guess. But I'm kind of nervous." She cleared her throat several times but couldn't seem to get it clear.

Meredith laughed. "Well, we won't get the whole thing done in one day. You're not even going to look like much today. I've already sketched you with light pencil and am about to put color to your shirt. Thanks for wearing the powder blue one. The blue brings out your eyes."

"Would you stop that?"

"Stop what?"

"Making me turn red. I'm probably going to ruin the painting."

Meredith smiled as Dani started blushing and picked up her brush. She looked at Dani for a moment and gathered in Dani's essence, Dani's energy. Most of her subjects never knew she did this, and she never told them. Meredith figured if her subjects knew she focused on them so intently, they would become more uncomfortable than they already were. Dani's energy, her aura, was strong and bright. Underneath the nerves, Meredith felt the rock-steady Dani she was getting to know. Meredith smiled again.

"What?" Dani asked with raised eyebrows.

"Oh, nothing. I was just thinking how amazing it is that Dani Lassiter, president of the senior class, is sitting here posing for me."

"And why should that be *amazing*?" Dani made air quotes when she said the word amazing.

"Well, a few weeks ago, I had no friends."

Dani smiled. "But you're changing that, aren't you?"

"Yeah. Seems that way." Meredith put a few brush strokes to Dani's shirt.

"Hey, that John Casey thing. You're the talk of the school, you know."

"I know. I'm not sure that's a good thing, though."

Dani shifted in her seat. "I moved. Sorry." She had a scared expression on her face.

"No, you're fine, but sit still, or I'll have to call you Mikey."

"Okay, okay. But I still think it's good that people know you can stand up for yourself. I, for one, am most proud."

"Well, thank you. Now shut up so I can focus." Meredith added an ear-to-ear grin to let Dani know she was teasing. She couldn't believe she had just told the senior class president to shut up. Several weeks ago, the thought of doing that would have seemed impossible.

A comfortable silence settled over the painter and sitter. Meredith kept an eye on the time, though, because she didn't want to make them late for their history class.

"Can I talk yet?" Dani murmured through closed lips.

Meredith laughed. "Sure. We've been at this a long time. You have excellent powers of concentration, by the way. Most of my subjects look bored after only a few minutes."

"Oh, I just took myself to another place. Honestly, if I didn't daydream, I'd be self-conscience the whole time and probably get an ulcer."

"Where did you take yourself?" Meredith dabbed her paintbrush in her cerulean blue mixture and put a few more strokes on Dani's shoulders.

"I daydreamed about the Hudson Pines Senior Center and thought about Esther and Millie. I thought about Gregory."

"Oh? And do you still think he's an okay guy?"

"Sure. And you're right. He is a hottie. If you like that sort of thing."

"What sort of thing?"

Dani looked down but then must have remembered that she was supposed to keep her head up. "Oh, sorry. Uh, I don't know. He's just not my type."

"What's your type?"

118

When Dani didn't answer, Meredith looked out from behind the canvas and saw that Dani had turned fire engine red. Meredith changed the subject quickly. "I hadn't really thought much more about Gregory, but it would be kind of fun to have Esther as an aunt, you know?"

Dani laughed. She sounded relieved. "Yeah, really. And Millie, too. I guess she'd be an aunt, too, right?"

"I wonder if either of them has ever been married."

"Well, they'll tell us if they want us to know, you know? We probably shouldn't get too much into their private lives. Unless they volunteer the info, that is."

"Yeah, you're probably right." Meredith put her brush in the jar of murky water and wiped her hands on her rag. She would clean the brushes more thoroughly in the sink after her AP class. "I think we'd better call it a day. I've got to clean up a little bit so Mrs. Levine can have her office back."

Meredith was about to pull the band out of her hair but, on a whim, decided to keep her hair pulled back for the rest of the day.

As they made their way out of the art room and up the stairs to their history class, Dani looked over her shoulder and said, "What do you think the other kids thought about us going into Mrs. Levine's private workroom?"

"Since when do you care what other kids think?"

"No, you're right. I don't really care what they think. We weren't breaking any rules, right?"

"Yeah, and besides, Mrs. Levine set up the whole thing. Probably because the sketch of your scissors was so amazingly awesome."

"Yeah, I know. Did you see my scissors?" Dani beamed. Meredith smiled but rolled her eyes at her friend.

Dani had taken to sitting in the back row next to Meredith, and as they walked past Ben Kinsey, Meredith caught the glare he threw at her. Mr. Dalton didn't assign seats, but usually, once kids chose seats at the beginning of the school year, they didn't change. How Dani got the guy who sat next to her to swap seats was still a mystery. Meredith would never have been able to do it.

The late bell rang to begin the class, and Mr. Dalton stood up from behind his desk. "Okay, people, settle down." He leaned on the front edge of his desk and waited for the din of student conversations to subside. "Okay, before we get into our topic for the day, I want to remind you that your typed proposals are due next Friday. And for you last-minute types, remember that mid-winter recess begins right after that, so make sure the proposals aren't late. I want to look them over during break. Yeah, I know. A fun vacation for me."

Dani smiled at Meredith, and Meredith smiled back. Their proposal was already typed up and ready to hand in.

"Okay," Mr. Dalton said. "Notebooks out. Pens poised. We're starting the American Revolution."

The students groaned, but Mr. Dalton laughed because he'd obviously been expecting that exact reaction.

Mr. Dalton, apparently, was a real fan of New York's role in the American Revolution. He shined an overhead of an old map of Fort Ticonderoga on the pull-down screen. Meredith had been to the old fort once since it still sat on the New York State side of Lake Champlain.

"This whole area," he said, making a wide circle around the areas, including Lake Champlain and Lake George, "was critical in the war."

As her teacher continued his lecture about the war, Meredith thought about the mountain town of Lake George, only a couple hours north of Albany, just inside the Adirondack Park. Meredith's family had taken a week's vacation there when she was twelve and

Mikey was six. She remembered the big lake and the boat tour, but the thing that stuck with her most was not the lake itself but the Canadian flags that flew everywhere in the town. She even received a Canadian penny in her change when she bought some candy in one of the local shops. She smiled because she still had that penny in her cigar box of treasures. She wondered if Dani had ever been to Lake George. Maybe they could take Mikey up there during the summer.

Mr. Dalton explained that the French built the Fort, originally called Fort Carillon, in 1755, but the British, threatened by a fort so close to their land, gained control in 1759. The British promptly changed the name to Fort Ticonderoga. Still, oddly enough, they only held onto the fort for sixteen years because the Green Mountain Boys from Vermont, led by American colonists Ethan Allen and Benedict Arnold, captured it in 1775. In 1776, Arnold, still an American patriot, constructed the very first American navy on Lake Champlain in an attempt to prevent British retaliation from Canada. Unfortunately, British General John Burgoyne, coming from Canada, recaptured the fort for the British in 1777.

Mr. Dalton explained that the only way for big ships to travel to the seemingly landlocked Lake Champlain was along the St. Lawrence River bordering the present United States and Canada. A question suddenly occurred to Meredith. Was Canada its own country at that time? She thought Canada was affiliated with England in some way back then and was curious to know its role in the war.

Meredith often had questions like this during class, but she was never the kind of student who raised her hand. She would wait until a classmate asked the question, or she would look it up later. Raising her hand and actually speaking in front of other students terrified her. She had no idea how Dani did it. She wanted to slip the question to Dani in hopes that Dani would ask, but Dani would probably tell her to ask for herself.

Meredith took a deep breath and slowly but steadily raised her hand. She could feel rather than see Dani's surprise. Meredith didn't dare look at her because she might lose her nerve otherwise. Mr. Dalton stopped in mid-sentence and said, "Oh," with surprise in his voice. "Meredith, you have a question?"

"Uh, yeah. Was Canada a country? Was the American Revolution against both England *and* Canada?"

Mr. Dalton nodded his head. His nod seemed to say that she had brought up a valid point. But before Mr. Dalton could answer. Ben Kinsey coughed into his hand and said, "Stupid."

Meredith reacted before she could stop herself. "Ben Kinsey," she blurted, "I wasn't talking to you."

The class went completely silent for a moment and then erupted in cheers for the quiet girl in the back of the room. Meredith heard things like, "Way to go, girl," and "It's about time she stood up to him." She couldn't believe the support she heard. She thought everyone hated her. Dani reached over and patted her arm, but Meredith barely felt it. She could not believe what she had just done. She looked up at Mr. Dalton in apology and waited for him to take control of the situation. He was about to say something when the bell rang to end the class period.

The students got up from their seats, and Meredith feared that, once again, she would be the talk of the school or at least the talk of the senior class. She wasn't sure that was a good thing, and she wasn't sure how Ben would take her public tongue-lashing. Some people, she knew, could dish it out but couldn't take it.

She put her notebook and history book in her bag and slowly stood up.

Dani said, "Who are you, and what have you done with my

friend, Meredith?"

"Oh, stop. He just hit the wrong button today, I guess."

"Well, I think—"

"Miss Bedford, would you come up here, please?" Mr. Dalton walked behind his desk with his arms folded.

Dani whispered, "Uh oh. I'll catch you later. Tell me what he says."

Meredith shouldered her book bag and walked up to her teacher. She shouldn't have blown up to Ben, but she'd had enough. And she had restrained herself, too. She wanted to say so much more but didn't dare. She felt the blood rise to her face and spread down her neck.

Mr. Dalton waited until all the students had filed out the door. Once the last student crossed the threshold, he looked her in the eye and stuck out his hand. "Miss Bedford, it's good to *finally* meet you."

Meredith smiled. She shook Mr. Dalton's hand and apologized for being disrespectful during class.

He continued to shake her hand. "Meredith, I've been waiting so long for you to stand up for yourself, and you did it tactfully." He let go of her hand. "I'm just glad I was able to witness it. Brava, Meredith, brava. By the way, Canada was still a primitive territory of England at the time and wasn't yet recognized as its own separate force. I'll pick up the thread of your question on Monday. But, anyway, I'm very proud of you."

~~~

The middle of February had arrived, but winter had not quite given up on the town of Whickett. The just-above-freezing temperature and the nasty drizzle would make the three-quarter-mile walk home miserable. As she and Mikey made their way toward the front doors of the high school, Meredith was relieved there was only one more day of school before the mid-winter recess vacation.

After standing up to both Ben and John Casey, Meredith had no trouble with either of them. John steered clear of her while Ben did his best to ignore her.

"Ready, Mikey Nikey?" Meredith pulled the green hair band out of her hair. She pulled her knit hat out of a pocket of her pea coat and plunked it on her head. She double-checked Mikey to make sure he was bundled tight for the weather. She opened the door and cringed at the cold. Would winter's gray, barren, muted colors ever become green and bright again?

They made their way toward the main circle of the school driveway. Meredith kept her head down to keep the wind-blown rain out of her face. Out of the corner of her eye, she saw a pickup truck pull into the circle. She put an arm in front of Mikey to stop him. Meredith readjusted her scarf, waiting for the pickup to pass, but when it didn't, she looked up and saw Dani waving to them from the driver's seat of the now-familiar white truck.

Dani opened the passenger door and said, "Get in, you guys. I'll drive you home. It's too gross to walk today."

Mikey, it seemed, didn't need a second invitation. He dropped his book bag on the wet pavement and crawled into the warm cab of the truck. "Hi, Dani," he shouted.

Dani laughed and whispered, "Hey, dude. What's up?"

"What up?" he whispered back.

Meredith shrugged and climbed in after her brother with both book bags in tow. She shut the door and said, "Don't you have lacrosse practice? Pre-season workouts or something? She reached down to help buckle Mikey in and then put on her own seatbelt.

"Uh, yeah, but I haven't been late yet this year. I'll drop you guys off, and then I'll head back. I was thinking about you and figured I'd try to catch you before you went home." She put the truck in drive, and they headed off school property.

"Well, Mikey and I both thank you. Our cold noses and toes thank you, too. Right, Mikey?"

"Right, Merry."

"Say thank you to Dani, Mikey."

"Thank, Dani."

"No problem, dude."

They drove in silence for a few moments, and then Dani said, "I can't believe how fast this school year is flying by."

Meredith laughed to herself. She had thought the exact opposite. The school year wasn't speeding along fast enough for her taste. "By the way, what is the latest countdown figure toward graduation? And freedom?"

"Ah, freedom. I haven't looked at my countdown calendar lately, so I really don't know." Dani glanced at Meredith and then back toward the road. "I always wonder if sixth-period teachers hate me because we take away one period every other month for our senior class meetings."

"That's probably why they schedule a lot of study halls and elective classes, like our art class, during sixth."

"Yeah, probably." Dani turned onto Center Street and reached down to hold Mikey's hand.

Meredith smiled at the sight of her brother holding her friend's hand. "So, do you know?"

"Know what?"

Meredith laughed. "How many days of school are left?"

"Got you hooked, don't I?"

"Yeah. I need to know how many more days of torture I have left." About a month earlier, Meredith had been dead serious about the "torture" aspect of high school, but things had changed a little since meeting Dani.

Dani's voice took on a serious tone. "Meredith, I don't think Ben will bother you anymore."

"I'm not so sure about that. I mean, I embarrassed him. He might resent that."

"He deserved it. He's been pissing me off all year. He's so immature. I called him last weekend after the big Bedford-Kinsey fight."

Meredith reached over Mikey's head and smacked her friend playfully in the arm.

"Hey!" Dani exclaimed.

"It wasn't a fight."

"Fine. The battle. Just kidding. Anyway, we talked, and I told him to lay off you."

"Really?" Meredith was a little skeptical. "And what did he have to say to that?"

"Oh, I don't know. He seemed to be okay with it. I told him that if he got to know you, he'd see how nice you were and what a good friend you could be."

Meredith raised her eyebrows. "Thanks, Dani, but I really don't foresee me and Ben Kinsey ever being friends. I mean, no offense because I know you guys are good friends, but with all those things he's said to me, I just don't see it."

"I know. I know. I'm just saying. And it's around eighty."

"Eighty? Eighty what?"

Dani laughed. "I think we have about eighty days of high school torture left."

Only eighty? The small number surprised her. Maybe she wasn't in such a hurry for high school to end after all.

Dani pulled the truck into the middle turn lane of Center Street. A car passed them on the right side, and Meredith pointed excitedly. "Dani, look. Isn't that Gregory?"

Dani craned her neck to look in the car. "The passenger? Grandnephew Gregory? Yeah, he's got that same rust-colored hair. It says Cayuga Commercial Real Estate on the side. Why is grandnephew Gregory here in a real estate car?"

"Good question. Doesn't he live somewhere in New Jersey or something? I don't know, but I think it's time we visit Esther and Millie again. We have to get those pictures from them anyway, right? Then we can ask them about the whereabouts of said grandnephew."

Dani laughed. "Sounds like we're private detectives or something. Right, Mikey? Detectives?"

"'Tectives, yeah, Dani. Yeah, dude." He flashed his heart-melting smile at Dani.

Dani returned his grin and then smiled at Meredith, causing Meredith's insides to turn to jelly. *Why does her smile disarm me? If she asked me to go bungee jumping off the Brooklyn Bridge, I'd probably jump if it meant I could spend more time with her.*

Meredith smiled back and hoped her blush wasn't too revealing. Lately, Dani made her feel funny inside. It was a little embarrassing.

Dani looked back to the road, but Meredith could still see her smiling. Dani pulled into Meredith's driveway and put the truck in park. She kept the engine running.

Meredith took off her seatbelt and helped Mikey off with his. "Thanks for the lift, Dani."

Meredith was about to reach for the door handle when Dani said, "Wait." She reached under the front seat and pulled out two heart-shaped boxes. She handed one to Mikey and the other to Meredith. "Happy Valentine's Day, you guys."

"For us?" Meredith's heart sped up. She and Mikey had exchanged Valentine's cards and candy with their parents that morning, but she hadn't expected anything from Dani. She focused on Mikey to hide her discomfort. "Look, Mikey Bikey, Dani gave us candy. Say thank you."

"Thank you." Mikey looked up at Dani and flashed his million-dollar smile again.

"You're welcome, dude."

"Welcome, dude," Mikey mimicked.

"Yeah," Meredith agreed. "Thank you. We uh. I didn't get you anything."

Dani shrugged. "That's okay. I just wanted to get you something. You *and* Mikey."

Meredith wondered whether Dani's pink cheeks were solely from the cold. She didn't think so. Although Dani still smiled, her eyes had become tender, almost vulnerable. They looked at each other in silence for a few moments. Dani's gaze made her feel warm, like the first sip of hot chocolate on a cold day. She reluctantly broke eye contact and opened the truck door. "See you tomorrow?"

"I'll call you tonight if that's okay."

"Okay." Meredith trembled, and she wasn't sure why.

They got out of the truck, and when they reached the front door, Meredith let Mikey go inside first. She lingered on the landing, holding her box of candy tight against her chest, and turned around slowly to face Dani, who was still watching her from her truck. Meredith waved, and Dani nodded but didn't back out. Yes, Dani gave her that hot chocolate feeling from head to toe. Meredith stepped into the house and smiled as she listened to the now-familiar

sound of Dani's truck in her driveway.

Chapter 10
Fish Sticks

Meredith watched Dani and Mikey race from the bowling alley to Dani's pickup truck. This had been their third bowling trip during winter break, and Meredith was positively worn out. Even though Mikey had thrown a lot of bowling balls for her that morning, she was still bushed from the unfamiliar physical exertion. But despite achy muscles, she hustled after them because she wanted to get out of the February cold as soon as possible. The sky was a hopeful powder blue, and the sun was brilliant but deceiving. The late February temperatures made spring seem a year away, not a month. Meredith laughed when Dani played the sore loser because Mikey touched the back of the pickup truck first.

Mikey did his happy dance and taunted, "I win. I win. Beat you."

"Oh, fine," Dani muttered. "You run too fast. It must be all that taekwondo, dude."

"Dude." He gleefully took Meredith's outstretched hand and walked to the passenger side of the truck. Dani walked to their side as well and unlocked the door for them.

"Thanks." Meredith let Mikey climb in first. "We're not late, are we?"

"No, Millie said one o'clock, and it's quarter 'till."

Meredith got in. "I can't wait to see those old pictures of the house, you know?"

"Definitely. They'll be great for our project."

Dani made her way back around the truck, and Mikey scrambled into his usual spot in the center. He found both ends of his seatbelt and snapped them together cleanly.

Dani had just gotten in on her side of the truck and shot an amused glance at Meredith. "He's amazing, isn't he?"

"Yeah, he's a cool kid. I'm going to miss him when I go to college." Meredith buckled her own seat belt.

"I can't believe I never asked where you applied." Dani put on her own seatbelt.

"Well, I never asked you, either," Meredith said. "I applied to some schools around here, like Union, but I really want to go to Syracuse."

"No way."

"Yeah, my dad loves anything and everything related to Syracuse. My father's watched so many Syracuse Orangemen. What do they call the women's teams? Orangewomen?"

"I think they call everybody 'Orange' now." Dani chuckled.

"Really? Well, we've had so many *Orange* sporting events on in the house that I got curious about the school. They have a great art department. I sent them my portfolio in January. I should hear back in about a month."

Dani stared at her, mouth open.

Meredith smirked and started to feel around her nose. "What? Do I have a booger?"

"Booger." Mikey giggled. "Merry said booger."

This made Dani laugh, too, and she said, "No, I just can't believe we both want to go to 'Cuse. I want to play lacrosse there. The coach isn't recruiting me, so I'll have to try and make the team as a walk-on, but I don't care. Oh, my God, Meredith. Wouldn't that be so cool if we went to the same college?"

"Yeah, that would be awesome. It'd be nice not to have to start completely over." Meredith laughed to herself because she had spent the last year and a half wanting to get away from all things Whickett High School. Going northwest across the state to Syracuse University was part of that plan. The plan where no one would know her. She still wanted to start over, but a friend like Dani in a new school would be nice. Dani put the truck in gear and pulled out of the parking lot. They headed toward the old painted lady, which was a few blocks down Center Street.

Dani opened the drive gate, jumped back into the truck, and pulled up the long driveway. Meredith looked back and made sure they'd left enough room for Esther and Millie's car.

Dani said, "Should we wait here or go in?"

"Well, I don't think Esther and Millie are here yet. I mean, I don't see another car." Meredith shivered from the cold and made the decision. "Yeah, let's go inside. But let's wait on the first floor. It's still their house, after all."

"Yeah, that sounds cool." Dani looked down at Mikey, who'd finally figured out how to unbuckle his seatbelt. "Hey, Mikey, want to go in the scary house?"

Meredith shot Dani a look, but Dani had already turned away to hop out of the truck. Meredith hoped Mikey would be okay inside the 'scawey house' because Dani had fallen off the front porch the first time they were there. And then they'd heard a door slam inside the house, which sent the three of them running to the truck.

Meredith said to Mikey, "It's okay. Dani and I went inside once, and it wasn't scary at all. It was nice. Really big. You should see the big fireplaces. Do you want to go see?"

"Okay, c'mon." He pushed his sister so she would open the

passenger door and let him out.

"Okay, okay, pushy Mikey." She opened the door and pulled her coat tighter around her. Meredith grabbed her brother's right hand while Dani reached for his left. They walked like that for a few yards, but then Mikey suddenly pulled his hands together, so Meredith's and Dani's hands touched. He let go and said, "Dani hold Merry. Dani hold Merry." He laughed and ran ahead of them toward the front door.

As Meredith pulled her hand away, she was surprised to see the look of utter panic in Dani's eyes. She rolled her eyes for Dani's benefit. "He's silly. Come on. We'd better catch up to him. The railing's gone on the front porch. Remember?"

Dani cleared her throat. "Okay."

Mikey tried to open the front door, but his gloved hands spun around the knob.

"Hey, Mikey, we need the key." Dani leaned the heavy flower pot back with one hand and reached under with the other. She held up the key. "See? You put the key into the lock like this." Dani turned the key and let the door swing open slowly.

Meredith grimaced at the slow and steady squeak of the hinges.

Dani must have seen the grimace. "I know. It's still creepy, isn't it?"

Meredith nodded and followed her brother and Dani into the house.

Meredith fanned her nose. "Oh, my God. It stinks like cigarettes in here. Do Esther and Millie smoke?"

"I don't know. I hope not, but you're right; it's gross. I don't remember it smelling bad like this last time."

Meredith shook her head. "It didn't."

Dani shrugged. "Well, at least it's warmer inside."

"Yeah, I'm glad about that." Meredith walked into the sitting room, and Mikey followed her. "Hey, Mikey, let me turn up the heat, and then we'll look at the fireplace." At the mention of the word fireplace, Mikey let go of his sister's hand and scurried into the fireplace.

Meredith laughed. "Or you could go now." She moved the lever on the thermostat to sixty-eight degrees.

Mikey tipped his head and stood up inside the fireplace. As they waited for the two older women to arrive, Mikey made sure Dani and Meredith saw him in the fireplace at least a half dozen times.

Meredith took a couple of pictures on the first floor. She walked to the window in the sitting room and looked out over the auto parts store. She frowned. *How sad it must have been for them to see their neighborhood turn into stores and traffic. Progress,* she thought with a sigh, *isn't always.*

"Hey, Merry," Dani called from the bottom stair.

Meredith raised an eyebrow. "Um…'Merry'?"

Dani shrugged. "I don't know. It sounds so cute when Mikey calls you that."

"Okay, but don't let anyone at school hear you call me that." She grinned and rolled her eyes.

"Sure thing…Merry." Dani's eyes were playful. "Let's go check out the kitchen. I think it's in the back of the house." She pointed behind her.

"Sounds good. Hey, Mikey? Get out of the fireplace and come check out the kitchen with us."

They heard an "Okay" echo off the stone inside the sitting room. Mikey came running into the front foyer. "Okay, Merry, c'mon." He grabbed her hand and led her back toward the sitting room. He stopped in his tracks and said, "Where?"

Meredith and Dani laughed, and Meredith steered him back around toward the kitchen. The door to the kitchen swung both ways on its hinges, like a door that might be found in the kitchen of a busy restaurant. It was also one of those doors that could knock you out if you didn't pay attention.

Both Meredith and Dani stopped dead in their tracks when they saw the mess. Beer cans covered the kitchen counters and floor. The cigarette stench overwhelmed their nostrils. Whoever had smoked the cigarettes couldn't find ashtrays but had at least used make-shift tin foil ashtrays instead.

Meredith let go of Mikey's hand to inspect the damage more closely. The sink was loaded with balled-up shop towels like the ones her father used in the garage. An empty pizza box sat discarded on the counter. "What happened in here? This is gross." She picked up a couple of beer cans from the floor and put them on the counter. "Do Millie and Esther drink beer?"

"I don't know, but this is way too much beer for just two people." Dani reached down and picked up one of the foil ashtrays. "This is really weird. If we were real detectives, we could send these to the lab and get DNA samples, and then we'd know who had this party."

Mikey reached for the other foil ashtray.

"Cigarettes are foul, right dude?" Dani picked up the other ashtrays and put them both in a high cupboard out of his reach.

Mikey whined, but Dani said, "You don't want to get that stuff on your hands, Mikey. It's gross." To Meredith, she said, "Maybe a few kids got in and, I don't know, had a party or something."

"Sure looks like it." Meredith felt a slight prickle at the base of her spine. She wondered if Dani was thinking the same thing she was. "Dani?"

"Yeah?"

"Do you think it was those guys?"

"What guys?"

"You know. Those guys from the auto parts store that night." Meredith enlisted Mikey's help picking up beer cans to get his mind off the cigarettes.

"Oh, yeah. They were smoking, weren't they?" Dani walked to the back door. "And, look. This lock is busted open, probably with a crowbar. Kids don't usually carry crowbars when they go out to party."

Meredith stacked the beer cans far back on the counter so Mikey couldn't reach them. "I'm just glad Esther and Millie weren't here when they broke in. This time or the last time."

Dani said seriously, "Do you think they were in the house the last time?" Her eyes were wide.

Something prickled at the base of her spine. "Oh, my God, Dani. I don't know. We didn't smell cigarettes last time, though. What do you think?"

Dani shook her head. "That front door didn't open itself."

"See? I told you I closed it tight."

"I know you did. I heard it click shut. And I still had the house key in my pocket, but I didn't want to scare you even more than you already were." Dani's tone was gentle.

Meredith was grateful Dani had been so thoughtful. "I think I'll take all the pictures we need today and never come back. Ever." Meredith put the last of the cans on the counter.

"I hear you," Dani muttered.

Mikey strained to reach the cupboard for the cigarettes since he could still see them through the clear glass. Meredith gently pushed his hand away. "Mikey, no." She looked at the tray of cigarette butts and said, "Hey, Dani, look at these. Does something look weird to you?"

Dani came over and looked closely. "Yeah, you're right. Something's not right."

Meredith pulled out one of the makeshift ashtrays. She nodded her head quickly. "Wait, I know. My grandfather used to mash his cigarettes out in the ashtray. These look like they were left to burn out on their own."

"Yeah," Dani added as if she, too, realized the same thing. "You're right. They don't look smoked. Look at the long cylindrical ashes. And look at this one." She pointed to one that hadn't quite burned all the way down.

"Yeah, I think they were lit and left to burn." She felt a slight prickle of fear run up her spine.

They heard the front door open, and Millie called, "Yoo hoo. Are you girls here?"

Dani called out, "Yeah, we're in the kitchen."

"Are you smoking in here?" Millie called.

"No, not us," Dani called back.

When Esther and Millie opened the swinging door, Dani raised both hands and said, "It wasn't us. We found it this way."

Millie looked instantly upset. She picked up an empty beer can off the counter and set it down again. She looked at Esther, who stood in the doorway leaning heavily on her walker, obviously tired from the trek up the driveway. "Esther, someone has violated our painted lady."

Meredith went to the back door. "They broke the lock."

Millie patted Meredith on the arm and said, "Honey, we can fix this." She turned to Esther, who still stood in the doorway. "I think I need to come by here more often."

With effort, Esther used the walker to shuffle into the kitchen.

"Yes, that's probably a good idea, dearest."

"Dani," Meredith said, "why don't you and Mikey get those plastic chairs from the upstairs balcony?"

"Good idea. Come on, Mikey, let's get the chairs, and then you can show Esther and Millie how you fit in the fireplace, okay?"

"Okay." He reached for her hand and pulled her out the door. "C'mon."

Millie and Esther laughed. Esther said, "He's darling."

"I'm sorry. I should have introduced you. That's Mikey, my brother. I hope it was okay to bring him. He loves being with Dani."

Millie rinsed out another beer can and said to Meredith, "You do, too, I imagine."

"Millie!" Esther scolded.

Meredith felt herself blush. Why did Millie have to make comments like that about her and Dani? Millie was complicated, very complicated, Meredith decided.

Millie smiled and focused on the beer cans. "I'm going to take these back to the store and get the five-cent deposit for each and every one. I should make…," she counted the beer cans, "whole dollar twenty."

Esther shuffled over to the broken lock. "Millie, you'd better get down to the hardware store and get a new lock, too."

"Yeah, I'll take Dani with me. I'm sure she's handy with tools." Millie winked at Meredith.

Yes, Meredith thought, Millie was complicated, indeed.

Before Millie and Dani left for the hardware store, they examined the broken lock and the splintered wood around it for a good ten minutes. The wood needed some metal plating for reinforcement in case the hoodlums, as Millie called them, came back.

While Millie and Dani were out getting a new lock for the back door, Meredith and Esther looked over the old photographs. Meredith reached down into the cardboard box between their chairs and pulled out another photo album. "These pictures are wonderful. Thank you so much for letting us borrow them. Dani has a scanner she'll use to make digital copies, and as soon as she does that, we can get these pictures right back to you."

Esther patted Meredith's hand. "That's fine, honey. You go ahead and keep them as long as you like. It's nice that someone's taken an interest in our old house. I'm anxious to get the Randall-Bradley House going. We've just got to work out a few more things, like the proper zoning. Once we do that, this old house is going to become part of the Women Helping Women Network. Millie found out about it a few years ago. It's a nationwide network of homes for women."

"That's so cool." Meredith rubbed her hands together. "And thanks for turning the heat up even more. I think I can finally take off my coat. Hey, Mikey Bikey," Meredith called to her brother. Mikey had taken to tromping up and down the stairs after showing Esther repeatedly how he could stand in the fireplace. "Do you want to take off your coat?"

"Okay." He bounded back down the stairs and stood in front of his sister with arms spread out.

Meredith laughed and said, "You can unzip your own coat."

"Okay." He grabbed the zipper and pulled it down hard, but it didn't budge. He tried several times, but the zipper just wouldn't go down. He groaned in frustration.

"Here, let me help you." Meredith reached over to grab the zipper, fearful that Mikey's whines would bother Esther.

Mikey shouted, "No," and flopped to the ground. He scooted across the floor on his backside to the fireplace and then turned away from them so he could work at the zipper by himself. After several long and nerve-wracking minutes for Meredith, he finally got the zipper undone.

"Hooray, Mikey," Esther congratulated him.

"That's awesome." Meredith gave him a thumbs-up. "Can you hang your coat over the railing?" He was obviously confused, so Meredith got up and draped her own coat over the stair railing. He put his coat right next to hers.

Esther stood up and took off her coat as well. Mikey came up to her and said, "Hang up." He reached for Esther's coat.

Esther smiled and said, "Why, yes, young man, you can hang up my coat for me. Thank you very much." Mikey smiled and ran to the railing, where he flung Esther's coat next to his own.

Meredith said, "Sorry about Mikey's little outburst. I think he's tired. He's probably hungry, too."

"Oh, he's fine, honey. Don't worry."

Just then, loud footsteps sounded on the porch. Esther's face lit up. "That's my Millie. I've missed that step on the porch."

She was right. The front door to the house opened wide, and Millie yelled, "Lunch is ready." She held out a bucket of fried chicken.

Dani came in behind Millie with several bags from the hardware store and the Price Chopper grocery store.

Esther's face lit up into a huge grin. "You got lunch? How sweet. Dearest, we don't have any plates or silverware."

Dani held out a Price Chopper bag. "We took care of that. We got paper plates, plastic utensils, napkins, big trash bags for our lunch trash, and the debris in the kitchen."

Meredith got up and took the chicken bucket and the other fast food bags from them. "Thanks for getting the food, you guys. Hey, Mikey, look. Dani and Millie brought us lunch. Say thank you."

Mikey ran to Dani and hugged her around the middle. "Thank,

Dani."

"You're welcome, dude."

"Welcome, dude." He giggled.

"Thank Millie, too," Meredith directed.

Mikey let go of Dani and ran over to Millie as if to hug her, too, but he stopped short and looked up at her. He said shyly, "Thank, Mill."

Millie laughed. "You're welcome, young one." To Meredith, she said, "He doesn't know me well enough, I guess."

Meredith nodded and smiled.

"Hey, dude." Dani reached into one of the grocery bags. "I've got something else for you."

"Okay." He came over and took the book Dani offered him. "Thank, Dani." He sat cross-legged on the floor and opened up his new book.

Meredith looked at Dani questioningly. Dani said, "Oh, we were in Price Chopper, and I saw one of those *Harry, Dog Spy* books and thought he might like it. That was okay, wasn't it?"

"More than okay," Meredith said, relieved. "This'll give him something to do. Thanks." She took the plastic wrap off the paper plates and unwrapped the paper napkin stack. While they ate, Meredith told Dani about the pictures Esther was going to lend them for their project.

After their quick meal, Dani and Millie went into the kitchen to start repairs while Mikey settled on the floor near his sister to read his new book. He was so absorbed in it that Meredith and Esther were able to look at more photos uninterrupted. Meredith saw pictures of Esther as a young girl, Esther's family, and the house when it was much newer. The house had been splendid in its day. At one point in the parade of pictures, she got a sense of the time period when Millie entered Esther's life. She couldn't help but smile because Millie and Esther were obviously great friends.

Esther closed the last of the photo albums and sat back in the resin chair. "Oh, I'm going to miss this old house. But time marches on, and Millie and I need to pare it down a bit. I know I'll be okay once I see the Randall-Bradley house open and helping people. And you girls have been so helpful. Millie and I missed out on not having children." She laughed loudly. "Maybe we can adopt you two, but I guess you'd have to be our grandchildren at this point. Can you adopt grandchildren?"

Meredith smiled. "We'd love to have, uh, adopted grandmothers. That's sweet. And I think what you and Millie want to do with the house is awesome. I want to give you a gift for the Randall-Bradley House if you and Millie are willing, that is."

"Oh?"

"I want to paint your portraits for the front hallway." She pointed toward the front door. "You know, somewhere in the entryway."

"Meredith, oh my." Esther put a hand on Meredith's arm. "That would be so nice. Let's go tell Millie. I need to get up and walk a little bit, anyway."

Meredith helped Esther out of the plastic chair and pulled the walker over. She then reached down and tousled her brother's hair. "Hey, Mikey, Esther and I are going to the kitchen to check on Dani and Millie, okay?"

"Okay." He didn't look up from his book.

Meredith opened the kitchen door just in time to hear Millie proclaim, "That ought to hold 'em. Belts and suspenders."

Meredith held open the door so Esther could shuffle through.

"Belts and suspenders?" Dani asked, confused. Meredith hadn't understood the comment either.

Esther laughed. "They're too young, Millie. Aren't they?"

"Pah," Millie said. "C'mon, youngsters. Belts and suspenders. It means you overdo something like wearing both a belt *and* suspenders to keep your pants up."

Dani clapped Millie on the back. "I get it. That's cool." Apparently, Dani and Millie had become old friends in one afternoon.

Meredith checked out the repaired back door. She never would have known what to do. They had replaced the back door lock and the doorjamb hardware, reinforced the wood with metal sheeting, and then secured a two-by-four barricade across the door. Meredith assumed the barricade was the "and suspenders" part of the project.

Millie leaned close to Meredith and whispered, "Your girl is quite handy with the tools. I'd hang onto her." Millie winked and turned back to Esther. "My work here is done. How's the hip, hon?"

"A little sore, dearest. I think we should get going. Did I tell you, girls? They let me go home for good two days ago. You should have seen how much work my Millie did to unpack the new apartment. It's so cozy, and she did everything. We must have you girls over some time. Oh, which reminds me, Millie. I've informed the girls that we're adopting them as granddaughters."

"Ho, ho. That's excellent." Millie clapped Dani on the back.

Dani looked pleasantly surprised. "We are? Hey, Meredith, we've got new grandparents. Grandmoms? Hey, can I borrow the car?"

They chuckled over the new leaves in their respective family trees as they made their way out of the kitchen toward the front foyer.

Esther stopped in the foyer and said, "And, dearest? Meredith wants to paint our portraits for our Randall-Bradley house. Isn't that wonderful?"

Millie, for once, seemed incapable of responding. Meredith saw Millie's eyes get moist. For all her confident mannerisms and gruff ways, Meredith decided that Millie Bradley was an old softie.

Millie blinked back her tears, cleared her throat, and said, "Thank you, Meredith. This is a wonderful thing you're doing." She turned to Dani and said, "See? I told you she was a keeper."

Dani turned away, obviously embarrassed, but turned back around just as quickly. Her eyes grew wide. "Where's Mikey?"

Meredith looked where she had left him, only to find his book abandoned on the floor. She spun around in a panic. "Mikey?" She called. "Where are you?" There was no answer.

Dani took charge. "Millie, will you look outside for him? Esther, will you please stay here in case he comes back? Meredith, you and I should go upstairs." Dani bounded for the stairs before anyone could agree or disagree with her plan. "You take the second floor. I'll take the third."

Meredith was frantic. She knew her brother tended to wander, and she had left him alone. She tried to reason with herself that she had only left him for a minute, but she knew she had messed up. She sprinted as best she could up the stairs and into the primary bedroom on the second floor. She didn't see him and started to leave but turned back around to double-check the fireplace. He wasn't there. "Mikey," she called out. When she didn't hear him answer, she unlocked the doors to the balcony. Nothing. She saw Millie walking the fence by busy Center Street. Her nerves jangled. What if Mikey had wandered out onto the busy road?

"Millie?" Meredith shouted and heard the panic in her voice. "Anything?"

Millie looked up to the balcony and shook her head no.

"Okay," Meredith called. Her heart pounded as she made her way out of the primary bedroom. She was about to go to the room she had dubbed her art studio when Dani called from the third floor. "He's

144

here, Meredith. He's here. He's okay. He's…" She popped out of a door near the top of the stairs and laughed. "He's sleeping in the fireplace."

"He is?" Meredith ran up the stairs past Dani. Her brother was indeed sleeping in his usual fetal position. She watched his chest slowly rise and fall. She exhaled in relief and willed her pulse to slow down. "Oh, my God. That was a close call. I know I can't leave him like that. What's wrong with me?" She fought back tears and struggled to keep her composure.

When Dani moved beside her, Meredith let her sudden exhaustion consume her and leaned heavily against her friend. Dani's arm went around her, and Meredith liked the warmth she felt from her friend.

"He's okay, Meredith. We'd never let anything happen to him."

She liked Dani's comfort. It felt safe. "Thanks." Meredith lifted her head. "I think we need to get him home, okay?"

Dani nodded. "You're right. I'll go tell Millie and Esther that we found him."

Dani bounded back down the stairs, and Meredith leaned beside her brother. "Mikey? Time to get up. We have to go home now." She shook his shoulder gently.

He blinked and sat up. He blinked several more times and looked confused.

Meredith brushed the hair out of his eyes. "Are you okay? You scared me. I didn't know where you went."

He took a deep breath, clearly trying to wake up. "I'm okay, Merry." He crawled out of the fireplace and stood.

"Why did you go upstairs?"

"Look for Merry. Merry and Dani." He made his way toward the door and grinned back at her. He said, "Dani hold Merry. Dani hold

Merry." He laughed gleefully, fully awake now, and hopped down the stairs.

Meredith tried to keep up with him as best she could. When they got back down the stairs, she watched Dani on her knees, hugging Mikey anxiously. Meredith had never felt such relief.

Millie walked in the front door. "Oh, look at our three grandchildren, Esther."

"We lucked out, didn't we?"

Meredith struggled to gather up Mikey and the box with Esther's pictures without losing either. Dani relieved Meredith of the box, and they made their way out the front door. Meredith held Mikey's hand as they went down the front steps together.

Although the winter afternoon sky had darkened, Meredith clearly saw the Cayuga Commercial Real Estate car move slowly and with purpose past the house. Meredith nudged Dani in the side and pointed to the car.

Dani's eyes flew open wide. She whispered low so only Meredith could hear. "Fish sticks."

"Fish sticks?"

"Yeah. There's something fishy going on here."

Chapter 11

Don't You Know?

Meredith put two colors, brown and yellow ochre, on her pallet and mixed them with her palette knife. Today was Dani's first hair day, so she would only use browns and yellows. Later, she would add greens and grays for shadow; then, cadmium yellow mixed with white would become Dani's light blond highlights. Meredith was very pleased with Dani's portrait, even though it was only their third session.

Dani looked out the window of the workroom, obviously lost in thought. The only thing she could possibly see was the early March mud. Meredith smiled when she saw Dani distractedly flick her head to toss a lock of hair out of her eyes. She had seen Dani do this a thousand times. The movement was as familiar as that hot chocolate feeling that regularly crept into Meredith's core these days.

Meredith mixed the colors and, out of the corner of her eye, saw her friend smile. The hot chocolate feeling that always started near her belly spread through her again, and she felt her face get hot. She moved quickly behind the canvas so Dani wouldn't see her blush. She didn't understand why Dani's smile made her react so oddly. Maybe, no, probably, because Dani had been the only one to show her compassion over the last two years.

Meredith took a deep breath in an attempt to get herself together. She tried to focus on the painting in front of her but couldn't, so she asked, "Why are you smiling?"

Dani didn't answer.

"C'mon. Why were you smiling just then?" Meredith peeked out from behind the painting.

"I'm just happy, that's all. Lacrosse started. We've got a great team, and Coach Pratt has me at first home again. I'm so psyched."

"First home. Is that a good position?" Meredith reached for a round brush. She had to remind herself to keep painting while they talked.

"Yeah, you get to score a lot. I hate playing defense."

Meredith laughed. She stroked Dani's painted hair. "Yeah. Offense fits you. I don't see you as the defensive type."

"Exactly."

"So what else made you smile just now? You weren't smiling that big because of lacrosse."

Dani looked down at her hands. "Pah...just stuff."

She sounds just like Millie. Meredith waited, but Dani didn't finish her thought. Meredith pushed. "You're not going to tell me, are you?"

"Nope."

"Oh, my God, Dani Lassiter. You like someone. That's it, isn't it?" Meredith knew she had hit the nail on the head when Dani cringed and put her head in her hands to hide her smile. Meredith was surprised when a shot of jealousy torpedoed through her.

Meredith put her palette down and folded her arms. "Okay, who is it? That cute guy in history? What's his name? Brian? Is it him?"

Dani looked up, this time with only a hint of a smile in her eyes. "No, I don't like Brian. I mean, I like Brian, he's a nice guy, but I don't *like* like him."

"I'll get it out of you, Danielle Anne Lassiter. You just wait and see." Meredith picked up her palette again.

Dani just nodded and looked out the window again.

Meredith shook her head, confused by the jealousy she'd felt at Dani liking some guy. It seemed like a betrayal somehow. She took another deep breath and reminded herself that she had a job to do. The portrait wasn't going to paint itself. They settled back into their usual comfortable silence.

Meredith leaned back to take in the day's work. She still had a lot more to do, but at this point, anyone who looked at the portrait would definitely know who the subject was. She cleaned off her brush and made mental notes for their next session the following Friday. She made another mental note to thank Mrs. Levine for letting them steal time from their regular art class. She didn't know when they would have found time to do the portrait otherwise.

Meredith fully intended to give Dani the portrait once Mrs. Levine photographed it for her portfolio. Still, Meredith had become attached to it in a way she had never been to any other. She wanted to keep those blue eyes, that smiling expression.

Dani broke the silence. "Now it's my turn to ask what *you're* smiling about."

"Oh, uh...nothing, really." Meredith didn't realize she had been smiling. "I was just mentally thanking Mrs. Levine for letting us use her workroom. She's pretty cool."

"Yeah, she is."

Meredith put the paint palette back in its plastic box. She stood up to restore order to the workroom and found Dani watching her intently. Meredith marveled at her expression, how Dani could, on the one hand, appear to smile but, on the other hand, look so completely serious.

But as the silence grew between them, Meredith began to feel uneasy to the point of uncomfortable. Meredith attempted to tease her friend again. She said quietly, "So, who are you thinking about? Hmm?"

The hint of Dani's smile waned. She said, "Don't you know?"

Confused, Meredith searched her brain for who or what she was supposed to know. "I don't. You'll have to tell me."

Dani withdrew, and Meredith felt a sudden void in the small room. As an artist, she was keenly aware of the energy surrounding people, and the abruptness with which Dani retreated felt almost like a physical blow. The tiny workroom suddenly didn't have enough oxygen. She said, "I think we'd better quit for today."

"Sure." There was resignation in Dani's voice.

~~~

Meredith tried to get comfortable on the hard, cold bleachers. She pulled her winter coat tighter. The third week in March was no time to sit outside watching a sporting event, yet there they were at Dani's first lacrosse game. Meredith tried to follow the game but basically took her cue from the many fans and from her father, who had been able to switch his shift at work to be there that afternoon. He seemed to know an awful lot more about lacrosse than he ever let on. After all, he was the one who had once said that lacrosse wasn't a sport. She had researched the game online, but what she read did little to shed light on the fast-paced game on the field below.

Meredith still hadn't figured out what had happened to cause that brief uncomfortable moment in Mrs. Levine's workroom two weeks before, but Meredith was relieved that she and Dani hadn't strayed from their comfortable routine. They still met at their lockers every morning and told each other everything they had forgotten to tell each other during their phone call the night before. Meredith even got a little lonely during the school day because she had to wait until sixth period to see her. Meredith liked having someone to walk with in the hallways, and she particularly enjoyed sitting next to her friend in two classes. Meredith was absolutely positive that Mr. Dalton had caught them passing a note once but had overlooked their indiscretion. She had never had a friend who passed notes to her. Oh, she used to get notes passed to her, but they were never the kind she wanted to read.

Meredith cheered, clapped, and stomped her feet with the other fans when Dani scored her second goal. The Whickett High School Wolves now led by a score of 3-2. Meredith watched proudly as Dani celebrated her goal by sprinting back to midfield, holding her lacrosse stick high in the air.

Mikey and her father seemed equally proud as they continued to clap. Her father finally sat down when the game began again at midfield. "Dani's quite an athlete. That Syracuse coach would be crazy not to take her."

"Yeah, I know. She's so quick."

"And, speaking of Syracuse..." He reached inside his coat and pulled out a thick envelope. "This came in the mail for you today." He held out the envelope so she could see the Syracuse University return address.

Meredith's jaw dropped open, and her eyes got wide. She reached for the envelope carefully as if it might disintegrate. "Dad! Why didn't you tell me?" She ran her fingers over the return address and flipped it over.

"I was waiting for just the right moment." He smiled, his eyes bright with pride.

She reached a finger under the flap. "It's thick. That's a good sign, right?"

"There's only one way to find out, daughter. Open it."

She took a deep breath and exhaled forcefully. She teased open the flap and pulled out the thick set of papers inside. She scanned the first paragraph and caught the words "pleased to accept." She stopped reading and threw her arms around her father. "I got in! I got in!" A few people looked in their direction, but Meredith didn't care. She had just gotten accepted to Syracuse University. "I can't believe *I* got in."

"Of course you did. You've got the Bedford genes working for you. Congratulations, honey." Her father beamed at her and opened his arms for another hug.

Mikey naturally wanted a hug, too. Meredith obliged, but her thoughts quickly turned to Dani. "Do you think Dani got in? We might room together. Oh, my God. I hope she got in. She probably doesn't know yet."

"Ask her after the game."

"I will."

"Too bad your mother couldn't be here for this."

"Let's call her."

"Already done. I told her I'd call if it *weren't* an acceptance letter. She said she'd see you tonight after her shift."

"I can't believe you both knew before I did. But who cares? I got in."

Her father smiled. "Of course you did. Since we're on our own for dinner, where do you want your old man to take you? We should celebrate."

"Really? Okay, uh, how about Fiesta Loca? You know, near the old house we're researching for our project?"

Her father's eyes followed the action on the field. "Sure. How about it, Mikey? Are you up for some Mexican?"

"Mekin! Yeah, Dad."

"Excellent. Ooh—" A Whickett player received a hard push from a player on the opposing team. "You can't check in girls' lacrosse, can you?"

"Dad, you're asking me? I have no clue. Ask Dani."

"Yeah, what was I thinking?" He rolled his eyes. "Let's see if Dani wants to go to dinner with us, okay?"

"Okay. That'd be cool." Asking Dani to have dinner with her family suddenly made her nervous. "I'll ask her after the game." If Dani got into Syracuse, they could have dinner together every night. Meredith swallowed hard around the lump forming in her throat.

The horn blew for half-time. The Whickett players ran to their team bench and sat down. Dani told Meredith that the Whickett High School coach, Ms. Pratt, had only been coaching for two years but was very cool. Cool like Mrs. Levine. Meredith watched the young coach push her long dark brown hair out of her eyes and then address the team. She referred to her clipboard as she talked to them.

Meredith stood up and stretched. "Hey, Mikey Pikey? Do you want to walk around the track?"

"Okay, Merry, c'mon." He reached for her hand.

"Dad, I'm going to take him for a lap around the track to tire him out a little."

"Good idea. I'll go see what they have at the concession stand."

Meredith and Mikey walked down the steps of the sizable bleachers. Meredith opened the gate to the track surrounding the football-turned-lacrosse field and smiled when Dani looked up from her team's halftime huddle. Meredith chanced a small wave, and Dani nodded ever so slightly back. Dani had announced at the March senior class meeting that very afternoon that there were only fifty-nine school days left of high school. Fifty-nine. Although Meredith yearned for freedom, she felt a bit of nostalgia for the routine she and Dani now shared, but if Dani got into Syracuse, they would have a different routine, one that would be even better.

Meredith held onto Mikey's hand tightly. At the three-quarter mark on their trip around the track, a lacrosse ball shot in front of them, narrowly missing Mikey. Unfazed by almost getting hurt by the small hard ball, Mikey struggled out of her grasp and ran for it.

Sarah, Dani's supposed best friend, stood with one hand on her hip, waiting for Mikey to get the ball. Without saying a word, Sarah rudely snatched the ball from his hand and stalked back onto the field.

Surprised at Sarah's rudeness, Meredith called after her, "He was just trying to help, Sarah."

"Yeah, whatever," Sarah said without turning back.

The words were said with such venom that it made Meredith wonder if maybe the ball had been thrown at them on purpose.

Meredith stewed as she and Mikey made their way back to their starting point behind the Whickett team bench. Meredith spotted Dani on the field with a water bottle in her hand. Mikey must have spotted her, too, because he yelled, "Gooooo, Dani," and ran up to her. He hugged her with all his might.

"Hey, dude. What's up? Are you having fun?"

"Fun."

"Excellent." Dani looked up from the twelve-year-old wrapped around her middle. "Hi, Merry."

"Hi." Meredith took a deep breath. She didn't want Dani to know that Sarah had made her angry. She forced a smile and said, "You're awesome. I had no idea."

"Well, thanks." Dani seemed embarrassed by Meredith's praise.

"And you've created a monster with my father. He's having a

blast. He's teaching me everything he knows about lacrosse."

"That's cool. The rules aren't that complicated, really. But I'd better get ready for the second half. Coach might pitch a fit if she thinks I'm goofing off."

Meredith was dying to ask Dani about Syracuse but decided to wait until the game was over. Dani might not know yet. Or worse. Maybe she hadn't gotten in. She reached for Mikey's hand to extract him from Dani's waist. "C'mon, Mikey. Let's go find Dad."

"No." Mikey squeezed Dani even tighter.

Dani had a slightly panicked look in her eyes.

"Mikey," Meredith tried again, "Dani has to go play. We have to go back to the stands. And, besides, I think Dad bought some snacks. You want some snacks?"

"No! Stay Dani."

Meredith shrugged her shoulders and shook her head, embarrassed. "He can be so stubborn when he gets something in his head. Why don't you try?"

"Okay." To Mikey, Dani said, "Hey, dude? Do you want to sit on the team bench? You and Merry can watch from there."

Meredith whispered, "Are you sure? Won't your coach get mad?"

As if silently called to end the controversy, Coach Pratt strolled over to the girls. She said, "Uh, Dani? Have you put on some weight? Around the middle?" She pointed to Mikey, who had buried his face in Dani's midriff.

Dani laughed and said, "Coach, I think he's having a little separation anxiety. Do you think Mikey and Meredith can sit on the end of the bench?"

The coach considered the request for a moment and asked, "Are we sure he won't run onto the field?"

Meredith nodded. "He won't. He's scared of the fast pace."

"Okay," Coach Pratt nodded, "but maybe we can do better than that. How about we put Mikey to work? We can make him an assistant manager. He can run after stray balls and fill up water bottles with Christopher. Hey, Christopher—" Christopher walked over carrying a crate of recently-filled water bottles. "I've got an assistant manager for you."

Christopher didn't appear to be the athletic type. His shaggy hair fell into his eyes, and his large belly indicated more of a videogame lifestyle. According to Dani, though, Christopher was an excellent team manager and made sure the players and coach had everything they needed.

Christopher put the crate on the bench. "Yeah, sure. I could use the help. What's your name, big guy?"

Mikey still held on strong to his grip around Dani's waist, but he turned his head toward Christopher and said, "Mikey. Mikey Bikey."

Christopher laughed.

Dani patted Mikey on the head and said, "So, do you want to help Christopher?"

Mikey finally released his stranglehold. "Hep Krifer," he said to Christopher.

Christopher raised his eyebrows in question.

Dani laughed. "He said, 'Help Christopher.' So, yeah, he's ready to help." Meredith beamed. Dani was getting pretty good at translating "Mikey-speak."

Christopher laughed and tousled Mikey's hair. "Okay, big guy, let's put these warm-up jackets back on the bench. See how they're on the ground? Messy."

"Messy." Mikey followed Christopher and helped him pick up the jackets.

Meredith smiled and said, "Thanks, Coach. This is all he's going to talk about for weeks. I'm sure."

"No problem. Dani can get you a schedule of our home games. We'll expect him at every home game, okay?"

"Every game? Wow. Wait until he hears that. I'll sit on the end of the bench to make sure he's okay."

"Great." The coach turned from Meredith as the two-minute warning sounded.

Dani flashed Meredith a thumbs-up and jogged over to her teammates.

Meredith looked for her father in the stands and pantomimed that she and Mikey were going to watch the second half of the game from the team bench. He nodded his understanding and sat down in the bleachers by himself.

The second half started, and Meredith found herself more engrossed in the game than she ever thought she would be. A couple of times, the fast-moving athletes frightened her when they came close, but it was thrilling just the same. She was quickly becoming a girls' lacrosse fan and wished she had brought her camera. At the next game, she'd get some action pictures of Dani Lassiter, #5, Whickett High superstar.

~~~

Dani walked back to the restaurant table, cell phone in hand. Her shoulders drooped, and she sported the biggest frown Meredith had ever seen. *Oh, no. Syracuse turned her down.*

Meredith held her breath. Even though the answer seemed obvious, she asked anyway, "What happened?"

Dani's frown popped into a big grin. "I got in! My mom didn't want to open the envelope, but I made her. And, get this, the lacrosse coach sent me a note telling me to email her."

Meredith couldn't believe their luck. She had gotten into the art program, and Dani was going to play lacrosse at Syracuse. "Oh, my God, Dani. This is so exciting."

Dani sat back down at the table next to Meredith. She turned toward Meredith's father. "Thanks for dinner, Mr. Bedford."

"No problem. Anyone who can score five goals in one game deserves to be taken out for dinner."

Dani smiled. "Thanks. I wasn't sure we were going to win that one. We were supposed to win but only had a one-goal lead at the half."

Meredith's father took a sip of coffee. "Oh, I had no doubts. So, Syracuse is recruiting you now?"

"I guess so." She shrugged her shoulders as if she didn't believe it herself. "Meredith and I might even room together. Right, Meredith?"

Meredith looked up from wiping Mikey's hands and smiled. "Oh, yeah. It'll be great having a friend already built in. Somebody to take out the trash, clean the room, and—Hey! You don't have to kick."

"We'll take turns taking out the trash." Dani's face looked stern, but Meredith saw the mirth dancing in those crystal blue eyes.

"Fine, fine, we'll take turns." Meredith looked at the old painted lady through the window. She had explicitly asked the hostess for a booth with a view of the house. The colored lights from the restaurant reflected off the house, creating an eerie carnival look. Meredith smiled when she thought about the changes the house would go through once Esther and Millie got their rezoning permits. She smiled bigger when she thought about the changes her life would go through once she and Dani got to Syracuse.

Her father touched her arm from across the table. "Well, my little girl will be in good hands with her new roommate. That I can tell for sure."

Meredith sighed. Her father always found new ways to embarrass her.

"Well, it's true. Dani's a good find. Keep her around, okay?"

Despite the mortification she felt from her father's embarrassing statement, she couldn't help the warm feeling that rushed through her. She tried to catch Dani's eye in apology for her father's comment, but Meredith's father asked Dani another question about lacrosse, and the conversation turned. Dani loved to talk about lacrosse. That was more than obvious to Meredith. And Meredith loved that about her. Dani was passionate about everything she did. Meredith couldn't help but wonder why she felt that warm sensation more and more lately. Dani had become a really close friend. That was it. Right? Just a close friend. But their closeness was starting to feel like something else. Something more. Maybe *best* friends were like this with each other, like Esther and Millie. Meredith had never had a best friend before.

As they left the restaurant, Dani held the door open for her and smiled. This time, Meredith's knees got jittery, and the warm feeling lasted all the way home.

Chapter 12

Anything for a Sister

"Do you want to see it?" Meredith peeked at Dani from behind the canvas. She swirled her paintbrush in the jar of water next to the painting.

Dani's mouth dropped open. "Really? It's done?"

"Just about. I'll probably work on the background more, but it's pretty much finished. Come look." She grabbed her rag to wipe her hands and stepped back.

Dani stood up hesitantly. She looked scared for some reason.

Meredith laughed. "C'mon, chicken. Take a look."

Dani took a deep breath and went around to the other side of the canvas. She didn't say anything for so long that Meredith began to wonder if she hated it. Maybe Dani just didn't know how to tell her how bad the portrait was. She saw Dani swallow hard, but before Meredith had a chance to get even more nervous, Dani said quietly, "You're amazing. People don't know how amazing you are."

Meredith felt her face color while that wonderful hot chocolate feeling radiated outward from somewhere in her middle.

"I feel so honored to be the subject of your painting. It's almost like looking in a mirror, but better. You've made me look so, I don't know, like majestic or something." Dani's voice was reverent. She shook her head as if she couldn't believe what she saw.

"No," Meredith said simply. "That's just you. That's what I see when I look at you." *And why does that sound so weird now that I've said it out loud?*

Dani swallowed again. "This is how you see me?"

"Yeah," she said barely above a whisper.

Dani stared at her. "I don't know what to say except thank you."

"You don't have to thank me. I should be the one thanking you. I need this painting for my portfolio, so…" Meredith turned away and put her palette in its case. She turned back to face her friend. "Dani, you've been such a good friend to me. Even when I tried to push you away, you were so persistent. I never thought having a friend could feel so good, so freeing. I almost feel like everything's going my way now."

Dani took a step closer. "I make you feel all that?"

Meredith knew she was blushing and knew that Dani could tell. She was embarrassed about admitting her feelings but wanted Dani to know. "Yes. You forced me out of my shell. You forced me to stand up on my own two feet. And you're amazing with Mikey. He's so excited about being the lacrosse manager with Christopher. You have no idea what it means to him. And to me." Meredith cleared her throat to cover her embarrassment. "Mikey loves the lacrosse sweatshirt Coach Pratt gave him. He wears it all the time." She looked away to turn off the extra lighting. "And remember what my dad said at Fiesta Loca a couple of weeks ago? He said something like, 'Find a way to keep her.' Well, I hope that you and I can be friends for a long time." *And why am I telling you all of this? You must think I'm really sappy or something.*

Dani's face took on a serious expression. Her voice was thick when she answered, "Me, too."

"I think we'd better get our stuff together before we turn into a Hallmark card right here in Mrs. Levine's room." She'd said things to

Dani that she hadn't thought through, and her sudden openness scared her a little.

Dani laughed. "Yeah, yeah. You're right. Phew, it's getting way too serious in here. Come on, let's tell Mrs. Levine that the masterpiece is practically finished."

~~~

Meredith, Dani, and even Mikey were excited because spring break officially began that very afternoon. The first portrait was finished, and Dani's lacrosse team had won its game. Dani drove Mikey and Meredith home after the win, and Meredith's mother insisted that Dani stay for dinner, which she gladly did after she called home to ask her parents.

After dinner, Dani stood up to help clear the table. "Let me help you with that, Mrs. Bedford."

Meredith's mom smiled. "Thank you, Dani. But don't worry about it. Mikey and I will finish up. Why don't you two go celebrate the big win?"

Dani put her plate down. "Okay, thank you. The stew was great. I'm so full I don't think I can move anyway."

Meredith's mother smiled. "You're sweet. Now, go on, both of you. Get out of the kitchen and leave the fun stuff to me and my son." She turned to Mikey and said, "You want to use the sprayer?"

His eyes lit up, and he bolted out of his chair, almost knocking it over. "Brayer! Come on, Mom." He scraped his chair across the floor toward the sink. He and Dani almost looked like twins in their matching green and yellow lacrosse sweatshirts.

Meredith laughed and pulled on the sleeve of Dani's sweatshirt. "C'mon, we'd better get out of here. This is going to get messy."

Dani laughed. "You don't have to ask twice."

As they made their way into the living room, Meredith debated for a split second but then asked, "Hey, do you want to come to my room? I want to show you the pictures I chose for Esther and Millie's portraits. I even started a sketch of Esther."

"Yeah, sure. That'd be cool."

Meredith grabbed her book bag from the base of the stairwell and flung it over her shoulder. "I hope my room's not too messy. I wasn't expecting company today." *Or ever.*

"I'm sure it's fine," Dani said as they made their way up the stairs.

Meredith detected a puzzling hint of nervousness in Dani's tone. Meredith hesitated a moment at the threshold and scanned her room. Her desk was littered with books and colored pencils, but the rest of her room was fairly neat. Luckily, she had made her bed that morning but cringed when she saw the juvenile comforter with the overlarge roses. She'd had that comforter for as long as she could remember. She made a mental note to ask her mom for a new one before heading to Syracuse in the fall.

She walked in and gestured for Dani to sit on her desk chair. "Have a seat. Let me put my book bag away." She put the bag in her closet and closed the door. "Thank God I don't have to take that out for a whole week."

Dani spun the offered chair around, sat on it backward, and rested her arms on the backrest. "I could definitely use the break. Don't our teachers know it's the spring semester of our senior year, and we don't want to do any more homework?" She sighed loudly.

"I know. I'm just glad I have two periods of art." Meredith thought about all the times she'd had Dani to herself in Mrs. Levine's workroom. That thought made her think about all the time they would have together at Syracuse. The hot chocolate feeling that had become so familiar but surprised her every time pulsed through her. She turned from Dani, slightly embarrassed, and quickly thought of something else to say. "Oh, I finished Mikey's portrait, too."

"You painted Mikey?"

"Yeah, that's what I work on during my AP class. I should have shown you. It's on the rack with my other AP stuff. I'll show you when we get back to school after break." Meredith reached behind Dani on the desk and pulled out the pictures of Esther and Millie she had decided to use for their portraits. She handed the photos to Dani. "I love this picture of Esther," she said softly.

"Yeah," Dani agreed. "She's looking right at the camera. It looks like Thanksgiving dinner or something."

Meredith leaned in closer to get a better look at the photograph. When her arm touched Dani's, she was pleasantly startled when that warm feeling welled up inside her again. She took a micro-step back when she realized their arms were still touching.

Dani handed Esther's photo back. "Are you going to use the dining room as the background?"

Meredith looked at the photo again, still pleased with her selection. "No, I'll probably paint her in front of a bookshelf or something. Something dignified. She'll be one of the founders of the Randall-Bradley House, after all."

"It sounds so official when you say it like that." Dani examined the photo of Millie. "Millie looks a little more serious in this picture. She's usually laughing or joking around."

"That's why I like this one. It shows her serious side, I think."

"Are you going to paint my serious side, too?" Dani looked up at her.

"Of course. I've got that sketch of you with the angry fire in your eyes. I'll probably work on that during AP now that Mikey's done.

You don't have to pose for that one."

"How come?" Dani looked disappointed.

How can I tell her that I never ever want to be on the receiving end of her anger? Meredith swallowed. "Well, because I think I've had enough practice by now." *Not exactly a lie.* "And, besides, you have your own stuff to do in class."

Dani groaned softly. "I have to figure out what my Whickett Days' project is. Mrs. Levine said we have to start on Monday when we get back. How come all our teachers want some kind of Whickett Days' project? They must have had a meeting or something to decide how to make our lives as busy as possible."

"Oh, I know." Meredith took Millie's picture from Dani and put them both back on her overflowing desk. She went over and sat on her bed. She leaned against the headboard. Dani was in her room, and it felt weird. Weird, but good. Dani had only been in her room once before to look at the sketches Meredith had made of Dani at that senior class meeting. That was a long time ago, the day they had met Esther and Millie for the first time at Hudson Pines. Dani had only stayed for about five minutes that day, and other than that, she had never had a friend in her room before. Meredith tried to act as if she had friends in her room all the time.

Meredith cleared her throat. "Mrs. Levine said she'd start taking slides of our AP work to send off to the College Board right after spring break. The slides are due the second week of May. Can you believe that's only four weeks after spring break?"

"Wow. And April's almost half over. Time's flying." Dani swiveled the chair back and forth. "Coach is making us practice over spring break, but she said she'd probably give us a day off. Do you and Mikey want to go bowling again?"

Meredith felt a flush of excitement at the prospect. "Yeah. That was fun. Mom has him scheduled with some play dates, so I'll have to call you back. Sorry, you have to practice." She rolled her eyes. "I mean, c'mon, it's spring break."

"That's okay. I like lacrosse."

"No. Really?" Meredith pretended to be shocked.

"Oh, shut up. God, I hope I make the team at Syracuse. I emailed the coach with my schedule and reminded her who I was. I even invited her to a game. My Dad said I should put that part in there."

"What game?"

"I don't know because I don't know if she's even coming. I know I'll play like crap if she comes here." Dani looked at the floor and exhaled forcefully. "God, if she actually comes here, I think I'll die."

Meredith sat up and crossed her legs Indian style. "Well, I doubt you'd die, but I can see how that'd be distracting."

"Speaking of distracting, how could you concentrate on your painting when I practically stared at you the whole time?"

Meredith laughed, suddenly nervous. "I used to get as self-conscious as my models, but once I get into my work, I don't think about it. And besides, I'm focusing more on the pieces and parts than the whole *you* part of you."

"You focused on my pieces and parts?" Dani watched her.

"Oh, c'mon, you make that sound so weird."

Dani picked up her feet and spun around in the chair. She grinned. "I guess it's not that weird. I mean, I even admitted that I went to the old painted lady in my mind a few times while posing."

Meredith smiled and pulled a pillow into her lap. "Yeah, I really like Esther and Millie. I know we still have the PowerPoint to do, but I'm psyched we finished our write-up. I wish Mr. Dalton had let us hand it in today."

"I know. He wanted the proposals to read over mid-winter break, but I guess he didn't want any final projects to read over spring break. He must have *big plans*." Dani put the emphasis on "big plans," which made Meredith giggle.

"Yeah, like going down to the Whickett Historical Society to schmooze with the goober smoochers."

Dani burst out laughing. Meredith had the warm feeling again. She loved Dani's laugh, especially because she'd been the one to make her laugh.

Dani stopped laughing long enough to say, "You're so funny. I'm glad Ben pissed me off that day, and I dissed him to be your partner."

"Lucky for us, right?" Meredith smiled softly.

"Best damn day of my life," Dani slapped her thigh in a perfect Millie imitation.

"Oh, my God. You sounded just like her."

"Thanks. I've been working on it." Dani waggled her eyebrows.

"Really?"

"No, not really." Dani smirked.

Meredith thought about the first time they had met Esther and Millie at the Hudson Pines Senior Center. She had wanted to ask Dani about Millie for a long time but couldn't figure out how to phrase a question. She still wasn't sure, but she went for it anyway. "Hey, do you find Millie confusing?"

"Confusing?" Dani flicked her head to get the perpetual lock of hair out of her eyes. "No. I mean, she's a real character, but no, she's not confusing. Why?"

"Oh, I don't know. She says things sometimes that I don't get. Like that first time we met, she said we could go in the old house any time we wanted to, and then she said something like, 'Anything for a sister.' What did she mean by that?"

"Uh..." Dani hesitated. "I don't know."

"Danielle Anne Lassiter, you're lying."

"What do you mean?" Dani seemed flustered.

"I know you well enough by now, and I can tell that you're not telling me the truth. You know what Millie meant, don't you?"

Dani fidgeted in her chair but, after a long pause, finally answered, "Um, kind of, but I think we should talk about something else."

Meredith remained quiet. Why would Dani keep something from her? Did Dani have a secret?

"Really, Meredith, another time. Please." Dani's voice had taken on a desperate edge.

"Just like how you won't tell me who you like? It's been over a month since you told me you liked somebody when we were in Mrs. Levine's workroom. You still haven't told me, you know." Both girls were quiet.

Meredith finally broke the silence. "You said I could trust you."

"You can."

"Well, you can trust me, too. So, what did Millie mean by 'sister'?"

Dani looked out the window. She pinched the bridge of her nose with her thumb and forefinger as if she had a headache. "Okay," she said slowly and released her nose. "But remember that *you* are the one who asked."

"Okay." Meredith wondered what was so earth-shattering to make confident and strong Dani Lassiter so uptight.

Dani cleared her throat and looked up at Meredith. "I think it means that...um, they're gay. They're lesbians."

The room became as quiet as a tomb. Meredith replayed silently what Dani had just told her. *They're gay. Esther and Millie are lesbians. Lesbians?* She couldn't quite grasp the concept. Finally, she said out loud, "No way. They're, like, in their seventies."

Dani chuckled, but Meredith heard the nervousness underneath. "I don't think that kind of thing has an age limit."

"How do you know they're…that way?" Meredith couldn't say the word. "Did Millie tell you? At the hardware store? Esther didn't say anything like that to me." Meredith heard the unease in her own voice and fought to keep it under control. She hadn't in a million years expected to hear that these two sweet old ladies were queer or whatever the word was. *This must be some kind of joke.* "Dani, are you kidding? Because it's not funny."

Dani watched her as if trying to gauge her reaction. She sighed and rested her chin on the back of the chair. With all seriousness, she said, "No, I'm not kidding. Millie hinted at it on the way to the hardware store, but I already knew."

"But what did Millie mean by 'anything for a sister?' I still don't get that part." As soon as she said the words, the realization hit her like a John Casey tackle. She hugged her pillow with both arms.

Dani looked at Meredith, and they stared at each other silently for a long time while Meredith tried to keep her growing panic from showing. Meredith hugged the pillow tighter. "Dani?"

"Yeah?"

"Did you know those things about Esther and Millie because you…because you are, too?"

Dani took a careful breath and said simply, "Yeah. I'm that way, too. I'm a lesbian, too."

Meredith inhaled sharply. She thought she had been prepared for the answer, but when Dani admitted it so quickly and openly, it took Meredith by surprise. She was also surprised to feel a little jealous. Dani, Esther, and Millie had shared a secret she hadn't been a part of.

Dani looked Meredith right in the eye and said defensively, "And now *you* know."

Meredith's heart lurched at how vulnerable Dani looked. She didn't know what to say. The only thing she could squeak out was, "Yeah." *Now I know.* Meredith's heart beat wildly. She didn't know what to do. This was...unexpected. *Okay, so Dani's a lesbian. Big deal. Why am I going all stupid and panicky? Get a freakin' grip, Meredith.*

But Meredith couldn't get a grip, and the uncomfortable silence spread. Her anxiety must have been obvious because Dani stood up abruptly, causing the desk chair to roll across the room. "I guess I should go." Her tone was distant.

Meredith remained frozen. She couldn't make her mouth move to say, "No, don't go. It's okay. I'm cool with it." For some reason, Meredith couldn't even say the word "Stay."

When Dani got to the doorway, she looked back at Meredith as if waiting for her to say something, but when Meredith simply held her breath, Dani turned and left quietly.

Meredith closed her eyes tightly, knowing she had just been on the receiving end of an expression she had never seen before—hurt. Dani's wounded expression tugged at her heart, yet Meredith still could not move. She blew out the air she didn't know she had been holding in her lungs and listened to Dani make her way down the stairs.

She heard Dani say, "See you later, dude," to her brother and almost bolted off the bed to run after her. That was, after all, the same Dani down there who had been her friend for over three months, but she couldn't get her legs to move.

Why did it take you so long to tell me, Dani? I thought I was your friend. As soon as Meredith got the thought out, she knew what a hypocrite she was. Dani was probably afraid to tell her because of the exact reaction she'd just had.

Meredith put her hands over her ears in an attempt to block out the sound of Dani's pickup door closing and the engine starting up. She uncovered her ears slowly, only to hear the sound of the now familiar truck fading into the distance.

The desk chair Dani had been sitting in had rolled across the room and now leaned against the closet door. Meredith got up and carefully placed it back at her desk. Deep down, she knew that putting the chair back was an outward attempt to undo the last few minutes. Dani was a lesbian. Why hadn't she known? And why did it paralyze her? As Meredith sat on her bed, an even bigger question formed in her mind. Had Dani been *after* her these past three months? Is that why they had talked on the phone just about every night? Is that why Dani gave her that Valentine's Day candy? Is that why Dani changed partners in Mr. Dalton's class? Meredith's head was spinning. How could this friend who'd made Meredith feel so good be a lesbian? And what did Dani think about all those things Meredith had given her? The art pencils, the lacrosse photos she had taken a few weeks ago, the brownies she'd made for the team? *Did Dani think I was coming on to her?* Meredith pondered that question for a moment. She had no answer.

Meredith also tried to wrap her head around Esther and Millie. She had known the two women were close, but she thought they were two old spinsters who'd become friends. Lesbians were scary people who had crew cuts and looked like men. Esther didn't look like a man. And even though Millie was fond of wearing jeans and flannel shirts, she didn't look like a man. And then there was Dani. Meredith had spent a lot of time looking at Dani. She had short hair and looked kind of boyish, but Dani definitely did *not* look like a man, and she wasn't trying to. Of that, Meredith was certain.

Her best friend had shared something very personal and serious

171

with her, and she had done nothing but let her walk out the door. *Why didn't I stop her?* Meredith leaped off the bed and yanked the cordless phone from its cradle. She held it in both hands against her chest and looked out the window in the direction Dani had gone. She closed her eyes. *Oh, God, what have I done?* She squeezed her eyes tight in an attempt to halt the flood of tears. To no avail. She cried with her forehead against the window for several minutes, but then, in resignation, she put the phone gently back into its cradle. She needed time to think. She would talk to Dani but needed to sort out this sudden upheaval in her life before she did.

Chapter 13

All It's Gonna Be

Meredith sat invisible at the end of the Whickett girls' lacrosse bench on the first day back after spring break. The Whickett team was losing to their rivals, Beverwyck High. She had so many confusing feelings inside her head about the bomb Dani had dropped on her over a week prior. Meredith had originally planned to spend the entire spring break with Dani. They had even planned to take Mikey bowling and to the movies, but Meredith hadn't called Dani once during the break. Dani hadn't called her, either.

Meredith was ashamed of the way she had reacted. She still liked Dani very much and wanted to be friends. She had been lonely without her. The weeklong break had been just enough time to work it out in her mind that having a friend who was a lesbian simply meant having a friend who was different than she was. Different was just that—different. The bigger issue now turning over in Meredith's mind was understanding why she hadn't known. She and Dani were supposedly good friends, best friends maybe, but Dani hadn't told her. That was big.

In art class that morning, Meredith could tell Dani was going through the motions. Her eyes seemed cloudy, not the brilliant blue Meredith was accustomed to. When Dani took her usual seat next to Meredith, she said, "Hey."

Meredith simply said, "Hey," in return. They didn't talk after

173

that, and the tension between them was as thick as oil paint. When the art class was over, Dani bolted out the door as fast as she could. Meredith figured Dani was waiting for her to make the first move, but Meredith couldn't figure out what to say to undo the hurt she'd caused her friend.

Meredith tried to stay present and focused on the lacrosse game in front of her. Keeping her attention on the game was painful, though, since she kept seeing Dani on the field. Instead, she tried to focus on the warm mid-April sun but winced when she saw Dani sail another shot well above the goal. Dani was playing poorly, and Meredith knew why. It was because she hadn't welcomed Dani with open arms after hearing her news. She hadn't done anything. She understood now. Her silence had been rejection.

~~~

The next day, Tuesday, a full eleven days after Dani revealed her secret, Meredith stood at her easel in Mrs. Levine's art room working on her portrait of Esther. She snuck a peak over her shoulder as Dani worked on a still life sketch of fruit. Meredith smiled when she noticed Dani using the colored pencils she had given her. She'd also overheard Dani tell Mrs. Levine that she was making the sketch to give to her friends Esther and Millie for the grand opening of the Randall-Bradley House. Dani told Mrs. Levine that the drawing symbolized the fruitful life the two women had led. Meredith kept smiling when she remembered how Dani didn't even know what a still life was at the beginning of the semester. And there she was doing one of her own.

Meredith desperately wanted to turn around and tell Dani that she wanted everything to go back to the way it was before. Instead, she looked back to her portrait with a sigh. She liked the photograph of Esther she had chosen because Esther looked extremely happy. Kind of the polar opposite of the way Meredith felt at the moment. Esther told her that she had been in her late forties when the photograph was taken. Millie added that was about the time Esther started getting her "character lines." But Esther didn't lose a beat and quipped that Millie was the cause of those character lines. *Esther is so regal*, Meredith thought. *Why am I having trouble accepting that she's a gay woman? No, no. It's okay to use the word 'lesbian.' Mille is a lesbian, too. And Dani. Wow, Dani is a lesbian. A lez-bee-un.* Why was there so much stigma and hate associated with that word?

Meredith had no answer for her unspoken musing and made a valiant effort to focus on the painting. She wasn't successful because she couldn't help noticing Dani's familiar mannerisms out of the corner of her eye. The way she flicked her head to get the hair out of her eyes or leaned back in her chair with her arms folded to get a better look at her drawing. Meredith noticed all of these things and more. The curve of blonde hair around Dani's ear, her strong chiseled chin, her lean athlete's physique. She had seen all of these things before, but not in the way she noticed them now. Meredith's chest tightened when she realized how much she missed Dani's blue eyes and the smiles meant only for her.

Meredith swirled her brush in the jar of water and stared out the window, knowing that Dani sat just five feet behind her. All she had to do was turn around and start talking. Tears filled her eyes when she realized how much she missed her friend. She missed talking to her during the school day and then after school on the phone. She missed hearing about lacrosse practice and student government stuff and everything. She missed how Dani looked after Mikey and brought him books and cookies. And Mikey. Meredith grimaced. He kept asking where Dani was. Where was his *dude*?

Meredith stabbed at the tears in her eyes and turned slightly to sneak a peek at Dani. Meredith took in Dani's tense shoulders and wan look. *You used to look so peaceful. Now you look...unsettled. Did I do that to you?* She cleaned up her easel. She couldn't work on Esther's portrait now, not with such a heavy heart.

She turned again only to find Dani looking at her. They both turned away quickly. Meredith took a deep breath for strength and slowly turned back around. Her heart clenched when she noticed the tired expression on Dani's face. Meredith got off her stool and sat in her usual chair. She looked down at her hands and said, "Dani, I'm sorry. I'm so sorry I reacted that way. I don't know what happened." She scratched at some paint on the table. "I got scared, I guess."

Dani regarded her as if thinking about how to respond. "Well, a wise person once told me she couldn't understand why everyone got so scared of people who were different. If they'd just take the time to get to know you, they'd see you weren't so different after all."

Meredith looked away. The words stung. Dani was quoting her. Her heart clenched, knowing she deserved Dani's hardened demeanor, but the pull to brush Dani's lock of hair off her forehead was powerful. *What's happening to me? I get so confused when I look at you. What is it about you that scares me to death?*

Meredith had hoped they could walk to their history class together and talk some more, but Dani bolted out of her chair for the second day in a row when the bell rang. Dani also ignored her during their history class, so Meredith spent more time watching the physical education classes play soccer on the field than listening to Mr. Dalton.

At the end of the school day, Meredith lingered in her AP Art class because she just couldn't deal with seeing Dani at the lockers. She'd stop at her locker after getting Mikey from his classroom.

Meredith forced herself to smile as she approached her brother's classroom and kept the fake smile while talking to Miss Stevens.

After leaving his classroom, Meredith said, "Mikey, I have to get my books out of my locker, okay?"

"Okay."

"Put your book bag down here until I'm done." Meredith spun the dial of her lock a few times, pulled up on the latch, and opened the door. She started to put her history book back in but then couldn't remember if Mr. Dalton had assigned homework. She couldn't remember much from that class except that Dani hadn't spoken to her, so she put the book in her bag just in case. Maybe she could work up the nerve to call Dani later and ask her if they had homework. What she would say after that, she had no idea.

Lost in thought, she barely noticed the shadow moving slowly across her locker. She whirled around and saw the army jacket first. She took a startled step backward when she saw Ben Kinsey standing right in front of her. Mikey, probably sensing Meredith's sudden unease, positioned himself between them. A granite stone formed in the pit of her stomach. Maybe Ben had finally come to get even with her for telling him off in Mr. Dalton's class. She looked frantically around the hallway. There was no one else in sight.

Ben stepped closer, and Mikey pulled his fists into a taekwondo sparring stance. Ben took a step back. "Hey, call off your pit bull. I come in peace."

"What do you want?" Meredith asked, her tone guarded.

"Look, I'm sorry I've treated you like crap this year. Dani says I'm kind of immature, and well, I guess she's right. So, I'm sorry."

Mikey stood rock still in his sparring stance, and Meredith stayed behind him. "Okay." Her tone remained cautious.

"I've wanted to talk to you since we got back from spring break. I don't know what you said to Dani, but she's bummin'. I know she told you she was gay, but I hope you know she's cool. She's, I don't know, she's just Dani."

Meredith relaxed, but only a little. Ben *was* here in peace. "You know about her?" For some reason, Meredith had a hard time believing that Dani had also told Ben.

"Yeah, she told me a long time ago, like in eighth grade or something. I know you're probably in shock about it, but I also know that you guys have been tight lately. I was jealous for a while, but I'm cool with it now. Look, before spring break, Dani was so happy. When you guys started doing that project, she just, I don't know, became a rock star or something. She likes you, I mean, *really* likes you, but if all it's going to be is a friendship between you guys, then she's okay with that. She told me. When she wasn't balling her eyes out, that is."

"She was crying?" Meredith's heart hurt instantly, knowing that she had been the cause of her friend's sadness.

Ben nodded his head slowly. "Yeah. She's a mess."

"I don't know what to say to her."

"She's still Dani. You know?"

It was Meredith's turn to nod slowly, "I know. I *do* know that. Does she know you're here talking to me?"

"Oh, my God, no. She'd kill me if she knew I said anything to you. No, this is just me trying to be cool for a change."

"Does she hate me?"

"No," he stated simply.

"I never meant to hurt her. I hope you know that."

"I guess."

"I gotta figure out how to fix this."

"Yeah, well, I hate to see Dani fall apart." He took a step closer as if to finalize his point but backed up immediately when Mikey pulled a fist back.

"Mikey," Meredith admonished. "I think it's okay now. This is Ben."

"Hi, Mikey." Ben stuck his hand out. "It's nice to meet ya."

Mikey hesitated. He looked up at his sister, who told him it was okay to shake Ben's hand. Mikey came out of his sparring stance and grabbed Ben's hand. He said, "Meet cha."

To Meredith, Ben said, "Look, I'm just gonna go, but think about what I said, okay?"

"Okay. Thank you. You're...you're an okay guy." *I think.*

"Aww, well, I'm working on it. I have to go. Later." He turned and walked briskly down the hallway.

Meredith sighed in relief. She had never expected Ben Kinsey to approach her like that. She never realized Dani would have told other people about being a lesbian. That seemed like something to keep quiet about. But then Meredith had a small moment of clarity. She realized she didn't have a realistic sense of any LGBTQ people, lesbians in particular. Why was that? Maybe because she hadn't seen many in real life or on TV. Lesbians probably kept quiet about their lifestyle or sexual preference or whatever it was called, just like Dani did. It must have been a catch-22 situation for Dani. All LGBTQ people. They had to keep quiet and be miserable all their lives, or they could say something and risk losing friends and even family. Or even worse. Meredith had heard of people getting beaten up or even killed just because they weren't straight.

Meredith's heart hurt. She closed her locker and steered Mikey toward the front doors of the school. She did wonder about one thing Ben had said, though. He had said, "She *really* likes you." That statement alone made Meredith wonder if maybe this was why she was so uncomfortable about the whole thing.

She stopped in her tracks when she realized something. Dani had that secret crush. *Was it me? Did Dani want me to be her girlfriend or something? Girlfriend.* Meredith frowned. She wanted Dani's friendship, nothing more.

~~~

After dinner, Meredith sat alone in her bedroom, trying to find comfort sketching Millie, even though her head still reeled from her talk with Ben that afternoon. She welcomed the knock on her bedroom door.

"Merry, can I come in?"

"Sure, Mom." Meredith put the sketch down.

Her mother opened the door and peeked in. "I'm not interrupting anything important, am I?"

"Nah, I'm just sketching." She pulled her knees up to make room for her mother to sit on the bed.

"How's school going? Only a couple more months left."

"I know. I can't wait. One more summer and then college." *Where I can start over once and for all.*

"Oh, Meredith. What are we going to do without you? You've been such a blessing to this family, taking care of Mikey at home and school. I don't know what I'm going to do next year. And you, I hope you won't be lonely so far away at Syracuse." Her mother's smile told Meredith this wasn't just a social call. Something was up.

Meredith smiled back. She would miss her family when she went to college, but she wasn't sure what her mother wanted her to say, so she said, "Well, Dani's going to be there, so I'll have at least one friend."

"Well, there's Dani. That's why I came up to talk to you. Dani hasn't been around lately. I thought you two were going to do all kinds of things over spring break."

Surprised that her mother had even noticed, she muttered, "Oh, uh, she's just really busy with lacrosse." What was she supposed to say? That she had freaked out over Dani's big reveal?

Her mother patted her hand and, with a sympathetic smile, said, "Okay. Well, if you need to talk, you know where I live. Okay?"

"I'm okay. But thanks." Meredith pushed her glasses back up onto the bridge of her nose. "Hey, Mom?"

Her mother turned around. "Yes, honey?"

"Can I get contacts? I hate my stupid glasses."

Her mother chuckled. "Okay. I'll talk to your father and see what we can do. Goodnight. We'll try to make it happen before you leave for college."

"Thanks, Mom. Night."

As her mother closed the door, Meredith knew she had to fix the breakdown in her friendship with Dani immediately. She had to try, anyway. What would Dani do if the situation had been reversed? With epiphany-like timing, she realized Dani had already shown her by example. Dani had stuck by her even when Meredith tried to push her away.

You believed in me when all I wanted to do was hide. Why am I having so much trouble believing in you? But, Dani, what do you want from me? And what do I want from you?

The questions tumbled around her mind, but in spite of her confusion, she made one important decision. She decided, no matter the consequences, she would attempt to salvage her friendship with Dani—even if Dani didn't think she was sincere. She picked up the phone on her bedside stand and hit Dani's number on the speed dial.

Chapter 14

Serendipity

Meredith sat on her bed, gripping the pillow firmly around its middle. Dani sat backward on Meredith's desk chair in an almost exact recreation of the scene eleven days before when Dani told Meredith that not only was *she* a lesbian, but Esther and Millie, too. The familiarity of the scene was not lost on Meredith. The fact that Dani had come over as soon as Meredith called made her feel optimistic about a reconciliation.

Unfortunately, the reconciliation would have to wait because Mikey sat on the floor in his Spiderman pajamas, staring up at Dani with rapt attention. His mouth hung open as Dani read to him from the first *Harry, Dog Spy* book she had given him in late February, almost two months before. Dani snuck a shy smile at Meredith and shrugged as if to say, "I guess I have to give him some attention before we can talk." Meredith simply smiled back and continued to clutch her pillow tightly.

After another five minutes of hearing about the exploits of Harry, the dog spy, Meredith finally had enough. "Hey, Mikey Bikey, how about you give me and Dani a chance to talk? You should go watch TV with Mom now because you'll have to brush your teeth and get ready for bed soon, okay?"

"Kay, Merry." He jumped up and hurried to the door. Turning around, he said shyly, "Bye, Dani."

"Bye, dude." Dani saluted him.

Mikey saluted back. "Bye, dude." He bolted out the door and stomped down the steps to the living room. Dani and Meredith both laughed. Meredith dropped her pillow, got up, and closed the door after him.

Now that Mikey was gone, the room became exceptionally quiet. *Now*, Meredith thought, *it feels just like the moment Dani told me she was a lesbian*. She sat back on the bed but didn't pick up the pillow this time.

"Dani?"

"Yeah?"

"I'm sorry." Meredith could tell Dani was going to let her lead on this one. Meredith wanted to laugh. So many months ago, Meredith was willing to let Dani take the lead on everything, but this predicament was of her doing, so lead she must.

"I overreacted. I know that now. I'm sorry. I wasn't expecting you to tell me you were a lesbian. I..." She sighed because she wasn't sure how to explain the rest.

Dani cleared her throat. "I took a risk coming out to you but thought you'd be okay with it. With me." Dani's voice cracked. "I thought we were close enough friends." The hurt in her voice made Meredith wince.

"We were close enough. I mean, we *are* close enough. And I *am* okay with it. With you. I really am. You just took me by surprise." She never realized just how vulnerable Dani was. "Knowing someone who's gay isn't an everyday thing for me. I was kind of sheltered, I guess, living in Greenspond. And the way the world views LGBTQ people, I guess I had all that stupidity in my head. I mean, I had this image of lesbians looking like men but hating men at the same time. And somehow, all gay people were child molesters and deviants. And when I finally sorted it all out, I realized that all that stuff is just plain bullshit. I let myself look at *you*. You aren't any of those horrible things, and I don't think gay people are any of those things, either. I mean, I'd never even met a gay person before. Well, I guess that's not true. Is it? I know Esther and Millie, don't I? And they are two of the sweetest old ladies in the world. But, to tell you the truth, them being lesbians still blows my mind."

Dani's eyes were sympathetic. "I know. Me, too. I couldn't believe it that first day we went to Hudson Pines. Millie's so obvious."

Meredith raised her eyebrows. "She's obvious? I couldn't tell."

"Well..." Dani hesitated. "I guess I kind of know what to look for. Esther doesn't really look the part. But that shows you can't judge a book by its cover, right? And I think if everybody could take that attitude and get to know me, they'd see I wasn't horrible."

Meredith was startled to see the raw emotion on Dani's face. She leaped off the bed and hugged her friend. She rubbed Dani gently on the back in sympathy and said, "You're *not* a horrible person. I judged you too quickly, and it was stupid. I'm sorry."

"It's okay. I guess I'll have this kind of thing my whole life. So maybe I should toughen up now."

Meredith's chest tightened. She had caused her friend so much needless pain through her fear. She moved back to the bed but sat on the edge. "You know in art today when you quoted that *wise person* who said something about being scared of people who were different? I know you were quoting me, even though I don't feel very wise right now, but back then, I was talking about how people react to Mikey. I'm just as guilty, though. I'm such a hypocrite."

"Oh, don't worry about it. It wasn't your fault."

Meredith reached over and swatted Dani playfully on the knee. "Oh, yes, it was. Don't you dare think you deserve to be treated that way. The problem was mine, not yours. When people make fun of Mikey, I always say it's their problem, not his. I've been thinking so much about this that my head hurts. And…"

"What?"

"I miss you." It was true.

Dani looked almost relieved. "I miss you, too."

"Oh, my God. I can be so stupid."

"Well, I can be stupid, too, I guess." Dani had an expectant look on her face. "So…are we friends again?"

"Absolutely. Now we'd better work on this PowerPoint. Our old painted lady isn't getting any younger, so fire up that laptop of yours, and let's get to work. Chop, chop."

"Okay, okay. I'm moving. I'm moving." Dani spun around to sit in the chair properly and then turned on her laptop. "Hey, do you think I can borrow your digital camera?"

"My camera? Sure." Meredith slid open the top drawer of her desk and pulled out the camera. "What do you need it for?"

"Oh, uh, I just thought I'd try to get a few more pictures of the house."

Meredith thought it was a little weird that Dani didn't want to go to the house together, but she decided not to push anything so soon after rekindling their friendship. She just said, "Keep it as long as you want."

"Thanks." Dani looked at the laptop screen and said, "Can you believe it'll be May when we do our presentation? I know I've been counting the days until graduation, but this is happening way too fast."

Meredith pulled her laundry hamper beside Dani's chair and sat on the closed lid. "Oh, my God. Tell me about it. You know, the weather's starting to get nice. Do you want to take Mikey to Bryant

Park with me on Saturday when he and I get back from karate?"

"Taekwondo."

Meredith laughed and slapped Dani's knee playfully again. "God, you're just like him. Just for that, *you* can ride the teeter-totter with him. I hate it."

Dani grinned. "Too much like exercise?"

"Oh, cut it out. I exercise. I walk to and from school every day."

Dani put her hands up in defense. "Okay, okay. I give."

"And speaking of May being right around the corner, did you know that my portfolio's due in three weeks, and I haven't even started on your scary portrait?"

"Please, never let Ben know you're painting my expression that I got pissed at him."

"Oh, believe me, I won't. I'll leave that up to you."

Meredith leaned closer so she could see the computer screen. Sitting there that close, in her room with the door closed, was surprisingly comforting. She took a deep breath to settle herself, but her breath caught in her throat as an awareness of Dani flooded her senses. Dani smelled clean, like baby powder. Meredith had missed that. Dani's thigh, inches from her own, was warm, and Meredith couldn't tear her focus away from that warmth. Something stirred deep inside.

Dani poked her in the arm. "Hey."

Meredith swallowed hard and looked up. She hadn't been listening to a single word Dani had said. Maybe this best friend thing was going to be trickier than she thought.

~~~

Meredith leaned against the windowsill in Mr. Dalton's

classroom as Dani invited their classmates to the open house of the soon-to-be-renovated Randall-Bradley House during Whickett Days. The open house was scheduled for the Saturday of Memorial Day Weekend, just over three weeks away. Mr. Dalton seemed pleased with their work, and their classmates had seemed fairly interested, too. Meredith knew Dani's outgoing personality was the main reason most of their classmates were attentive, but she couldn't help thinking that perhaps she had satisfied her classmates' curiosity about herself. And surprisingly, she hadn't been that nervous talking in front of them. Ben had helped in that regard. Right at the beginning of her part, he winked at her. She hoped Dani hadn't seen because she certainly didn't want Dani to know that she and Ben had talked.

Meredith smiled when Dani flicked her head to get a lock of hair out of her eyes and felt that oh-so-familiar warm sensation sneak up on her again. She watched the strong, athletic way Dani moved and the way she riveted everyone's attention. *How could I have ever let her out of my life? What in the world was I thinking?*

Dani powered down her laptop. Mr. Dalton stood up and said, "Thank you, ladies. That was an excellent presentation." Meredith and Dani returned to their seats in the back of the classroom. "I'm sure we've all wondered about that old house at least once. And what serendipity—discovering Esther and Millie at Hudson Pines. It sounds like it was meant to happen."

Ben raised his hand. "Uh, Mr. Dalton, what does 'serendipity' mean?"

Mr. Dalton laughed. "How can you be seniors in high school and *not* know what serendipity means?" He laughed again when the students protested his assessment of them. "Okay, okay. Uh, let's see. Serendipity is the effect of discovering something you needed when you weren't looking for it. For example, have you ever found something, like your lost car keys, when digging out a sock from behind the dryer?"

Every student, it seemed, had a ready story about serendipity. Mr. Dalton let the conversations continue for a few minutes, but then he called the class back to order and reminded them that the finalists would display their projects during the Whickett Days Celebration. He went behind his desk and pulled out a piece of paper that presumably held the names of the finalists. Attaching the list to his clipboard, he scribbled something on the bottom, walked to the front of his desk, sat on the edge, and said, "Now, before I name the finalists, I'm reminding all my classes that the final fundraiser for the senior class is this Saturday, nine a.m. at the Freezy-Frost. You'll be washing cars for a good cause—your senior prom. And Dani tells me this is the very last fundraiser. The prom should be all-systems-go after this." The students clapped enthusiastically, and Dani put two thumbs up toward Mr. Dalton for plugging the senior fundraiser.

"Okay, okay," Mr. Dalton continued. "Here are the finalists from this class. Finalists, please see me to discuss displaying your projects during the celebration." The class turned quiet. All eyes were on their teacher. "Sarah, Jeff, and Ben. Your interviews with the members of the Whickett Swing Band were top-notch. I had no idea that the Hudson Pines Senior Center even had a swing band. See me later, and we'll figure out how to display your project downtown. Maybe the band can play."

Meredith watched Ben lightly smack Sarah and then Jeff with the back of his hand as if to say, "Good job, project mates." Dani leaned forward and patted him on the shoulder. Ben beamed when he turned around. He smiled first at Dani and then at Meredith. Meredith smiled right back. Her smile faded when she felt Dani's gaze on her. Meredith turned to face her. In answer to the question in Dani's eyes,

Meredith just shrugged and said quietly, "What?" Dani shook her head but never lost the smile in her eyes.

"And," Mr. Dalton continued, "I will also need to see Joe and Palmer. Your rap about the History of Whickett will simply have to be seen by the entire town. Maybe we can squeeze you in after the swing band." Joe and Palmer looked pleased with themselves as they looked around the room, grinning at their classmates.

"And, finally, I hope that Esther and Millie are ready to have a lot of people at that open house because I think the entire town might just be curious about seeing the old painted lady. So, Meredith and Dani, let's talk with your new friends and see what we can do to help, okay?"

Ben turned around to give Dani a high five. Meredith hoped he didn't want a high-five from her. When he turned back around, she breathed a quiet sigh of relief. He must have realized he had almost given himself away earlier.

Meredith turned to look at Dani, and her stomach fluttered when she found Dani already looking at her with those crystal blue eyes. Meredith swallowed and somehow managed to smile back. *What is happening to me? Why did I spend those eleven days away from you?*

The bell rang to end the class period, and what Meredith did next was so impulsive it even surprised her. She leaned over to Dani and asked softly, "Walk me to class?"

Dani looked startled by the request. "You want me to walk you to your next class?"

Meredith's stomach fluttered again as she wondered what Dani must be thinking. Meredith nodded almost imperceptibly, and she said shyly, "Yes."

Dani pursed her lips together and said, "Okay, but there might be a surcharge for the service, ma'am."

Dani was kidding, of course, but Meredith would have paid triple the surcharge to keep Dani close for a few moments longer. She wasn't sure where this impulse had come from, but she felt incomplete without her friend nearby. Dani held open the classroom door and let Meredith walk through first.

~~~

A little over three weeks after Meredith and Dani patched up their friendship, they sat in what was becoming their regular booth at Fiesta Loca overlooking Esther and Millie's soon-to-be-majestic painted lady. Meredith motioned for the waiter. He came over and said in a somewhat thick accent, "What can I do for my two beautiful señoritas?"

Meredith smiled. "Can we please have a few extra napkins? My *beautiful* friend here spilled her soda."

"Aay, yes, right away."

He sped away in search of napkins, and Meredith laughed out loud. "Dani, stop laughing. You spilled your soda because you're out of control."

Dani continued to laugh and repeatedly smacked the tabletop with the palm of her hand. "I, I—" she took a deep breath and said, "I can't believe Mikey tried to take on Ben. Ben called him a what? A pit bull?" Dani started laughing again.

Meredith pointed her finger at her. "Stop that. I wasn't ever going to tell you that story."

"Oh, but I'm so glad Ben did. He's a good guy. Really."

The waiter handed Dani a replacement glass of Sprite and a stack of napkins to Meredith. After wiping up the soda spill with a damp rag, he headed to another table in the busy restaurant.

Meredith said, "Yeah, I might have to give him another chance. So, when did you tell him about you?"

"Tell him what?" The way Dani lifted her eyebrows, Meredith knew she was teasing.

"C'mon. You know."

"Well, he knew before I did."

"He did?"

"Yeah, he said he could tell. And then he just came out and asked me. Oops, sorry about the pun. He asked me a long time ago."

"Is he, you know, gay, too?"

"Ben? No, but he watches out for me like a brother. And nobody knows this except you now, but I've kind of hidden behind him throughout high school. I think that's why he's having such a hard time. He and I were always such good buds. But now I'm pulling away from him. I don't hang with him much anymore, you know?"

"Because of me." It wasn't a question.

"Well, yeah. But he gets that. He's okay with it. I mean, he even went and talked to you when we were, uh, having our misunderstanding."

"Misunderstanding. More like *my* misunderstanding. And I truly am—"

"Look, you have to stop apologizing. I'm just glad you came around. And look, we're here at Fiesta Loca, checking out the old painted lady, celebrating the completion of your portfolio. We've left the kids at home—no Ben, no Mikey—and it's supposed to be a Friday night with just you and me." She picked up her new glass of soda and saluted her friend.

Meredith saluted back with her glass of water. "That's right. We need to celebrate. The AP portfolio slides were mailed today, and I tell you what, I'm finished painting portraits for a while."

"I like how my angry eyes portrait turned out, but can you *not* hang that anywhere? I prefer the world not see me like that."

"Why? I was going to hang it in the front hall of the house, right beside Esther and Millie. You mean you don't want it there greeting destitute women and children?"

"Uh, no, they've probably seen enough angry eyes for an entire lifetime. But, um, speaking of Millie's portrait." Dani tapped her index finger on the table.

"Oh, God. Don't remind me. I guess I'm not done painting portraits after all. But I've got two weeks left with nothing to do in AP Art except work on Millie. Okay? Happy? Nag, nag, nag."

"We're sounding like an old married couple."

Meredith laughed and swatted Dani playfully on the forearm.

"Hey. That's going to leave a bruise. I'm going to be the first client at the Randall-Bradley house, I think." Dani rubbed her forearm.

"I didn't hurt you. You're just wimpy. But, hey, speaking of artwork. Mrs. Levine loved your still life. I do, too. You've really blossomed as an artist."

"I've blossomed. How nice. Like a marigold. Just call me Marigold Lassiter from now on."

"Now listen here, Marigold." Meredith smacked her on the forearm again. "You *have* blossomed. If Mrs. Levine had gotten hold of you a few years earlier, who knows? We might have been in the same AP Art class together."

Dani turned her head away. Meredith was sure she had just made Dani blush. Dani said, "Now it's your turn to stop. Let's talk about something else. Thanks for coming to the car wash last Saturday. We made way more than we needed for the prom."

"Mikey and I had a great time."

"He sure washed a lot of cars."

"That's because you were there." Meredith grinned at Dani.

"Aw, cut it out. You're going to make me blush again."

"You're an old softy. Just like Millie." Meredith teased.

When Meredith mentioned Millie, they both looked at the house through the restaurant window. Most of the house was cast in shadow except for the third floor, which was still bathed in the weakening sunlight of late evening. Meredith imagined the house full of life and new beginnings. She looked at her friend and said, "I can't wait to see the old lady with her facelift. Esther said they should get all the legal papers they need next week. They can probably start renovations right away."

"Millie and I are going to fix the banister tomorrow. What are you and Esther going to do?"

"I think we're going to give the place a nice deep clean. With no furniture, we can get to all the walls and floors. We've only got two more weeks to get ready, but with so many people traipsing through for that open house, we'll have to turn around and clean it all over again. And since Esther can't move very well, I'll probably be doing most of the work."

"I hear you. Millie's got all kinds of things planned for me, too. According to her, I have an 'aptitude for tools.'"

Meredith smiled but then turned serious. "I think it's sad that they don't have any children. Or grandchildren, either. Who do they have, besides us, their adopted granddaughters, to help them?"

"Well, there's grandnephew Gregory," Dani said with a hint of disdain.

"Aha," Meredith accused. "You've been talking to Millie. You don't like him either, do you?"

Dani pushed her plate away. "No, I don't. Millie doesn't trust him big time. She told me she's civil to him for Esther's sake."

"Well, he's Esther's family, I guess. That was weird when we thought we saw him in that real estate car. I could have sworn it was him."

"Yeah, me, too. But Esther said he was back home." Dani stacked Meredith's discarded plate on top of her own and pushed both plates toward the edge of the table.

"We must have imagined—"

Meredith couldn't finish her thought because the Fiesta Loca mariachi band strolled over to their booth. The four heavyset men wore matching black suits, white shirts, and floppy sombreros. One of the biggest men held a huge guitar against his ample belly. Meredith wondered how he could reach his chubby arms around his belly and the guitar. The smallest of the men stepped up to their table and asked, "Sweethearts?" in a teasing fashion.

Dani's mouth dropped open, but Meredith smiled back at him coquettishly. "Uh, no." She placed her hand over Dani's and said, "Just friends."

"Ahh, jes friends," the man said and winked at her.

The band launched into a seductive-sounding song anyway. Meredith and Dani laughed even though neither of them understood the Spanish. As the band played, Meredith realized that her hand still covered Dani's. Oddly, she didn't let go. She didn't want to. The intimacy of their shared meal and the familiarity of Dani's company made Meredith want to be close to her friend. She continued to smile at the musicians as if nothing was happening on the table with their hands. She didn't dare look at Dani because she didn't know what her eyes might convey.

Dani, Dani, Dani. What are you doing to me?

Chapter 15

Fireworks

Meredith flung her book bag on her bedroom floor and then flopped on the bed. She couldn't help the smile permanently etched on her face. The warm feeling that had taken over her lately had returned double fold that afternoon. She removed her glasses, put them on her bedside stand, and then laced her fingers together behind her head on the pillow. She stared at the ceiling without seeing it. Dani had announced that afternoon at their very last senior class meeting that there were nineteen days of high school left. And with the end of the day-to-day routine of high school came an entire summer of vacation days she could spend with Dani. And Mikey, too. During the summer, Mikey pretty much became her responsibility.

She grinned in spite of herself. This last month since she and Dani had become friends again had been amazing. Two weeks ago, the mariachi band played that song for them. Two weeks ago, Meredith's hand covered Dani's. And two weeks ago, Meredith developed a permanent fluttery feeling in her stomach whenever Dani was around. She didn't really understand what was happening to her. The emotions were becoming so intense that she had trouble keeping them at bay—especially after what happened earlier that day.

After history, Dani walked with her to AP Art, which she had done every day since Meredith first asked her to. Meredith started to enter the art room but turned back when she sensed Dani lingering at the door. She went back to see what Dani wanted and couldn't help herself. With one lingering motion, she reached up with the tips of her fingers and gently lifted the lock of hair out of Dani's eyes. The movement had been so intimate that Meredith was surprised she had even done it. Meredith read the look in Dani's eyes loud and clear. In that moment, Meredith finally understood what she had been afraid to admit. She was in love with Dani Lassiter. And had been for quite some time, probably since Valentine's Day when Dani gave her the candy. Valentine's Day was the first time she had felt that all-encompassing warmth—that first hot chocolate feeling. She barely remembered to breathe in the hallway outside the art room as her heart hammered in her chest. She wondered if the same look she saw in Dani's eyes was reflected in her own. The shrillness of the school bell snapped them out of the moment.

Meredith leaned back deeper into her pillow. She sighed and looked at the framed portraits of Esther and Millie. Meredith and her mother had gone shopping earlier in the week for solid wooden frames. She would hang the portraits early the following day before people arrived for the Randall-Bradley open house. Dani and Millie had already installed the sturdy hooks. And Mayor Taylor Brown, Whickett's longstanding mayor, was going to unveil the portraits during his dedication speech. Mr. Dalton had been right. Serendipity had brought the four of them together, she was sure. Meredith laughed when she thought that fate brought new granddaughters to the two older women, and fate had brought Dani to her, too. *I like you so much, Dani. And, I think I even kind of love you, but am I like you?*

A soft knock on her bedroom door broke her out of her thoughts.

"Honey, may I come in?"

"Of course, Mom. I'm doing absolutely nothing for a change."

Her mother opened the door and stepped into the room. She looked at the portraits on the desk and said, "You do such beautiful work, and those frames are perfect. I can't wait to meet Esther and Millie tomorrow."

"I'm so glad you guys are coming." Meredith sat up on the bed.

"We wouldn't miss it. After Dad and I take Mikey to karate—"

"Taekwondo, Mom."

Meredith's mother laughed. "Okay. We'll stop by the house after we take Mikey to his taekwondo demonstration. We can't wait to see what all the fuss has been about. I'm sure Esther and Millie are wonderful."

"They are. They even gave Dani and me a key to the house. Millie didn't want to leave a key under the flower pot anymore."

"Because of the vandals?"

"Yeah, she said she didn't want to scare Esther, but she told us she was glad they had moved out when they did."

"You and Dani just be careful, okay?"

"We will."

"So, can we bring anything tomorrow?"

"No, Esther and I went shopping for fruit punch and cookies. They rented a couple of tables and lots of chairs for inside the house. So, we'll be okay. Mayor Brown is dedicating the house at one o'clock, so just be there by then, okay?"

"We'll be there. Oh, and next week, I made an appointment for you to get those contacts you wanted."

"You did?" Meredith jumped up and hugged her mother. "Thanks, Mom. I think I'm ready to lose those stupid things." She gestured at the black-rimmed glasses on the bedside table.

Meredith sat back down on her bed, and her mother joined her. "Once again, I'm sitting here thinking my baby is almost a high-school graduate."

"Oh, Mom, don't get all misty on me. And, besides, I'm not your baby. Mikey is."

"I know. But you've looked so happy lately, and I've been so happy for you. You and Dani patched things up, I presume?"

Meredith marveled at her mother's sixth sense. "Yeah, we had a falling out, and it was my fault. All of it. I was pig-headed and stupid."

"You?" Her mother sounded like she couldn't believe her daughter could be pig-headed.

Meredith frowned. "Yeah, me. Well, I'm going to tell you this, Mom, but it's in confidence, okay?"

"Oh? Okay."

Meredith took a deep breath. She wasn't sure why she was about to tell her mother what she was about to tell her, but her instincts told her that she should. "Dani's gay. She's a lesbian. And I reacted badly when she told me. I'm really ashamed of myself. I didn't talk to her for like eleven whole days."

"Over spring break?"

Meredith nodded her head in shame.

"I thought something had happened. But Meredith, she's still the same person she always was."

"Believe me. I've been through all that in my head. I snapped out of it finally. I don't know why I wigged out. But we're okay now. Except..."

Her mother waited for her to continue but finally prompted Meredith by saying, "Except what, honey?"

Meredith pulled the pillow out from behind her and hugged it. She looked down at the pillow because she couldn't look her mother in the eye. Things were finally making sense in her head. She had sort of known for a while now, but as she talked to her mother, everything clicked into place. Although she had barely said the words to herself, she decided to take a chance and say them out loud. "I think I might be that way, too."

Meredith didn't look up. The clock ticking in the hallway outside her room maddeningly filled the growing silence.

Meredith almost jumped when her mother finally spoke. "Maybe you just have a crush. Girls get crushes on other girls. You admire her, we all do, but maybe it's just because you've had such a hard time adjusting to life here in the city. It'll pass."

"Maybe." She blinked back the tears welling in her eyes. "But Mom?"

"Hmm?"

"What if it doesn't pass, and what if I'm that way, too?"

"Well..." Her mother seemed to think about it for a while and said, "Well, it's not what your father and I pictured for you, but you know we'll love you no matter what. And Dani *is* very charming. Your father loves her. She's the brother he always wanted for Mikey." They both laughed. "And Mikey just lights up when he sees her. She's so good with him. I have to admit, I like her, too. But more importantly, I like how you light up around her. How can you fight that?"

Meredith covered a smile with her hand but kept her head down.

"So, honey, if you are *that way,* we'll simply adjust. You know we love you, and we'll accept you any way you are. The Bedfords are good at adjusting."

Meredith, overcome with emotion, threw her arms around her mother. The tears she had been trying to hold back let loose. She let go after a minute and sat back against the headboard. The pillow had fallen to one side, but she didn't reach for it again. Instead, she reached for a tissue from her bedside stand and chuckled when her mother reached for one, too.

"Mom, even if I'm not *that way*, I still kind of love her."

Her mom smiled. "I understand, honey. I think your father and brother feel the same way."

There was no possible way her father or her brother felt the same way she did about Dani. To be away from Dani hurt. Meredith smiled at her mother and said, "I hadn't even planned on saying anything to you about any of this, but you just sensed it, I guess."

Her mother stood up and turned to go. "It's that motherly thing, I suppose. Well, when you get yourself together, come down and help me get dinner on, okay?"

Meredith couldn't help but notice her mother's worried brow. "Okay, I'll be right down. I just need a minute." *I think I'm going to need more than a minute because I think I just told my mother I might be a lesbian.*

Meredith felt a little dizzy, so she put the pillow behind her head, closed her eyes, and wondered what she was going to do about Dani.

~~~

When the Whickett Days crowd finally dissipated, Esther, Millie, Dani, and Meredith had the old house to themselves again. Meredith and Dani moved two of the rented chairs out to the front porch of the old Victorian house.

Meredith patted one of the chairs and said, "Here, Esther, have a seat. I think the fireworks will go off any minute now. Which way's Whickett Park?"

Millie sat in the other chair. She pointed across Center Street in a northerly direction and said, "I think it's over that way. They're shooting them from Whickett Park?"

"Yeah, that's what my dad said." Meredith leaned on the back of

Esther's chair. "I'm so tired. What a day."

Esther turned in her chair. "We couldn't have done this open house without you girls. Right, Millie?"

"Nope."

"You girls are the best granddaughters we could have adopted. Right, Millie?"

"Yup. Why don't you kids go upstairs to the balcony and watch the fireworks from up there? Me and my girl need some alone time."

"Millie!"

Meredith laughed and looked at Dani, who shrugged and said, "Okay, we'll be upstairs. Just yell if you need us."

Meredith and Dani made their way up the staircase to the second-floor primary bedroom and onto the balcony. They could hear Esther and Millie talking below them but couldn't quite make out what they were saying.

Meredith moved to the railing and looked in the direction Millie had pointed. "I don't see anything yet."

Dani moved next to her. "I'm sure we'll hear the fireworks once they get started. We should have brought a couple of chairs up. Oh, well. I'm too tired to go back down. What a day. I never saw so many people in my life. Wasn't it cool to meet Mr. Dalton's wife? She seemed really nice."

"She did. And she was so pretty, too. Speaking of meeting people, I'm glad I finally got to meet your parents and your sister. They were really nice."

"Thanks. I grew them myself." Dani laughed and added, "My mom said you were pretty."

"Ack. Oh, please." Meredith knew she was blushing.

"My sister agreed with her. And so do I."

Meredith hid her face behind her hands and decided to change the subject as quickly as possible. She lowered her voice. "Esther looks tired, doesn't she?"

"Yeah. So does Millie. I don't think any of us were ready for the interest the town had in the Randall-Bradley House. I think you upstaged the mayor's speech."

"Noooo." Meredith dragged the word out for emphasis. "Oh, my God. Do you really think so? He must hate me."

"Well, he *was* kind of boring, and then everybody clapped so loudly when your paintings were uncovered."

"I know. Did you see Mikey cover his ears?" Meredith smiled at the memory.

"That was cute when he hugged you in front of everybody. You're, like, a big celebrity now."

"I doubt that highly." Meredith snorted.

The first of the big booms diverted their attention. The fireworks show had begun.

Dani craned her neck. "Can you see them?"

"Yeah, move over here behind me." Meredith motioned behind her since she was shorter than Dani. "The tree's in your way."

The first few fireworks lit up the clear night sky, and although Meredith enjoyed the burst of color against the dark sky, she lost interest. She lost interest because she could feel Dani's body heat behind her. Meredith stood perfectly still and listened to Dani's soft breathing. She imagined Dani's breath on the back of her neck. She imagined moving her hair out of the way so Dani could lean down and kiss her there.

Meredith jumped when Millie yelled, "How're my granddaughters doing up there?"

Dani cleared her throat and called down, "We're fine, Grandma."

Meredith shouted, "Everything okay down there?"

"Just peachy," Millie called back.

Meredith sighed. She wondered if Dani had any clue the effect she had on her lately. Maybe she should find out. She swallowed, trying to find the courage. She shuffled back slowly, almost imperceptibly, inch by inch, until she felt Dani's folded arms against her back. Meredith's heart was pounding. Part of her was in denial, but the other part, the part that was winning, pressed against her friend more firmly. Dani let out a small whimper, but Meredith persevered and kept contact.

Meredith stayed rock still against Dani, barely breathing. The fireworks in the night sky went unnoticed in front of her. She only registered Dani's arms against her back and wondered what Dani must be thinking. She hoped Dani couldn't feel her trembling.

Meredith's breath caught in her throat when Dani's arms slowly encircled her waist. Dani linked her hands over Meredith's stomach. Meredith let out a slow and controlled breath as she covered Dani's hands with her own. She was sure Dani could feel her trembling now, but she didn't care. She leaned back and let her head fall onto Dani's shoulder. Dani sighed in her ear. God, being this close to Dani felt so right. Dani's arms around her made her feel secure, safe, and protected. But, no, it was more than that. With Dani's arms around her, she felt loved. She wanted to keep Dani's arms around her, not just for a moment or an evening, but forever.

The thundering of her heart matched the thundering of the fireworks. Meredith couldn't restrain herself any longer. She swiveled around and put her arms around Dani's neck. The intense blue eyes gazing back answered her unspoken question. Meredith tilted her head back in invitation. Dani leaned down and touched her lips gently to Meredith's. With that hot chocolate feeling surging through her veins, Meredith pulled Dani closer and kissed her back. She had never felt anything like this before, and there was no question that Dani returned her kisses with matched emotion. When they finally broke apart, Meredith ran her fingers through Dani's hair and rested her head on Dani's shoulder.

"Dani?" she said thickly.

Dani cleared her throat. "Mmm?"

"I hope that was okay."

Dani laughed shyly. "Uh, yeah, I..." She stopped as if trying to figure out what to say. She cleared her throat again before continuing. "I've kind of wanted to do that for a long time. Ever since we first came here to the old house. When the banister broke, and I fell off the porch."

Meredith giggled, surprised. "It's been that long?"

"Yes," Dani said quietly. "But I'm patient."

Meredith nuzzled against Dani's neck and then pulled back so she could look Dani in the eye. "I guess I'm the slow learner this time. You were right there in front of me the whole time."

"Remember when you sort of held my hand at the Loca?" She nodded in the direction of their favorite Mexican Restaurant.

"Yeah, that was kind of an accident."

"Accident, my eye. I almost stopped breathing right there in front of the mariachi band. And remember when you did this to me outside the art room yesterday?" Dani brushed a lock of hair off of Meredith's forehead.

Meredith looked down, embarrassed. "I wasn't planning that. It just happened."

"Well, I almost died. I wanted to kiss you so bad, but, come on, we were at school, in the hallway. I think I knew at that moment that you had crossed over."

"Crossed over? Is that what we're going to call this?" Meredith drank in the affection she saw reflected in Dani's face.

"I guess. It doesn't matter though, Merry, because I really like you. I have for a long time." Dani reached out, placed her hands on either side of Meredith's face, and kissed her again.

Meredith returned the kiss. Her heart pounded in her chest while her stomach did excited flip-flops. When they reluctantly pulled away from each other, Meredith took a shaky breath. "Dani, I think...I think I really like you, too." She put her head back on Dani's shoulder, and it felt like she belonged there. The fit was perfect. Dani wrapped her arms around her again.

Meredith whispered, "You've made me feel more a part of the world than I've ever felt before. I'm sorry I didn't see it sooner. I guess I always figured I'd fall in love with some guy. I never considered a...I never considered *you*." *Oh my God, did I just say* fall in love? *Oh, my God.*

Before Dani could say anything, Millie called up the stairs. "Hey, what's going on up there? The fireworks have been over for five minutes already."

Meredith grinned and whispered, "No, they haven't. I think the fireworks just got started."

Dani matched her grin and said, "C'mon. Our grandmothers call."

"Don't you dare say a word to them. I'm...I'm not ready yet."

"Your wish is my command, madam, but you'd better wipe that grin off your face, or they'll know instantly." She waggled her eyebrows.

Meredith walked down the stairs of the old house a very changed person.

Chapter 16

Weasel

Meredith and Dani arrived at the old Victorian house about a half hour before Esther and Millie were supposed to arrive. They wanted to get to the house early enough to finish cleaning up after the open house the weekend before. Dani held the dustpan while Meredith swept the last of the debris into it. The kitchen was officially swept and ready for mopping.

Dani picked up the now-full dustpan. "When did Esther say they were coming?"

Meredith looked at her watch. "Oh, any minute now, I think. I wish we could have finished cleaning last weekend, but I don't think we had the energy after returning the chairs and tables on Sunday." She pulled a bucket from the kitchen closet and put it in the sink under the faucet. She turned on the hot water and added some floor cleaner she found under the sink.

Dani flicked her head to get the hair out of her eyes. "Esther and Millie can't do all this alone," Dani agreed. "And I just didn't have time to get over here this week, what with school and lacrosse and all. You know how it goes."

Meredith lifted the heavy mop bucket from the sink and put it on the floor. "Mikey and I are so proud of you for making the all-county lacrosse team."

"Thanks." Dani looked at her, eyes sparkling. "It's awesome. That

Syracuse coach had better notice me *now*."

"Well, duh."

"And with the team making the playoffs and open houses and new girlfriends, I'm kind of worn out," she teased.

Meredith smacked Dani playfully on the arm. "I can't believe I'm somebody's girlfriend. I never thought it would ever happen. But I like it. And, Miss Lassiter, one of these days, we'll have that talk about your *old* girlfriends, but for now, at least have the decency to kiss me when you insult me."

"You really have crossed over to the wild side." Dani grinned and pulled Meredith into an embrace as instructed. Meredith marveled at how amazing she felt in Dani's arms. She felt like she had found a lifetime supply of hot chocolate.

When they separated, Meredith said, "Mmm. That's more like it. I think...I think I'm okay now with telling Esther and Millie."

"Yeah? Are you sure?"

"Yeah. But not my folks. I'm not ready for that yet. I think my mom probably knows, but I want to wait. But let's tell our grandmothers today." Meredith looked down. "Could you do it? I don't know if I can."

Dani smiled and said softly, "Okay. But let's mop this floor before they get here."

Floor mopped and the kitchen sparkling, Dani and Meredith sat on the front porch steps and waited for Esther and Millie to arrive. Meredith reached for Dani's hand and held it tight.

June was days away, and the seasonably warm May weather promised a comfortable summer. During the past couple of months, the yard had bloomed brightly with various colors. The delicate crocuses had come first but were gone quickly. The regal tulips followed them, and then the king of all gardens—the daffodils. And now, as if timed to keep the yard bursting with color, the azalea bushes bloomed bright. The fuchsia, red, pink, and white blossoms assured that summer was close. Meredith's khaki shorts and red short-sleeved shirt with a tiny polo player on the front were also testaments to the warm and sunny day. She had taken to wearing the polo shirts since Dani said they looked good on her. In fact, Dani almost looked her twin with her own blue polo shirt and khaki shorts.

When the Ford Taurus pulled into the driveway, Dani jumped off the porch and raced to the car. Meredith waved to them from the porch.

Esther made her way slowly up the porch steps, leaning on Dani's arm. "Ah, my grandbabies. I wish we'd had you earlier. But I guess fate brought us together when we needed you. Right, Millie?"

"Yup." Millie followed behind them and grabbed the banister railing. She gave it a good tug. "Good work, Dani. It's rock solid." She turned to Meredith and said with a grin, "I told you she was a good catch."

"Millie!" Esther glared at Millie.

Meredith laughed. "Esther, it's okay. She's right."

"What?" Millie's mouth dropped open.

Esther slipped her arm out from Dani's and negotiated the doorway by herself. This allowed Dani to grab Meredith's hand. Dani grinned at Millie and said, "Uh, yes, Meredith crossed over to our side."

"She has?" Millie slapped her leg and said, "It's about time, girl." She reached over and stole a hug from Meredith. "Welcome to the club."

"Thanks, I think." Meredith felt a little nervous.

They walked into the house, and Esther reached for a hug from Meredith. She said, "Congratulations, Meredith. You and Dani make a wonderful couple. And we saw it right away when you visited me at Hudson Pines. I have to admit, though, that when you first walked in the door, I thought such a pretty girl like you might be a good match for Gregory."

"Pah, Gregory." Millie looked like she wanted to spit.

"Millie, come on now. Don't get these girls involved in our family stuff."

Millie shook her head and looked like she had eaten something nasty. "Okay, fine. Let's look over the renovation plans."

Dani said, "Thanks for including us in the process. This means a lot to us."

"Hey, you're our grandkids, aren't you? You're a big part of this." Millie shook the bundle of drawings in front of her for emphasis.

Esther sat down heavily in a resin chair. "We wouldn't dream of keeping our new granddaughters out of this. Without your energy, that open house never would have happened."

Meredith said, "We're happy to be part of the team."

Millie took the contractor's plans and spread them out over the table they had brought down from the upstairs balcony. For about an hour, they talked about the scheduled renovations. Each bedroom on the second and third floors would be remodeled so that a woman and her children could have their own private room and bathroom. The first floor would be renovated to include a visitors' area separate from the rest of the house. The stronger security would include magnetic locks on each outside door. Someone inside the house would have to hit a release button to let someone in. This ensured that the wrong person wasn't let in by mistake. Esther insisted that the women using the Randall-Bradley House feel safe, so extra strong doors were going to be installed, as well as alarms on every window and door. Security cameras would also be placed strategically around the house and yard.

Meredith knew the strict security steps were necessary to ensure the safety of the people living there, but the house was still starting to sound like a prison. But the house was going to help a lot of people, and she was about to say so when she saw movement at the front door. Dani must have also seen the movement because she looked toward the door.

Dani said, "Millie, I think our guest has arrived."

Meredith looked at Dani. "What guest?"

Esther looked as confused as Meredith felt. "I don't know either, honey. This must be something these two cooked up on their own."

Dani went to the front door and shook hands with a tall, lean man with thinning dark hair. His dress pants and sport coat looked as old as he was—about forty. Millie introduced herself to Mr. Jim Blayne from the Cayuga Commercial Real Estate Company. Meredith shook hands with the real estate broker when she was introduced as one of Esther and Millie's granddaughters.

Mr. Blayne said, "It's so nice to finally meet you all. I've had some serious interest in this house for a few months now. A potential buyer suggested to me that the house was to be turned into a professional building. He said that there'd be big bucks flowing through here."

Esther glanced at Millie and then looked back at Mr. Blayne. She asked calmly, "Oh? Big bucks? Please do go on with your story, Mr. Blayne. I find this quite interesting."

Meredith hid a smile at Esther's sarcasm, but she also clenched her fists in anger. Mr. Blayne had some nerve coming up to the house trying to convince them to turn their charming home into some profit-making venture for someone else. *Everyone in Whickett must have heard about the plans for the old house by now, so how could he—*

Dani must have picked up on her angry thoughts because she whispered in her ear. "It's going to be okay. Just listen."

Meredith tried to keep her anger under control, but she was getting worried because Millie was way too calm.

"You see, the potential buyer contacted me over a year ago, and in that time, I've been the middle man between him and a local contractor who would be developing the property. But lately, as I drive by, I've seen a lot of activity. I've seen the two young ladies in and out of the house." He gestured toward Meredith and Dani. "And I've also seen you two more seasoned young ladies coming and going. And who hasn't heard about the big dedication this past weekend for the Randall-Bradley House? So, it finally occurred to me to do some more checking. It seems that the potential buyer of the property may have, to put it simply, overstepped his bounds."

"Mr. Blayne," Esther said with a serious tone, "who would this *potential buyer* be?"

The real estate broker pulled an official-looking document from the inner pocket of his sports coat and handed it to Esther.

Esther opened the papers and read, "Gregory Sheridan."

Meredith's mouth flew open in shock. Millie and Dani exchanged a knowing glance. Esther calmly glanced through the rest of the document and handed it back to the real estate broker. She turned to face Dani and said, "Dear, may I borrow your cell phone? Could you dial the number for me? I don't know how to work those infernal things." Dani punched in the number Esther gave her and then handed the phone to Esther.

"Bernice? It's Esther...I'm fine, honey, I'm fine. Listen, I have a few questions to ask you."

At this point, Meredith and Dani walked onto the front porch to give Esther privacy as she talked to her sister, the sister who also happened to be Gregory Sheridan's grandmother. Meredith turned to Dani. "What's going on?"

"I'm sorry I couldn't tell you, but Millie wanted it that way. Remember when we were getting ready for the open house, and Millie and I were outside fixing the banister?" She gave the banister another firm tug.

"Yeah?"

"Well, Millie told me she thought Gregory was up to something, but she just didn't know what. She couldn't talk to Esther about it because you've seen Esther; she's so loyal to her family that she'd never believe it. But then I remembered we saw Gregory in the Cayuga Real Estate car, and we both knew it was him. It's too bad we cleaned up those beer cans and cigarettes so well. The police said we destroyed evidence."

"The police?"

"Yes, Millie had me call them because she couldn't find a way to call without Esther hearing. Millie asked me to come back and take pictures of the broken banister, the grease stain, and anything else I could find that would point to Gregory. I took more pictures for our project, too. Meredith, I really wanted to tell you, but Millie didn't want to worry you."

"That was thoughtful, but I would have been okay."

Dani leaned closer and said softly, "I know. I know. But I didn't want to break my word to her, you know?"

"That's okay," Meredith relented. "Go ahead."

"So last week, I came to the house by myself. I went that day Coach let us out from practice early. I parked at our favorite restaurant and walked over because I didn't want to deal with the drive gate. I'm so glad I did because I saw him before I got to the house."

"Gregory?"

"Yeah, he was inside the house. I snuck up to a window and took pictures of him inside."

"Oh, my God. That was kind of dangerous. Don't you think?" She hugged Dani quickly.

"For sure. My heart was pounding. When Millie and I went down to the police station last week and showed them the pictures from your camera, they said they could probably get him for criminal mischief, trespassing, or burglary. Something like that. Anyway, I called the real estate office, and Mr. Blayne didn't want to tell me anything over the phone, so I arranged for him to meet us today. I'm learning a lot of this for the first time, too."

Meredith looked at her wide-eyed. "My stomach hurts thinking about anyone taking advantage of Esther."

"Me, too," Dani agreed solemnly.

"And her own nephew—grandnephew—whatever." Meredith threw her hands up in disgust.

Dani squeezed Meredith's hand when Esther called them back inside.

"Here, honey." Esther handed the cell phone back to Dani. "I'm not sure if I hung it up right."

All eyes were on Esther. She cleared her throat and said, "Well, Millie, it looks like you've been right all along about my grandnephew. He *has* been up to no good. Bernice told me that Susan, that's Bernice's daughter and Gregory's mother, told her that Gregory has been spending more and more time away from home. Susan said that Gregory was investing in real estate somewhere upstate."

Millie punched the air. "I tried to tell you he was up to something."

"Dearest, I know you did, but I can be a stubborn old lady." Esther turned her attention to the real estate agent sitting on the staircase. "What do we do now, Mr. Blayne? I do *not* wish to convert my home into a professional building to make 'big bucks.' Oh no, Mr. Blayne. I have much better plans for this house."

"Miss Randall, I understand, and that's why I'm here. I don't like being lied to, either. Your grandnephew misrepresented you. He told me that you and he had a verbal agreement and that this was a joint venture."

Meredith shook her head in disbelief and watched the others do the same.

Mr. Blayne continued, "But, as it turns out, your granddaughter's call came just in time." Dani raised her hand when he looked questioningly at them. "And here's the fun part. I'm scheduled to meet Gregory at my office in about twenty minutes. How about I ask him to meet me here?"

Millie slapped her leg. "Oh, boy. This day is turning out much better than we thought. Right, Dani?" She had an evil grin.

"Absolutely," Dani agreed with glee in her voice. "Hey, let's move the cars to the Loca next door. That way, he'll think no one's here except Mr. Blayne."

Millie said to Esther, "She's sneaky. She must take after my side of the family."

Esther smiled, but Meredith could see the sadness underneath.

Mr. Blayne said, "Ladies, my professional integrity is on the line here. Miss Randall, I assure you that he assured me that he was acting on your behalf. He said you didn't want anything to do with paperwork and contracts. He assured me you would sign on the dotted line when the time came."

"What a weasel." Meredith put a hand to her mouth and couldn't believe she had said it out loud. "Oh, Esther, I'm sorry. I didn't mean to say that."

"Oh, honey," she said with a sigh, "you're fine. And you're right. I have to face up to the fact that I have a weasel for a grandnephew. Now, all of you, go on and move the cars. I have to collect myself before he gets here."

After moving the cars, Dani and Meredith hid themselves on the second-floor balcony so they could watch grandnephew Gregory's entrance. When they saw him pull up in his rust bucket of a car, Meredith watched with a mixture of anger and glee. She marveled how those two emotions could ever be felt together. They slunk quietly from the balcony and repositioned themselves at the top of the stairs so they could hear everything.

"Aunt Esther, what a surprise." Meredith heard the genuine surprise in Gregory's voice. "I thought you'd be at home resting. You shouldn't be on your feet."

"My hip, Gregory, is the least of my problems at the moment. Mr. Blayne tells me you want to turn my house into a professional building."

"Aunt Esther, you know I wouldn't have done anything without your consent. I was just trying to get everything set up so you wouldn't have anything to worry about. And I thought you'd be pleased. Grandma Bernice told me you were moving out anyway, so I came up here to help you."

Dani whispered to Meredith, "He's lying."

"How do you know?"

"You can hear it in his voice."

Just then, Meredith heard the swinging door to the kitchen bang open. Right on cue, Millie stomped into the sitting room. "What about that banister, Gregory? Who cut that?"

Dani and Meredith slowly made their way down the stairs. This was their cue. Meredith calmly but forcefully said, "And who slammed that door inside the house after Dani fell because of that broken banister, Gregory?" Her heart was pounding.

Gregory didn't have a chance to answer because Dani then said, "Yeah, Gregory, and who trashed the kitchen with beer and cigarettes? Were you trying to scare us?"

Meredith watched uneasily. Gregory's face turned bright red, matching the color of his hair. He stammered, "Yeah, I put that stuff in the kitchen, but I was trying to keep you meddling girls away. You had no business being here."

Like you did, weasel? Meredith thought.

"And yeah, I cut the banister. I wanted this house to be too much for you to take care of Aunt Esther. Can't you see? It's time this house moved on with the times, with fresh ownership and fresh—"

"Money?" Esther broke in. "These girls were our guests, Gregory. It's bad enough you've messed with me, but now you've really crossed the line. This young lady," she pointed to Dani, "could have been seriously hurt."

"I wasn't trying to hurt *her*, Aunt Esther."

Meredith jumped at the sudden volume of Esther's response. "Then who *were* you trying to hurt, Gregory?"

Gregory didn't answer. His silence was answer enough.

Mr. Blayne looked down and shook his head as if he couldn't believe he had gotten involved with someone as low as Gregory Sheridan.

Millie said, "You have majorly crossed a line, Gregory Sheridan. Why did you put axle grease on the floor? Who were you trying to hurt then?"

His eyes widened, and his head whipped back and forth from Millie to his aunt Esther. He looked like a caged animal. He took a quick step backward.

Millie whispered urgently to Dani, "Did you make that call?"

"Yes," she whispered back. "They should have been here by now."

Gregory turned to run out the front door just as two uniformed police officers stepped into the foyer. He saw them and recoiled, but the female officer grabbed him by the back of his shirt collar before he could change paths.

The male officer said to Millie, "Is this the one?"

"Oh, yes."

"Okay then. Sir," he directed his attention to Gregory, "it seems you've had quite a few accusations thrown at you. We'd like to take you back to the police station with us so we can ask you a few questions. Would that be all right with you?"

When Gregory didn't answer, the female officer tightened her hold. She said, "Sir, we'd prefer you cooperate of your own free will. Seriously, it'll go much easier if you cooperate."

"'kay," Gregory mumbled.

"How's that?" she demanded.

"O-kay," he barked and let himself be led away by two of Whickett's finest.

Mr. Blayne, Esther, and Millie left the house minutes after Gregory's unceremonious departure with the police officers to give their statements at the police station. Dani closed the front door once they'd gone and turned the latch. Meredith wrapped her arms around Dani's neck and leaned her head on her shoulder. "What do you think will happen to Gregory?"

"I don't know, but he's not so *grand* anymore, is he?" Dani held her tight.

"Esther looked so heartbroken. And did you see how upset Millie was? She didn't like doing this to Esther, but I don't think she had a choice, did she?"

"No, she didn't. I'm glad Esther learned about her weasel of a grandnephew before it got even more complicated. You picked the perfect word for him." Standing in the foyer, Dani gently rocked Meredith in her arms. "I can't believe that jerk tried to hurt Esther and Millie. I hope he gets locked away forever."

"At least Esther and Millie are through with him and can focus on getting the Randall-Bradley House up and running." Meredith was pensive for a moment, thinking about Esther's double-crossing grandnephew. Needing to change the subject, she pulled out of Dani's embrace and grabbed her hand. She led Dani up the stairs of the darkening house into the small bedroom Meredith had dubbed her art studio. They walked to the window. Still holding Dani's hand, she looked out the window at the bright lights of Fiesta Loca. "Are you sorry?"

"Sorry?" Dani asked, clearly perplexed. "Sorry about what?"

Meredith turned to face Dani. "Sorry that this is prom night, and you're not there?"

"No." Dani smiled gently.

"I mean, you raised all that money for the senior prom. You're the senior class president. Won't it look weird that you're not there?"

"Nah. I didn't want to go to the prom anyway. I never really liked those hetero exhibitions."

"Hetero?"

"Yeah, you know, heterosexual. Ben always went with me so I wouldn't feel out of place, but I always felt out of place, anyway. Not that anybody could tell, but I didn't fit in."

Meredith smiled. "I know the feeling."

"I know. Maybe that's why I was drawn to you in the first place. And when we landed in the same history class, I was so psyched. I was finally going to meet the cute new girl, but you really made it hard to do that. God, you're so pretty, but you were always hiding."

Meredith knew she was blushing. Only her parents had ever called her pretty. She swallowed around her embarrassment and said, "Some artists have their blue period. I had my invisible period, I guess."

"And I guess by *not* going to the prom together, we're still kind of staying invisible." Dani reached for Meredith's free hand.

"Hypocrites, aren't we?"

"I guess." Dani kissed the palm of the hand she had just taken. "But I'm here with my girl on prom night and having the best time of my life." She kissed the inside of Meredith's wrist and forearm and then the soft skin inside the bend of her elbow.

Meredith's breath caught in her throat. "Dani, I can't believe how you make me feel."

"Mmm." Dani continued to trail kisses up Meredith's arm and then kissed her on the neck.

Meredith's breathing got heavy. "Dani..."

"Mmm?"

"Maybe we shouldn't..."

Dani pulled Meredith closer and used her right hand to caress Meredith's cheek. She leaned closer and kissed her again.

Meredith forgot why she had begun to protest and threw her arms around the one person in the world who seemed to understand her.

~~~ The End ~~~

Newsletter Signup

Sign up for Barbara L. Clanton's newsletter to keep up with new (and revised) releases. She also likes to provide writing tips for writers and recommend books to read (other than her own, of course).

Sign Up on Barbara L. Clanton's Official Website:

www.BLClanton.com

Resources
lgbt national help center
https://lgbthotline.org/

From the lgbt national help center website:

"All of our support volunteers identify as part of the LGBTQIA+ family, and are here to serve the entire community, by providing free & confidential peer-support, information, and local resources through national hotlines and online programs."

LGBT National Hotline: 888-843-4564

LGBT National Coming Out Support Hotline: 888-688-5428

LGBT National Youth Talkline: 800-246-7743

LGBT National Senior Hotline: 888-234-7243

About the Author

Barbara L. Clanton

Barbara L. Clanton is a native New Yorker who left those "New York minutes" for a slower-paced life in central Florida. While in middle and high schools, she played any sport she could find— softball, volleyball, basketball, and field hockey. During high school, she could even be found in the upstairs gym playing handball with her friends. She played softball at Princeton University and was the team captain during her Ivy-league champion senior year.

She has spent her career teaching computer science and mathematics at college preparatory schools in New York and Florida. She also coached softball and basketball in both states as well. As an amateur softball player, she was inducted into the ASANA's (Amateur Sports Alliance of North America) Hall of Fame.

Somewhere in adulthood, she picked up a new hobby. "Dr. Barb" plays the bass guitar and has been in several pop-rock bands, playing in notable events such as Gay Days Orlando.

When asked why she started writing, she said she was writing the books she wished she had in high school to help her make sense of her "differentness." Although the world is evolving, it's still not easy to come out to yourself or the world. She hopes her books will help.

Barbara L. Clanton's Website:
http://www.blclanton.com

Barbara L. Clanton's Instagram:
https://www.instagram.com/barbara.clanton14

Barbara L. Clanton's Facebook:
https://www.facebook.com/BassGuitarGirl

Barbara L. Clanton's Goodreads Page:
https://www.goodreads.com/author/show/3072442.Barbara_L_Clanton

Barbara L. Clanton's Author Page on Amazon:
https://www.amazon.com/Barbara-L-Clanton

Books by Barbara L. Clanton

THE WHICKETT SERIES (Young Adult & New Adult)

The Whickett Series follows two young women who discover a close friendship. For Meredith, their friendship has always been about friendship and nothing more. For Danielle, it has always been about more, but she respects the friendship and resigns herself to remaining friend-zoned because it's a way to keep Meredith in her life. This series starts following the two young women in their second semester of senior year in high school. Book one is the young adult novel: "Art for Art's Sake: Meredith's Story." The series continues into their first semester of college in the new adult novel: "More Than Roommates: Dani's Story." Somewhere along the way, their definition of friendship changes.

Art for Art's Sake: Meredith's Story
(Book One in the Whickett Series)

A young adult lesbian romance.

High school senior Meredith Bedford is a social outcast. Her family recently moved from the Catskill Mountains to the sprawling suburbs of Albany, the capital of New York State. Shy and self-conscious about her acne scars, she stays to herself and tries to remain invisible. Her twelve-year-old brother, Mikey, has Down Syndrome, and she tries hard not to blame her troubles on him. Despite verbal and sometimes physical harassment, she survives because she has her art. She was selected to be part of the elite Advanced Placement art class and is quite good at capturing the emotions of her subjects in her portraits. Besides her family, art is the one thing that helps her cope with her outcast status.

One day, at a senior class meeting, she sees Dani Lassiter, president of the senior class and captain of the lacrosse team and knows that she must paint this enigmatic young woman. One class period later, Dani manipulates things to have Meredith as her partner for a history project. Meredith is suspicious of Dani's motives but takes a chance. And it pays off. Meredith slowly sheds her invisibility cloak and allows Dani in - a little at a time. They explore an old Victorian house for their history project and become close with Esther and

Millie, the two older women who own the house and who've lived together for about forty years. But, when Dani reveals to Meredith that she is gay, Meredith simply can't deal with the news. How had she not known? What is it that won't allow her to come to terms with this unexpected news? Will Meredith control her own homophobia, or will she reject the one person who had taken a chance on her and made her feel human?

ISBN: 978-1-953734-34-1 (eBook)
ISBN: 978-1-953734-35-8 (Paperback)

More Than Roommates: Dani's Story
(Book Two in the Whickett Series)

A new adult lesbian romance.

This new adult lesbian romance is the story of Danielle (Dani) Lassiter as she heads off to Syracuse University for her freshman year of college. And as far as any of their new college friends know, she and her girlfriend Meredith are just roommates and nothing more. And for a little while, they are able to keep it their private secret.

Dani has goals for her college career. She wants to get involved in campus politics and get elected as one of the freshmen representatives of the Student Association. She's also set her sights on improving her lacrosse skills so she can be good enough to make the varsity women's lacrosse team.

Reality hits hard and fast, though, when she discovers that things aren't coming as easily to her in college as they did in high school. An older female student assaults her. A lacrosse coach tells her she isn't good enough. And, the worst thing, her relationship with her not-just-a-roommate Meredith lands on shaky ground from both sides.

Dani accidentally starts an informal after-school program teaching young neighborhood children lacrosse. At one point, she advises them to just "be themselves." She tells them that good things will happen if they do that. It is only when ten-year-old Natalie reminds her to do that for herself that she becomes unsure of what it means to "be herself." Who is Danielle Lassiter, really? Unsteady and unsure, Dani has difficult decisions to make. And one of those decisions includes whether or not she should stay at Syracuse University. Running away to Albany State might be easier on everyone, including herself.

ISBN: 978-1-953734-36-5 (eBook)
ISBN: 978-1-953734-37-2 (Paperback)

THE CLARKSONVILLE SERIES (Young Adult)

The Clarksonville Series follows four high school girls in upstate New York as they maneuver the difficult process of coming out to themselves, each other, and their families. And it doesn't always go well. The four friends have a mutual love of softball, which helps them bond and find love. Each book is from a different character's point of view, but all four main characters are present in each book. There are currently eight books in the series.

Out of Left Field: Marlee's Story
(Book One in the Clarksonville Series)

A young adult lesbian romance.

High school junior Marlee McAllister lives and breathes softball. She's the pitcher for the Clarksonville Cougars in the North Country of upstate New York. With the season opener approaching, Marlee and her best friend, Jeri D'Amico, go to scout their rivals, the East Valley Panthers. The Panthers' star pitcher, Christy Loveland, took the All-county pitching title the preceding year. It is a title Marlee covets. Marlee and Jeri settle in for the game, but as the Panthers take the field, Marlee finds herself staring at Susie Torres, the Panther left fielder.

For reasons Marlee doesn't understand, she's drawn to Susie. Over the next few weeks, Marlee and Susie will slowly act on their mutual attraction. But suddenly, Susie pulls away without explanation, and Marlee realizes it has to do with Christy. Susie won't explain the bond she and Christy share, but whatever it is, it threatens Marlee's burgeoning relationship with Susie.

Struggling to maintain her grades, dealing with the ever-increasing estrangement from her best friend Jeri, and handling the pressures of the All-county pitching competition, Marlee also has to confront the bittersweet realities of what it might mean to be gay.

ISBN: 978-1-953734-04-4 (eBook)
ISBN: 978-1-953734-16-7 (Paperback)

Tools of Ignorance: Lisa's Story
Book Two in the Clarksonville Series)

A young adult lesbian romance.

Lisa Brown is the starting catcher for the Clarksonville Cougars High School softball team, and she has a major crush on her pitcher, Marlee. Lisa continues to carry her torch for Marlee, even when Sam, a rival softball player, flirts sweetly. However, Lisa becomes more confused than ever when Tara, the first girl she ever kissed and the first girl who ever broke her heart, resurfaces. Since Marlee doesn't know Lisa's alive, should Lisa give up on her once and for all?

Sam seems to have secrets of her own, but Lisa wonders if she should overlook them and allow her fledging attraction to grow for the pretty blonde, or should she fan the tiny flame still burning in her heart for Tara? Lisa faces these problems and deals with society's tools of ignorance in her quest for love and acceptance.

ISBN: 978-1-953734-06-8 (eBook)
ISBN: 978-1-953734-17-4 (Paperback)

Going, Going, Gone: Susie's Story
(Book Three in the Clarksonville Series)

A young adult lesbian romance.

Susie Torres planned to spend most of the summer before her senior year of high school with her girlfriend, Marlee McAllister, but that's proving to be quite challenging. Marlee works at D'Amico's restaurant, and Susie babysits for Mrs. Johnson, her mother's boss. Susie hates the job because she not only works like a slave but almost gets paid like one. Susie is desperate to take her physical relationship with Marlee further, but she knows she has to go at Marlee's slower pace. Complicating things is the attention that a pretty blonde softball player from another team shows Marlee, and Susie falls into a funk when Marlee seems to enjoy it.

On top of that, nothing she does seems to be good enough for her summer softball coach. Frustrated with life, Susie accidentally, on purpose, comes out to her mother. It would be an understatement to say that her mother didn't take it well. Can Susie deal with a girlfriend whose head has possibly been turned by another, an employer who treats her like dirt, a coach who doesn't respect her, and a mother who tells her she is unnatural? Can she get her life back on track before senior year starts?

ISBN: 978-1-953734-05-1 (eBook)
ISBN: 978-1-953734-18-1 (Paperback)

Stealing Second: Sam's Story
(Book Four in the Clarksonville Series)

A young adult lesbian romance

Samantha Rose Payton likes girls, but her parents don't know that. And Sam would like to keep it that way because her parents are ultra-conservative Republicans. They live in a mansion and have servants and chauffeurs. However, instead of playing the dutiful debutante who plays the violin and still has a nanny at age seventeen, Sam would rather watch ice hockey on TV and play second base on her summer softball team. Having to hide her relationship with her girlfriend, Lisa, from her parents is becoming an agonizing struggle. Not only are her friends pressuring her to come out to her parents, but they are also trying to convince her to attend a very public gay pride festival at the local college.

At least she has her nanny Helene to confide in, but for how much longer? Sam is acutely aware that the time for Helene to move on may be fast approaching. And if that isn't enough, Sam's summer softball coach gives her no end of grief after an error-filled game and isn't afraid of making an example out of her. Will Sam remain the perfect princess her parents expect? Will her beloved nanny leave her forever? Will her girlfriend get fed up about being kept hidden? Will her friends continue to pressure her about coming out? Will Coach Greer make her life miserable? All of these questions are answered in Stealing Second: Sam's Story.

ISBN: 978-1-953734-07-5 (eBook)
ISBN: 978-1-953734-19-8 (Paperback)

Out at Home
(Book Five in the Clarksonville Series)

A young adult lesbian romance

Marlee McAllister just wants to fit in. She didn't know she didn't fit in until Kate and Rita – the prettiest girls in the senior class - pointed it out. Even Marlee's grandmother declared that Marlee was too old for "this tomboy nonsense." All the other girls at school have long hair except Marlee. All the other girls wear something other than jeans, a T-shirt, and sneakers to school every day. Except for Marlee. All the other girls fit in except Marlee.

Marlee decides to grow out her short hair, buy femmy girly clothes, and pretend she has a boyfriend named Ronnie. Really, though? She has the most amazing girlfriend in Susie Torres. Susie is everything Marlee hoped for - sweet, sexy, kind, athletic, pretty. And best of all? She loves Marlee as much as Marlee loves her. Although their parents know about their relationship, not many other people do.

Marlee is out at home but not to anyone else. And if anyone else finds out she's into girls, Kate and Rita especially, the entire school and her grandparents will know within a day. Life as she knows it will be over.

Out at Home is the story of Marlee McAllister's life-altering struggle to fit in.

ISBN: 978-1-953734-20-4 (eBook)
ISBN: 978-1-953734-24-2 (Paperback)

Tools of the Devil
(Book Six in the Clarksonville Series)

A young adult lesbian romance

Seventeen-year-old Lisa Brown loved going to church. Oh sure, sometimes she'd rather sleep in, but she liked the calming and empowering strength of her faith. Sundays revitalized her spirit when she thanked God for the wonderful things in her life, like her loving family and amazing girlfriend, Samantha Rose. One day, she hoped to marry Sam, have a house and yard, and have babies together. One day.

But then it happened. That fateful Sunday, the guest preacher stepped behind the pulpit and spoke four words that would change Lisa's world forever. "Homosexuality is a sin," he said. Had she heard him right? She knew she had when her mother put a hand on her forearm. Every muscle in her body tensed, and she forgot to breathe. What was happening?

The church she'd been baptized in, grown up in, and wanted to get married in had, in one instant, turned against her. Still not quite believing what she'd heard, she mumbled, "Ignorance is a sin, Reverend." Never one to back down from a challenge, she scanned the congregation but didn't find a single soul who looked upset by his statement. On the contrary, many nodded in agreement. Under her breath, she muttered, "Game on, people. Game on."

ISBN: 978-1-953734-21-1 (eBook)
ISBN: 978-1-953734-25-9 (Paperback)

Going Under
(Book Seven in the Clarksonville Series)

A young adult lesbian romance

Susie Torres is a second-semester senior with devoted friends and an amazing girlfriend in Marlee McAllister. Susie's father has a job that takes him away from home on frequent business trips, but lately, his trips seem to be longer and more frequent. Tensions rise at home when Susie's mother challenges him about that. At first, Susie and her younger brother Miguel hide in her room when their parents' frequent squabbles elevate to out-and-out yelling matches. But as her parents' war escalates further, Susie finds other ways to escape the tension.

A fake ID becomes a clear and easy way to anesthetize herself with alcohol. Her crumbling home life becomes momentarily forgotten whenever she swims in a sea of peaceful drunken bliss. Unfortunately, Susie doesn't realize she is alienating everyone around her with her attempts to cope with her parents' possible divorce, including Marlee. Her best friend Sam tries to warn her that her excessive drinking is driving away all her friends, but Sam's well-meaning advice isn't heard. Will Susie finally realize that it is her own actions that are making her life fall apart around her? That her new love of drinking is getting in the way of everything good in her life? That her amazingly patient girlfriend isn't going to put up with much more?

ISBN: 978-1-953734-22-8 (eBook)
ISBN: 978-1-953734-26-6 (Paperback)

Stealing Hope
(Book Eight in the Clarksonville Series)

A young adult lesbian romance

Sam Payton is a high school senior with a bit of an identity crisis. Raised in a well-to-do family, she dutifully plays the role of Samantha Rose Payton, the wealthy debutante. Now, almost one full year into her life-changing relationship with Lisa Brown, Sam is hit with many life-challenging events. Her best friend, Susie Torres, struggles with alcohol addiction and a wrecked home life as her parents go through a bitter divorce, and Sam tries to help her friend keep her head above water. In another struggle, two friends cross the line between friendship and intimacy—a line that should not have been approached. Sam finds herself trying to make them see the incredibly egregious transgressions for all involved. And to top it all off, Sam's mother is diagnosed with a serious illness.

Through the love of her parents and her girlfriend, Sam navigates these challenges the best way she can, all while trying to fulfill everyone's varying expectations of her. Sam struggles to break free of the preconceived roles she seems bound by and figure out who she really is. It ultimately comes down to whether Sam can make everyone see that she is both a softball-playing, ice-hockey-loving lesbian named Sam as well as a classically-music-trained debutante named Samantha Rose.

ISBN: 978-1-953734-23-5 (eBook)
ISBN: 978-1-953734-27-3 (Paperback)

THE GRASSE RIVER SERIES (Young Adult)

Quite an Undertaking: Devon's Story
(Book One in the Grasse River Series)

A young adult interracial lesbian romance

Devon Raines, a sixteen-year-old journalism nerd, was happily minding her own business when her life was turned upside down. She struggled with grief when her grandmother died from a sudden heart attack. But it was at her grandmother's wake that she locked eyes with the most beautiful black girl she'd ever seen. No, Rebecca Washington was the most beautiful *girl* she'd ever seen, period. Would this beautiful dancer freak out if she knew Devon was gay and attracted?

Enter Jessie Crowler, Rebecca's basketball-playing best friend. Or were they only friends? Devon tried to hide her attraction for the ebony dancer, but would fate allow Rebecca to look her way? Would Jessie get in the way? Would the difference in skin color keep them apart? All this adds up to quite an undertaking in Devon's formerly quiet existence.

Rebecca's Story
(Book Two in the Grasse River Series)

< Coming Soon >

THE GIRLS' SPORTS SERIES (Children's Books Ages 9-12)

Bases Loaded

Sixth-grader Mackenzie Kelly's first love was soccer until her best friend talked her into playing summer softball. Now Mack is eager to be on her school's softball team and dreams of playing in the Olympics with her idol, Cat Osterman. But first, she needs to bring up her failing English grade to stay on the team. When she learns softball has been cut from the Olympics, she's determined somehow to get it back into the Olympic Games so she can fulfill her dream.

"I just wanted to let you know I received the book and
I think it is FANTASTIC!"
– **Jessica Mendoza,** *US Olympic Softball Team*

ASIN: B0094IT3RK (eBook)
ISBN 978-1-934452-79-0 (Paperback)

Side Out

Seventh-grader Dina Jacobs feels like she's landed on another planet when her family moves from Long Island, New York to Indiana. She tries out for the seventh-grade volleyball team, and her new friend, Christine, introduces her to Olympic volleyball. Now Dina dreams of playing in the Olympics like her newfound idol, Logan Tom. Indiana doesn't seem so bad until Dina's Jewish faith crashes against her coach's win-at-all-costs attitude. Miserable, Dina is torn between staying true to her religious customs or putting them aside to play the game she loves.

ASIN: B005HM9CUU (eBook)
ISBN 978-1-934452-65-3 (Paperback)

Live, Love, Lacrosse

Addie Coleburn, fresh out of the sixth grade, is spending the summer at her grandmother's house in Syracuse with her mother and brother. Kimi Takahashi, a girl who lives up the street, invites Addie to go to the park and play lacrosse. Addie hasn't the first clue what lacrosse is and would rather sit on Grandma's front porch eating potato chips, drinking sodas, and reading books. But then again, spending the summer dealing with her younger brother isn't appealing, either so she goes to the park with Kimi. Within a week, she's hooked on lacrosse. She's overweight and can't keep up with the faster, stronger girls. She has to find a way to lose her excess weight quickly or risk getting cut from the team.

ASIN: B09GPYMHDK (eBook)
ISBN 978-1-943837-50-2 (Paperback)

www.ingramcontent.com/pod-product-compliance
Lightning Source LLC
Chambersburg PA
CBHW061615170626
46811CB00001B/434